THE PASTOR'S Diaries

JOSHUA PRESSLEY

authorHOUSE®

AuthorHouse™
1663 Liberty Drive
Bloomington, IN 47403
www.authorhouse.com
Phone: 1 (800) 839-8640

Published by AuthorHouse 08/21/2017

ISBN: 978-1-5462-0584-5 (sc)
ISBN: 978-1-5462-0583-8 (e)

Chapter One

You could hear the sound outside if you listened carefully enough. On a cool Saturday evening the sound of hot sex in an old bungalow in the West End block of Atlanta. The panting and moaning sounds of sex and lust: hot passion steaming up the windows of an upstairs bedroom. Not the sound of love being made but lust being made manifest between a Pastor and a woman who was not his wife.

"Oh, Pastor Wright don't ever stop..." she whispered in between strokes as his thrusts drew her closer to the point of her peaking.

"Please don't stop; I am almost there..." she said again.

He hardly spoke. At times of passion, just as at times of purpose, he calmly focused on his mission as if he was a soldier and his mission was everything.

"Baby, I am almost there. Don't stop. Don't stop. I...I....am coming!" she screamed as her body collapsed off him. She laid there for a moment to allow her convulsions to subside. His position of choice seemed to always cause the desired reaction. What woman doesn't like the penetration that doggie style provides?

As she laid there enjoying her continued climax, he stood up and walked to the bathroom. The sound of Midnight struck on his clock downstairs as he began to wash his face. This was nothing new to him, the constant stream of women in and out of his bed, yet the thought of a future with any of them far from his mind. He knew that she would be just another of the many that have come this way and seen the inside of his bedroom and have felt and known him in ways that they shouldn't have.

Pastor William Fitzgerald Wright looked at himself in the mirror as he wiped his face. A shapely dark man with a gruff but approachable demeanor stared back at him. Just handsome enough to be noticed but not so much to be untouchable. As he looked at himself in the mirror, the vixen that exuded womanhood, slowly and seductively slid into his view from behind.

"Do you like what you see?" she asked, as she admired his nakedness and her nakedness together.

"Because I am liking what I see..." Tee said, sex dripping from every word. Will remained quiet for a moment. He was still concentrating on himself in the mirror. His eyes focused past the image of himself and the woman who was with him, to another place or another time. Though he heard and understood everything she said, he wasn't even in the room at that moment. His mind was somewhere else and that was a place that she could not be.

"Will? Will? Do you hear me talking to you?" Her voice slightly annoyed by the fact that he had not noticed her advances.

"Yes, Tee I heard you." William finally responded. You could hear it in his voice that he was not there with her.

"What is the problem?" she asked, perplexed by his distance after such a wonderful occasion of sex therapy.

"Nothing. I'm cool." he responded, without even looking at her in acknowledgement.

"You were beginning to scare me. Are you ok?" she asked as she slightly rubbed his shoulders with her soft smooth hands.

"I believe it is time for you to go," he said, still looking in the mirror.

"Wha...What?" she gasped.

"I believe it is time for you to go." He replied again. His focus finally changed as he stared her in her soft brown eyes through the mirror. She then understood that he was very serious.

"You know what? You are no better than the rest of them. In fact, you are the worst of the bunch because you are a Pastor!" Her voice trembled with anger as she slammed and gathered her things.

He heard her commotion but his temperament would not even allow him to explain. Nothing new just the same response, he thought.

"You are full of shit and God is not pleased." She yelled as she slipped her pants that were at the foot of the bed, back on.

Will laughed in his mind, because he found it interesting how she mixed her profanity with her beliefs.

"What do you know about God? What do you know, huh?" he said with a condescending tone in his voice.

'You got what you wanted. I got what I wanted. Now it is time for you to go. This is not algebra." He said.

"Mark my words, Will, you are going to see this again. Believe that. You will see this shit again." she said loudly as she walked down the stairs towards the door. William could have cared less.

The door slam echoed and resounded throughout the house and then, once again, the silence enveloped. She was gone. Now he, again, was alone. This was not how he wanted it to be but it was the only time that he could truly deal with what he was thinking after he had done what he had done.

This had always been the case for William Fitzgerald Wright. It was "William the Pastor" versus "William the man". "William, the child of God and professed defender of the faith" versus "William, the lover of sex and women". His demons continued to be the same. How do you overcome the drug that you do not have to buy or pay for, but it is given to you so freely by willing participants? How do you overcome something that was always there waiting for you and wanting you to take it?

Will walked from his bedroom to the end of the stairs and looked down at the light coming in through the side windows of the doorway. The moon was full that night and the blue rays of its light illuminated the foyer with a haunting ambient glow.

"Lord, they say reflection is good for the soul, but I don't want this life. I…" He stopped himself. The reflection that he had was of that fateful day. He had said those words so many times that he refused to say them again.

"I pray not for myself but for everyone that I have touched with the worst of intentions. Lord, please be with them that they may know you and not the man that touched them. I know that I didn't love them but Lord, I pray that my sin did not lead them astray. That burden I cannot bear. In Jesus' name, Amen."

Laying his burdens at the foot of Jesus was supposed to have relieved his mind of the pressure and stress of his past and present, but Will couldn't help but be affected. It was 3:09am, and the last words Tina said before she left were like a thorn in his mind. "You will see this again. Mark my words…" They ring out in his head, lingering even as he got up from his prayer and tried to lie down.

He began to try to think of the past, to a happier time, or rather a time of innocence; a time when he was at peace with himself. This was nothing new for him. This was his ritual, his way of getting over his flaws. Reminiscing allowed him to escape the moment if only for long enough to fall asleep.

He remembered the birth of Kristian, on that cold day in March of 1993. The snow that covered everything and the wind that blew on that day. The snow, the buses being covered and the blizzard that shut the city down. The Storm of the Century. Atlanta being a white mess and he the hero, on his way to save the day and help the mother of his child get to the hospital. The more he remembered, the heavier his eyes got.

The slipping and sliding of the taxicab as they made their way to Georgia Baptist Hospital; his eyes dimmed some more. Holding Tawanna's hand as she tried to squeeze blood from his and being okay with that because he knew that she was bringing their new life into a world that really wasn't ready for her, but was happy she was on the way anyway. And as he remembered that, he slipped away into that memory, and that memory brought him home to sleep.

Saturdays had always been the time for what had transpired earlier. Will was always on the prowl back then, seeking whom he may devour. Friday nights were the days when he would unload. Will would pick up Kristian from school and take her to her grandparents on weekends. His story was that Saturdays were the best days for him to go over his sermons and that he needed that whole day in order to get prepared. He knew exactly how to bend the truth for his advantage.

It was true that Will would use Saturday as his day of preparation. He would study the Word and prepare his sermons. He would build his argument and go through it with all due diligence and earnest effort. He would have his game face on and make sure that all the I's were dotted and all the T's were crossed. But, when it came to Saturday evenings, Will was able to find enough time to make things happen that were not centered in Christ.

Will had done it all, sexually, even as a pastor and his respect for the nature of sex was as a dog's respect for water. If he wanted it he knew how to get it. He didn't have the biggest dick, he was about seven and a half inches, which he considered long enough to handle any woman, but Will did know how to work his tongue better than most men. And women were not expecting a pastor to work them three ways over in the bed like he did. Will was never afraid to take it in a different direction and always creative if he got in that zone in the bedroom.

And who were these women to him? Most of them were

bumps in the night; conquests for the day and opportunities for the night. Few had come his way that he deemed worthy enough to know longer than he did. And his saying that he was a single pastor was like icing on the cake.

So many women didn't mind the fact that he was a Pastor, in fact that made it better for them. One woman asked him something that he had never thought of before then.

"Do you know how long I have wanted to do a Pastor?"

He was slightly shocked at the question but later his naïveté was overcome by the tremendous opportunity that this presented for him. 'I can fulfill my desires to be pleased and I can fulfill other women's desire to have their fantasies played out', he thought.

Of course he came to realize that you cannot deal with the women of your church for too long. He had already dealt with over seven women in his church alone, and none of them attended the church anymore. You would think that the word would have gotten out by then but it hadn't. His presence in his church was so large that it could not be ignored or overcome by the words of catty women. So each one that left First Baptist, left without destroying his reputation or their own because in their hearts they loved him and didn't want to ruin him and his reputation.

That is the part that saved him so often- they liked him. They liked him as a person, as a friend, as confidant. Sex with Will was an experience that often involved an opportunity to explain your most intimate feelings and problems. It was almost like going to a therapist after having an orgasm with the therapist, being ok with all of it all the while. That is why there were never hard feelings, but who could continue to look on knowing that he would continue doing this with other people?

But Will's heart had turned colder in recent days and the wonderful bedside manner that made for good tidings thereafter were no longer in vogue. His response which was once cuddly and attentive had become cold, distant, and disinterested. Will was no longer searching for Miss Right; Miss Now would do.

6:01 am. The blaring blast of the alarm clock awakened the mind and body of William Wright. Last night seemed to have taken its toll on his shoulders, as soreness seemed to bite when he began to stretch and yawn. The night always seemed too long when he couldn't sleep and too short when he could, he thought. Of course the mornings were never long enough. A cup of coffee would make for a better morning than he was having he murmured to himself in his mind. To make or not to make, that was the question. To make it meant that he would just place the coffee in the coffeemaker and let it run. To not make it meant that he would meet Rev. Al Williams at Pascal's for coffee and conversation.

That was the ritual for Sunday mornings. Pascal's had been a part of their Sundays for at least thirteen years. It was typical for people from Atlanta University to go to Pascal's on a Sunday morning before church. Al and Will had done this all through Seminary at the Interdenominational Theological Center, and nothing had changed since then, except the fact that they had gotten older and hopefully a little wiser. Al, Will's best friend and the jokester of the two, had always been the one that would make Will go to Pascal's. Will acted mostly like he didn't want to be there but deep inside he knew that he needed that to help break his nerves whenever he would preach or speak.

It had become a ritual alright. Previously it provided an opportunity for Will to explain the night before to his closest and dearest friend. However, the viewpoint had changed slightly. Before, Al was a single minister and his insights were more consistent with the viewpoint that Will exhibited. Now, after being married for about two years, his rhetoric was coarser in regard to Will and his philandering of women.

While Will was sitting in the bed still pondering whether or not to make the coffee, the phone rang. Startled slightly by the ringing, Will clumsily juggled the phone to answer it. "Hello?" He said still struggling as the headset slid in and out of position on his ear. "Hello?" He said again.

"Will, hey man, this is Al. Are you ready?" Al asked.

"Ready for?" Will replied still a little befuddled by the phone that was sliding down his shoulder at the time.

"Will, come on man! Do we have to go through this every week? You know what for, man. Pascal's, of course." Al's tone was a little as a matter of fact-like. They had done this for how long, he thought.

"Will?" Al said crisply.

"Yeah, Al?"

"How long have we been going to Pascal's?"

"Well let's see. Kristian is 14."

"Uh huh."

"And we met when she was one when both had just finished our first year at Morehouse."

"Uh huh."

"So I guess I would say that it would have to be about thirteen years."

"You are absolutely correct." Al said with a hint of sarcasm in his voice. He was not done with the questions yet though.

"So I have one more question?"

"Ok, shoot."

"Why is it then after thirteen years, you would still ask me this early on a Sunday morning where we are going as if it has changed?" Al laughed mentally. He already knew what the next response would be.

"Man, I don't know." Will responded, just as Al expected him to.

"Will, you are a trip. Still that same dude from undergrad and still that same dude from Seminary... You ain't neva gonna change boy. You ain't neva gonna change."

"Well if I did what good would I be to you? You like me for who I am anyway, dude."

"Who said that I like you Will?"

"Let's pretend I didn't hear you, shall we? Al, I will be there at 7:30, ok?" Will said as a means of cutting the banter short. He was still trying to figure out his coffee dilemma.

"The last time you said that you would be at Pascal's at 7:30 I waited for an hour before you showed up. I am not playing stupid again. I know how you black folks are. And church going black people are worse."

"What? You are so stupid, dude. Aren't you and I going to the same church?"

"So what, I know how to get to places on time. I am not black, I am white." Al said with a chuckle.

"So your punctuality makes you white, huh? Ok, white boy, I will see you at Pascal's at 7:30."

"We shall see, young grasshopper."

"Bye, Al..." Will said with a grumble.

Will hung up the phone and began to make the coffee. Everything except the coffee had been placed in its specific order so that he could be prepared to preach. His notes for his sermon were on the kitchen counter next to the coffee pot where he left them last night. His suit, a black suit nicely tailored, was pressed and ready to be worn. Shoes were lined up in the closet according to their color and the red power tie was hanging around the collar of the crisply pressed white shirt that he would be wearing that day.

The sermon was on 'Seeking the Source'. He thumbed through verses of scripture in his head to make sure that his topic and his references lined up. He mumbled a few lines to make sure that his voice was ready as he waited for his coffee to brew. Ring!

Coffee maker sounded off. The coffee was ready.

"Our plight is not to continue to seek after sin, but to seek after our Source. The Source of our righteousness, which is in Christ Jesus..." His full tone bellows throughout the house.

Will stopped to take his first sip.

7:00am.

As he looked at the time he realized that he was going to be late. He ran up the stairs stumbling and almost falling as he reached the top. He still had to take a shower, get dressed, lock up, and get his coffee of course, and head over to Pascal's and park before seven thirty. Also, he hadn't called his daughter that morning; so he had to do that before the day could even continue.

When he got to the bedroom he remembered that fact, so he picked up the phone and called his parents' house to see if everyone was up. The phone rang and Kristian, his daughter, picked up.

"Hi Daddy, what are you doing?" She said with a yawn.

"Getting ready for church Kristian, are you ready?" He asked as a father that knew how his daughter would answer. He knew that she wasn't.

"Uh…yeah, I am ready. Uh…yeah, got my clothes on and everything, Daddy." Her voice gave her lie away. He didn't even respond to her answer.

"Well, is Grandma CeCe up?"

"Yeah, she and Granddaddy are making breakfast."

"Ok. Well, tell them that I will see you all at church, ok?"

"Ok, Daddy."

"I love you Kristian."

"I love you too, Daddy.'

"Bye, baby."

"Bye."

With that call done, Will could then focus on the problems at hand. Like the fact that his behind was going to be late.

7:25am.

He was finally dressed and ready to walk out the door. He had everything that he needed and was ready to go. He walked out the door and got into his car. Will drove a Honda Accord coupe; a black one with charcoal interior. He liked his car but that was not as important to him right then as it was for him to make it to his destination on time. The problem with that was that it was going to take him more than four minutes to get from his house to Pascal's. Pascal's was located on the other side of the colleges in the West End and he lived closer to the church than to Pascal's.

Will's serial tardiness continued. No use in trying to make up time that had already been spent. He decided to appreciate the morning for what it was; a beautiful one. The air was crisp with a slight breeze. Just cool enough to let you know that it was autumn and just warm enough to let you know that it was still Hotlanta.

Will arrived at about seven forty five, not with a look of stress on his face, but with a look of expectation. As he walked through the door it became abundantly clear that the greeting would be more of the usual jokes. As well it should. He was late, and he in that vein, was adhering to the age old adage that black people can do no more than be late. So he waited for the stripes to come and they were coming.

Al laser beamed him with that 'I told you so' gleam in his eyes. The eye contact was enough; there was no need for words. The understanding had been made but Will was insistent in letting him know that the premise that he had come to was not always true.

"I had to call my daughter. I did. Had to call her..."

"Ok... Dude, trust, it's ok. I understand that you just can't be on time. I understand that. That is how it was in undergrad; that is how it is now. You haven't changed that much, dude. You are still you, man. It is what it is." Al said as he sipped his coffee. He had ordered his favorite blend of Mocha and Espresso before Will arrived. He figured he would be rather late, so instead of just one cup a carafe would be just enough. 'If I have to wait, I might as well enjoy it.' Al thought.

Al, of course, got there at seven twenty. His sensibilities had always kept him ahead. He really believed that heaven was to be a prepared place for a prepared people. He wanted to be prepared early.

"Ok, so what is the scoop?" Al asked. He knew that there was another one at the house last night. He knew the routine. The anticipation was killing him.

"What scoop?" Will questioned in a vain attempt to play coy. He knew exactly what Al was talking about.

"Dude, do we have to go through this every time? Ok... If that is what we have to do then let's begin. I will ask a question and you will answer it. Ok?" Al asked.

"Ok." Will responded.

"Did Tee come over last night?" Al asked.

"You already know the answer to that question."

"Why? Why do we have to go through this? Can't you just answer the question? Did she come over there last night?" Al vehemently implored Will.

"She came over." Answered Will in a low short tone. He knew that the inquisition would begin as soon as he got there but he was hoping that coffee and breakfast would beat the first question. Unfortunately, luck had other plans.

"And?"

"And we had sex. I mean you know what happened. We did what I always do; we had sex. Not made love, we had sex. That is what happens on Saturday nights. I have sex." Explained Will in a not so friendly tone. He was getting slightly agitated at this point about where the conversation was going. But, Al just kept it real.

"You need to find something better to do with your time because you are becoming numb to it." Al said as he continued sipping his Mocha Espresso blend. His personal carafe had steeped enough for him to drink it more quickly.

"Numb to what?" A flustered Will responded.

Al added a little cream to his mocha espresso blend as he crafted his words in response to Will's question.

"Numb to sex. It has truly become something to do for you. There is no feeling in it. No emotion. No joy. It is truly like a drug that you use to sedate that need or emptiness, or whatever within you." Al said adding a little more cream to his coffee.

"If you are going to be a whore, at least enjoy it."

"I am not a whore, I am a Pastor." Will answered with faux pride and a certain amount of sarcasm.

"No, William Wright. You are a whore." Al said as he closed his eyes to focus on his sip of coffee. As much as he loved coffee he would only allow himself to have his fix on Sundays. He always worried about the staining of his teeth. A once a week indulgence was moderation enough, he thought.

"Have been for many years now… You are just the last man to know it. Trust, everybody else does." Al said with a laugh.

"So you think this is funny, huh?"

"Yeah, dude it is." Al said laughing slightly with his head down, trying not to look Will in the eyes. He knew that he was not taking this as lightly as he was.

"You know that I am not in the mood for this right now right? You know that I am trying to get over my nerves as I go to preach." Said Will with an angry look on his face.

"Well, let me preach." Al fired as he sipped the last bit of his mocha espresso blend. He knew that statement would disrupt Will's train of thought because he would never give up his pulpit for the threat of losing it for good.

"Ok. Preach then." Will returned.

Al closed his eyes for a minute and counted down from five. "Four… Three… Two… One…"

"I am not giving up my pulpit. You don't really want it. If you wanted it then you would be the Pastor and I would be the evangelist." Will, stated his position. Al already knew that Will was just talking and that he wasn't going to allow his church to become the church of another. He knew Will, and in knowing him, he knew that he was possessive.

"The idea of giving up that pulpit still bothers you doesn't it?" questioned Al.

"No. I don't think that has ever been my issue."

"So, what is your issue? You seemed a little afraid to me. Like I was going to steal your thunder or something," stated Al as their breakfast arrived.

Al ordered his usual: pancakes and sausage with a side of buttermilk and sour cream grits and a large orange juice. Will ordered light- cheese eggs and a biscuit with yogurt and a side of fruit. Different styles of preaching, and definitely, different styles of eating.

"Why would I be?" Will declared.

"I am the Senior Pastor of First Baptist church by choice, not by chance. I was hand chosen by the founding Pastor himself, for nothing more than merit. I have served God with due diligence and I have received and am currently reaping the benefits of being in His will."

"Ok. But, let's keep it real, Will. You and I both know God is not pleased with your actions. You know that and I do too. So let's not make it seem like you are some goody two-shoes choirboy that has not sinned a day in his life. You are the chief amongst sinners." Al fired back.

"So you are saying that God has not used me?" Will inquired.

"God can use anybody." Al jested.

"Ok. I see where this is going."

"No, you don't see where this is going." Al cautioned.

"I am just saying that heaven is watching, and the eyes on the earth are not too far behind. Know that God is not pleased with the whole sex thing. I am only mentioning it because I have to keep it real with you. One, because I am your fellow minister; two because you are one of my closest friends and I care; and three…"

Al's words stopped in their tracks as his eyes followed a woman around the room. William could not see the woman without making an obvious turn around in his chair. Will tried figure out what three was but he couldn't help but notice the obvious fixation that Al's eyes had established. He didn't want to be noticed but the only way that he would even get a glimpse of this, what could only be a damsel, was to turn around and look. As he was beginning to fidget to make that turn Al murmured, "Don't turn around."

"What?" Will whispered.

"Don't turn around; I believe they are coming to you." Al said as low as possible but just high enough for Will to hear him.

In that very instant bam, there SHE was. Stephanie Flourencois in the flesh, with a man that appeared to be her man and at the place that she knew he would be. Al was right. They were coming to Will for reasons that he could have only dreamed of, or maybe only had nightmares over.

"Hi, Al!" greeted Stephanie. She gave him a hug and a kiss as if he were an old friend that she hadn't seen in a long time.

"Step, hey girl! How are you doing?" Al replied. He received the hug and kiss with open arms and with slight surprise, considering that she hadn't been that nice to him since she and Will broke up some time ago now.

"Al, you know my boyfriend Michael, right?" Stephanie asked. It was a funny question because there again they all went to the same church and though he had never formally met Michael Ross he knew his name through the grapevine.

"No, I don't think we have met. Hello, Michael, nice to meet you." Al shook his hand. The encounter was all too awkward. The interesting thing was, all of this took place right in front of Mr. Ex-boyfriend himself, William.

"So, Al, I was wondering if you had heard the news?" Stephanie inquired.

As if the blatant disrespect was not enough, William's heart began to race slightly. He knew that the question that she had just asked could only mean two things and neither was what he wanted to hear at that moment.

"What news?" Al and Will simultaneously responded. Al with interest. Will with fear.

"Well, Michael just asked me to marry him." She exclaimed with the excitement that only a new bride to be could implore. Even though this was truly William's situation to the core, both of their hearts dropped at the same time.

"Congratulations." Al sighed. He knew in his heart what it was all about, but he never in a million years thought that she would have the audacity to come up into Pascal's and do this.

"So when is the big day?" he continued.

"That is what we were hoping you could tell us. We wanted to get married around Christmas. Is that something we can do?" she asked waiting with bated breath.

"We will make the accommodations for you." Will added, barging into a conversation that he had been locked out of. He had said nothing up to that point. His heart was way too heavy for a response to the initial information.

He understood in his mind that they were no more. That part he had no problem dealing with. He also had seen her with this guy, this Michael Ross guy, and that he could get over as well. But in his mind he wondered, 'Why do this at Pascal's on an early Sunday morning? Why this guy as well? He wasn't even her type. He was not her norm or maybe he was.' The questions came from all sides of Will's mind. 'If this was who she was marrying then was I really her type?'

Will stood up and appropriately shook the hand of the man that was about to marry his former lover, and the closest thing that he had had to a wife. "Congratulations again..." He said to Michael. "Stephanie, can I talk to you for one moment about something?" he beckoned.

"Of course, Pastor," she replied stanchly.

Will walked from their table to the door pondering at his every step.

'This doesn't make sense.' he thought to himself.

'I know that we have been black history for a while but why am I feeling like this? I have seen her with this guy for a while at church, but why do I have this feeling?'

She trailed behind, still conversing with Al at the table. Will, in his mind, was still perplexed and having an emotional roller coaster ride. As he stood at the front of the restaurant, he tried to compose himself to save face. Organizing his thoughts enough to ask the questions that he felt he needed answers to.

With each step she took closer to him, Will was reminded of what he had thrown away. With each instance his composure was undone and redone. His will shifted and reassumed. Finally, she was in front of him, inches from his person, as she used to be. Her smell still cozy in his nostrils, her skin still glistened as if kissed by sunlight.

"What is it that you want to talk to me about, Pastor?" Stephanie said, as always, with a hint of attitude in her voice. There was still a disdain for Will that existed within her since they parted ways.

"You know very well what I want talk you about. This is about this wedding that you are planning. We don't have to play games, ok? I am just a little concerned about how quickly you are moving forward with this. Don't you think that you should think things through a little more?"

"I believe that thinking things through too much is what got you and me into the situation that we were in. Thinking things through is what left us so far apart and thinking things through is what ultimately ended our relationship wouldn't you say, Pastor?"

Stephanie's argument was very clear and concise and from him no rebuttal. There was nothing that he could say to that.

"Well, why at my church? Why not another?" he responded trying to be soft in his conversation.

"Why not, First Baptist? That is my home church, which is the church that I have given my time and my energy for the last six years. Why not there? I know you are the Pastor and all, but I am a parishioner. I deserve to be treated and allowed to do the things that all parishioners do."

Another good point, which Will could not ignore. She was right on everything, his own jealousy was blinding him and she knew that as well.

"You are jealous aren't you? I would have never guessed it, but you are, aren't you?" Stephanie asked, slightly chuckling.

"You knew I would be, that is why you did this. You didn't have to do this the way that you did. Why here and why now? You could have asked this question after church and you didn't have to ask it in my presence. You didn't have to go there."

"I know, but I wanted to see if I still felt anything for you and if you did the same. Obviously, I am over you but..."

"Oh, don't get it twisted." Will cut her short.

"I am over you but I am not over the fact that you are moving on this fast. I am honest enough to say that this just seems too quick for me and for you."

Stephanie stepped closer. She whispered in his ear.

"Let me tell you something, Will. I know what is best for me, and I am willing to move to do what is best for me. I know that I still care about you. I also know that there is no future with us. I am just making moves to have a future with someone that can love me and someone that I can love. So be happy for me and give me your blessings."

As she finishes, Will leaned in closer to whisper back.

"If you are happy then I am happy for you. But, I don't think that you are happy. I think that you are settling and if that is the best that you have, then ok, I hope you enjoy it. You can do better, though." He cockily ended his banter.

"Goodbye, Pastor."

She stomped away without a response. With every step he was rebuffed in knowing that somewhere in the midst of what he said there was a grain of truth. If she believed that what he said wasn't even the least bit true, she would have let him know what the truth was and would have crucified him with her words. But, somewhere in there, he was right.

As William returned to his seat, his mind was caught up in the fact that she was there, still in his heart after all this time. And the fact that she had brought this to his attention continued the possibility and hope that maybe it wasn't too late. But these things were but distractions. He had to regain some of his composure and try to prepare his mind for the things that he had to do, namely, preach. As he sat down he looked at Al and Al looked at him. Without saying a word they understood each other. Al had to say something, though. He felt compelled to let him know what he was really thinking.

"Man I couldn't live your life. You have to deal with some serious stuff. Just after dealing with the things that have transpired today, I would have been exhausted." An exasperated Al vented.

"If I had to choose between being single and a Pastor, or being married and a Pastor, I would choose being married. You just have way too much going on. How do you do it, man?"

"If it was up to me, Al, I wouldn't do it this way. But hey, I am having fun, right?" Will said sarcastically.

"I would be tired of having fun if I was you. Man, I know I am beating a dead horse but you are the Pastor of a fairly large church. God requires more from you, not less. You need to figure this stuff out before…"

"Before what??" Will cut Al's sentence short.

"Before I get caught? Before I lose my church? Are you the moral majority? I hate to remind you and I know that I am probably being devil's advocate with this but you were like me not too long ago. If you don't remember, it was I, Mr. Gigolo, who set you up with your wife. I was the one promoting you to marry her, and I was the one that was trying to make sure that you guys worked even after you cheated on her right before y'all got married. Then, again, right after you got married. Then, again, when she found out about that…"

"I know, yeah, you helped with all that." Al mumbled.

"I am just trying to return the favor, that is all. 'Cause all I see is that the writing is on the wall. I promise you brotha, if you don't change soon, it is going to get much worse before it gets better."

Chapter Two

10 am.

"It's time", rang clearly in the mind of William Fitzgerald Wright. Time to speak to the people of God about problems they faced. It's time. William was beginning to focus his mind once more on the sermon that he had prepared for the day. The time for allowing his mind to get the best of him was over. He regained his focus because in just about forty-five minutes he was going to be facing a congregation that had gone through some things throughout the week and needed a boost of energy to remain faithful and hopeful.

But, it was hard for William to remain focused when he had been tested and bested, even in the last few hours. He couldn't get the thought of Stephanie out of his head. She was still in his heart, but thoughts of the two of them were fleeting because their love was volatile. Even still, his thoughts were arrested by the newfound revelation of her pending nuptials.

Al and Will sat quietly for a moment as it continued to soak in for Will. Al, seeing that Will was focused on his sermon, focused his own energies on calling his wife to check on progress at home. Al's wife and two kids were still there getting prepared to go to church. Al's wife, Sharon, understood that long before Al had thoughts of her these rituals that her husband and Will entered in were sacred. It was more so that

Al made Will seem pathetic, and that was acceptable. Because she remembered how pathetic Al was prior to marrying her. So allowing him to spend time with his superior and friend before they went to church was understandable. And since Will was already a friend, she knew that if anything he would be leading Al on the straight and narrow.

Enough of the moment had passed for Will to make his mind up to head to the church. Focus in the Lord's house was easier for him.

"Al, I am going to head on over to the church, alright?"

"Yeah, man, that is fine. I am going to wait on the wife and kids to get up and we will be on over there, ok?"

"Alright then, dude, I will see you then. I will be going into some stuff and you are going to need the Word this week. And... we aren't going to be projecting everything on the walls for you lazy Christians so bring your Bibles with you. Alright?"

"Alright, I got you. See you in a few."

"Alright, Al, bye."

Will hopped into his Honda Accord and drove back to his house from Pascal's. His mind still all over the place, yet focused enough to realize that he needed to go over his sermon notes one last time before preaching. It was about a 10 minute drive from Pascal's back to his house. Then, about another 5 to 7 minute walk from his house to the church. He never liked to drive to the church, especially since he lived in the neighborhood.

A drive was to Gwinnett or Decatur. A drive was to visit a member that was in the hospital or at a nursing home. Walking when you are close enough to walk was always better in his mind. The walk to church was an opportunity to get closer to the Lord as he prepared to speak to His people for Him, he thought. Plus, if people pulled pop ups at his house, walking some of the time afforded him the privilege of not always being there when they expected him to be. So, in some ways it was strategic.

Will parked his car at the house. As he exited the car, and noticed that he dropped something in the driveway before he left to go to Pascal's. Will walked closer to see what the gleaming item was. To his surprise it was a glossy photograph of Kristian and Tawanna when Kristian was a baby.

The memories of an earlier time flooded back to the forefront of his mind. He realized and admitted to himself finally that he missed the time that he shared with Tawanna and he missed just that time altogether. Tawanna was not his wife and in the end things did get bad between them but he knew that things would have been a lot different; a lot better if she still were alive.

10:15 am.

William began his walk to the church. This had always been the time that he talked with God and questioned and expected the answers from Him.

"Lord, I come to you as humbly as I know how. I know that I am but a sinner but I need to understand some things, Lord. I am dealing with my, my issues and you know what they are. I need to understand why I am here left with so much but I always feel like I am the only one. I need Tawanna to be here for her little girl and I need her to be here helping me raise her. I know that everything happens for a reason- I know that. I understand that Ecclesiastes says "for everything there is a season, and a time for everything that is under the heavens". But Lord, you are a merciful God, so why not send mercy my way when I needed it, huh? Why leave me alone with this burden?"

The only response that was heard was the sound of the jaybirds singing their morning songs as the morning sun dried the dew from their feathers. The sound of cars driving down the street with music blasting the likes of T.I.'s latest and greatest. No clear word back from the Lord, though. Yet that had never kept him from continuing to ask.

"I... I love Kristian with all of my heart, but Lord, I am having difficulties with this. Then, on top of that, I have the congregation and the responsibilities of that. Then there is the other problem that I have and you know I can't keep dropping her off over my parents house while I do what I do on Saturday nights and someone not figure out what's going on. Help me overcome, Lord. Help me overcome. In Jesus' name I pray, Amen."

The closer he got to the church, the more anxiety he felt about things. This was a Communion Sunday and those sermons are supposed to be the ones that touch the heart just a little bit more than others. They are also expected to be the shorter sermons because no one wants to be in church all day. So as he went through the sermon in his mind he thought of both of those realities. Time... Relevance...

Sister Mattie Mathews was parking her car on the street where Pastor Wright was walking. The church parking lot had already become full enough for her to decide that her vehicle would be better suited for the street than the lot. As she was getting out of her car Pastor Wright decided to open the door for her.

"Good morning, Sister Mathews." William said as he patiently held the door for this beautiful older woman.

"Oh, Good Morning, Pastor Wright, how are you this morning?" She replied tipping her new church hat.

She was the sharpest lady to be seen at church that morning. Clean as a whistle and sharp as a tack. She was 67 years young but still the best dressed thing to ever set food up in First Baptist. her membership went back 30 years to 1977 whn she was then a 37 year old stewardess for the old Eastern Airlines in Atlanta. She was married back then to a pilot, which was unusual for an African American to be back then. They lived in East Point where most of the pilots at the time had found their home. Some things have changed in her life since then.

Her husband passed away in 1987 of liver cancer. She wanted to move but she couldn't. She just couldn't bring herself to leave and she loved this church that she was a member of. So, she stayed. Now she was one of the church mothers. She was respected by all and revered by some. Most believed that she was the first lady of the church when the first lady was away. But no one dared to ever let the first lady hear them say that.

Since Pastor Wright wasn't married, who would the first lady of the church be? Well, that would be Pastor Stovall's wife, Betty. Sister Betty was and had been the first lady of First Baptist Church for ages. She was a legend unto herself. She had a seat that was assigned to her. In fact she had a row that was assigned to her and her family. No one dared to take that row without the expressed written consent of the family of the founding Pastor.

She was a dame in every sense of the word. She carried herself in such an elegant fashion that her very presence exuded the essence of royalty. However, in the very same respect, she had no problem with speaking her mind whether it was in the appropriate or the not so appropriate environment. She would speak her mind and didn't care who was there. It was once said that if Jesus himself were to do something that Sister Betty didn't like, Jesus would not have to worry about reading the faces and minds of everyone. Sister Betty would let him know in 10 seconds flat.

"Good morning, Sister Betty." Williams said with a warm Christian embrace.

William always greeted his female parishioners with a warm smile and very tender embrace. He was very careful not to linger though. It is the same for the young and the old; not too much to seem fresh, but not too little to seem distant or unaffectionate.

"William, so how is my Pastor doing today?" Sister Betty replies.

"Ma'am, I am excellent and happy in Jesus this morning. I am so glad to be able to thank the Lord for another day."

"Well, that is good, son. Now, tell me something. How are you really doing?"

"Ma'am that is how I am really doing."

"Ok...Ok. I know I see something on your mind. I have been around you for long enough to know that you are not what yah said yah are but I won't press you. I know you have a sermon to preach and I am just going to rest my spirit in believing that the sermon has you looking like someone just killed your dog. I will rest my soul on that. Ok, son?" She said with an 'I am not stupid so don't act like I am' look on her face.

"Yes, Ma'am" He said knowing that she could have read him from a mile away.

"Ma'am?"

"Yes, William."

"Could we talk about this later? I do have some things on my mind and I do need someone to talk to that has no affiliation with the people or the things that I am dealing with. I need someone to talk to that will be able to give me an objective and unbiased opinion about everything. But, can we talk later, Ma'am?"

Sister Betty sighs. "You know that you don't have to ask. I love you like you were a son of mine and I don't mind talking with you later, ok?"

"Yes, Ma'am."

William again closes with a hug and continues his walk toward the entrance of the church.

He glanced down for a moment and reviewed himself and stepped back into the right frame of thought. "It's time," he said to himself. As he glanced back up, his eyes focused and were once again confronted with the beautiful hazel brown eyes of his ex's- Stephanie. William quickly glanced back down and slowed his approach as if he was a 747 trying to glide into the runway on slower crosswinds.

He slipped on into the church, knowing that the eye-to-eye transaction had taken place, but knowing also that the time for distant glances was over for the both of them. He had something that needed his undivided attention and that was the Word of God. So he ran through the Word in his mind remembering scripture.

10:30 am

Sunday school had ended. Testimony time had begun and this was when the Pastors and the deacons of the church assemble to pray and worship before the call to worship.

Pastor Wright was sitting in his study waiting and ready. He had finally gotten his focus back in the last five minutes. He was ready to deliver and he was also ready to get this day over. Time had been more of an enemy than a friend and things that would normally take moments seem to drag on for an eternity. The assembling began and Pastor Stovall walked in and prepared the assembly for a word of prayer and a word from on high.

They clasped hands one by one and kneeled as they always did for their prayer.

"Brethren, we have assembled here to worship this day. First we want to ask, that Lord You forgive us of our many transgressions. We are not perfect, but Lord we press toward the mark, for prize of the high calling In Jesus.

"Well!" bellowed Deacon Walters.

"We pray now for our choir that is preparing to sing today. We pray that their voices will be used to lift you up and you alone."

"Yes Lord," cried out Deacon Patterson.

"Now, Lord, bless our Pastor, Pastor Wright. He needs a double portion of your help and strength. He needs to be able to lean on your everlasting arms. He needs to know that you are on the main line he can tell you what he wants."

"Amen." yelped Deacon Jester.

"So, Lord, in the name of Jesus, come by here and make this place a resting place for your spirit. In Jesus' name we pray."

And they all said, "Amen."

"Pastor, can I speak to you for a moment before we march out?" Deacon Patterson asked as he slowly rose.

"Yeah, sure, what is going on?" Responds Will.

Deacon Patterson lowers his voice and quickly asks his question. "You didn't tell anybody about what we talked about did you? You know, about that stuff? You didn't' tell anyone did you?"

"I understand your concern Brother Patterson, but I don't think that is something that we should discuss right now. We can talk about that later, ok. Right now let's just praise God for what He has done for us, ok? I will speak with you in private about that later." Will said.

"But, Pastor…"

"No. Now is not the time." Will reiterated.

"I promise we will discuss it later."

One by one they filed out of Pastor Wright's office preparing for the beginning of service. One by one, each with his own take of why his position in the church made him more faithful and, in some cases, more holy.

Pastor Wright, on the other hand, came to service with much more care and much more reverence. He knew who he was. As high and haughty a position it was to be the senior Pastor of a successful church, his personal life would always make him humble.

10:45am

The call to worship ushered in the ministers and the deacons. The service always began with the sounds of the church choir and praise team leading out with praise and worship. This was the preliminary pomp and circumstance that was supposed to usher in the Spirit. The choir was forty-five men and women strong, lead by a very determined, yet very feminine director by the name of Antwon Voe.

Twon was unfortunately your typical choir director. He had a large footprint of feminism in his actions. He pranced around with such flair that he would make some women jealous. His high pitched vocals did not help his cause either. If you didn't think that he was gay by his dress then the voice would remove all doubt.

"Praise God from Whom, All Blessings Flow..."

The choir led and the congregation followed. Pastor Wright and associate ministers stood up from their seats facing the congregation as they continue in song.

You could tell by a glance at how power in the church was disseminated based on the pulpit arrangements. Pastor Wright sat in the center in the seat most appropriate for a king. He was the center attraction and the decision maker for the church. Pastor Al Williams sat to the right of the Pastor. He was truly his right hand man in the ministry and his most active Pastor who had helped in every way with the growth of the congregation.

To the left of Pastor Wright is Lil Junior, or Pastor Cleveland Stovall, Jr. His ministry was community service. He loved that because it helped him to make a name for himself outside of that church building. He knew that his day would never come in those walls, but he had his eyes always set on a split. If I can build a congregation, he thought, then I will be able to start and have my own.

To the right of Pastor Williams there sits the man who started it all. Pastor Cleveland Stovall, Sr. is the founding Pastor of this grand edifice. He has a dignified stature about him. Always down home but still very distinguished for a man of his age. He doesn't dress like he is a young man, but he also doesn't dress like he is an old one either. His very presence is always a reminder that the heritage is kept even in the transition of old to new, of former to current.

Finally, the last Pastor on pulpit is, as always, Pastor Davis. He has the least role in this church but he is a friend of the founding Pastor so you have to make concessions. In Pastor Wright's eyes, that is a small price to pay for the blessings of his ministerial mentor.

The head deacon and the second deacon were on the list. The head deacon, of course, sits at the far right hand of Pastor Wright and the second deacon sits at the far left hand.

"Praise Father, Son, and Holy Ghost. Amen." The song closes out.

11:00am

Announcements. Welcoming of Guests and Fellowship. It has always been a peculiar thing- the announcements at most southern Baptist churches. It seems to be common fare that the announcements were made by someone that had issues with public speaking but no one had let them know. This was also the case at First Baptist. There was always that one Sunday that Sister Staple would be doing the announcements.

She was an older lady about 68 but still kindly to look at. She still had her a young woman's swagger and spunk. She was the hat queen at First Baptist. Today's ensemble required a particular black hat with a front that flopped down over her right eye as she wore it. The penchant for flare and the flare for the dramatic was her personality in its simplest form. However, speaking was not what she was placed on the earth to do. There was her slight lisp. This lisp was her biggest issue by far, an issue that she would never acknowledge or even try to get help for. The greater evil was the fact that everyone heard it, and everyone had a problem with it. But no one, not even Pastor Wright himself, would bring it to her attention. Instead, whenever she would speak, the conversation of Sunday dinner would always lead to the laughable sounds of the lisping Sister Ida Mae Kincaid.

"Theses are your church announcemens" She said, always with an extra s sound at the end.

"There will be a church boards meeting at 5:30 pms. All board memberses are requested to attends this meeting. We will be discussins the upcoming budges and installation of new offices for the upcoming years.

Mass choirs will be meeting nexs Saturday to discuss the upcomings concert and celebration for Christmas. Please see Antwon Voe, ministers of music if you will not be able to attends the meetings. Its will only be for an hours.

Our fall revivals has been rescheduled for Novembers first through eighth. Please join Pastor Williams for his crusade entitled "Doing Right in Darkness." He is requesting your prayers your helps, and your supports.

Theses are your church announcemens."

Something that normally seems to be a moment in time this time around causes cringing. Yet Will was still focused on the things ahead for the day. His sermon was finished but the jitters were there. Sometimes he could appreciate the fact that he was always so frightened when he would stand up speak. Other times it was more of a bother than a blessing. This was one of those bother times.

11:05am

The welcome. Will and the founding Pastor, Pastor Stovall, head to the podium on the pulpit to welcome the guests to the church that he built. His gratitude for the growth is always shown in his welcome.

"I would like to say welcome to all who are visiting First Baptist for the first time. I am the founding Pastor, Pastor Stovall, but what you see now is the work of my senior Pastor and yours as well. That is, of course, this man standing next to me. Pastor William Wright." Pastor Stovall said gleaming with pride.

"Thank you, Pastor Stovall. And with all that said, will all of our first time visitors please stand."

About thirty people stood up and the congregation applauded the number with a few amen's mingled in for good measure.

"Amen." Will responded himself to the volume of visitors.

"On behalf of this body of Christ, known as First Baptist of West End, we would like to welcome you to our home, that we hope to make your home. If there is any way that we can assist you in your spiritual walk and development, please let us know. Now that you have been here once, we would like to welcome you back, because once you have been you are family.

Now, family, greet each other in the way that we do here at First Baptist."

Pastor Wright proceeded to make his way from the pulpit to the congregation to greet his daughter and talk with his parents first. This had been his routine since being a Pastor at this church. He spoke to his parents, then his daughter, and then the rest of the congregation, but most importantly, Sister Betty before the rest of the congregation. That was his order of operation.

"Mom, how are we doing today?" He asked.

"Well, you seem to be doing ok. Why won't anyone tell Sister Kincaid that she can't speak?" his mother asked sincerely.

"She is always getting up there to speak and everybody that hears her knows that she can't speak but still y'all let her prance her behind up there and..."

"Momma, I know. We all know. I was really just trying to make sure that Kristian has been behaving and ain't no boys been calling her on that cell phone she has." Pastor Wright interrupted.

"Well, I didn't know I was supposed to have her under

twenty-four hour surveillance. She is fine. She will be fine. She is not you nor is she her mother. You have to let that go, Son." His mother cautioned.

"We will talk about this later mom. I love you. Where is Kristian anyway?"

"She sat in the balcony with her friends. She is old enough to leave my side and I had you, so, I guess..."

"Yeah, I know, Mom. You have been doing this much longer than I have. Anyway, we will talk more about this after church today."

"Ok. Now, worry about the sermon, not Kristian," she said dismissively.

He moved on, rather quickly, giving Sister Betty Stovall a kiss on the cheek and making small talk with some of the other members of the congregation before returning back to the pulpit.

"Consider yourselves welcomed and at home," he closed.

11:20am

The choir sang 'Oh, Happy Day' and the church got into the groove while getting its praise on. You can tell how well a choir at this church has lifted the congregation based on the reaction of those in the balcony. The balcony is always the last to respond to anything that is going on. Twon did his job well. As he directed you could always see his feminine side come out. The most interesting part of it all is the fact that the more feminine he moved the more lush, vivid and soulful the choir sounded.

11:30am:

Tithe and Offerings. The choir sang some gift giving music as the collection plates were passed around, in some cases like hot potatoes rolled in foil. It has always seemed that no matter what church you go to when it comes down to the money, everybody has a very strong reason to give or not to. They can all justify it through the word of God as well. This church is no different.

Will was watching the collection plates as they are being passed around. He knew that it was almost his turn and then communion. As his mind turned to Stephanie, Will looked out into the congregation to see if he could see her and her man seated like the happy couple that they were supposed to be. When he didn't see them he was a little disappointed. 'No matter,' he said to himself, yet his expression says otherwise. Will's hands were cold and clammy. He had a slight shrill going down his spine. He was trying his best to be focused on the situation at hand.

'In about ten minutes I am going to preach about the goodness of the Lord and the grace that He has given through Jesus Christ, His Son. But, I can't get my mind off someone that I have been with, have broken up with and have moved on from. I need to get a grip' he says.

Deacon Jester motions the congregation to stand. "Let us pray," he says.

"Father, we thank you for this tithe and offering that has been collected for the continuing of your church for your purposes. Lord, bless those that gave. Please bless those that had the desire to give but had it not. And Lord, bless those that gave not but had it to give. May their hearts be changed by your mercy and your love. In Jesus' name we pray. Amen." The congregation repeated with a hearty amen.

11:45am

Hymn of Meditation and Sermon. The moment of truth had finally come and Pastor Wright was now ready. Forget everything that had happened that day. Forget everything that had happened that week, for that matter. It was time to speak to God's people about His plan for their lives. He was ready to make that transition and hoped to save a soul in the process.

He stood up, walked to the podium, and began to open his mouth.

"Good morning, First Baptist." Will said with his Pastor's voice in perfect form.

"Good morning," they replied.

Not as enthusiastic a reply as he expected, so he greets them once again.

"I said, Good morning First Baptist."

They replied with a louder roar, "Good morning!"

"Now that is a better response from the people of God in God's house on a Sunday morning. I am again, glad to be in the house of worship once and I hope that the Lord has kept you in good health throughout this week. Now, let us open with a word of prayer."

He pauses and swallows, lowers his head and begins to pray.

"Lord, as I live and have breath, I will follow you. Forgive me of my sins and always allow me to be used as a vessel to impart your truth to your people. Take me out of me, Lord, that I might only say and do those things that are pleasing in your sight. Allow your people to hear only the word that is from Thee. Let your Bible be our guide and your Holy Spirit our Mentor, in Jesus' name we pray. Amen."

Then he began his sermon. Vocally, he has a voice that can be as moving as Martin Luther King, Jr. His style has always been that of a teacher preacher, with charisma to spare. He would have it no other way than to have people learn something and write down what he says than to just go by what he says. In his mind he knows that empowerment is necessary if any group of people want to grow and succeed.

"The Bible says that any man having placed his hands upon the plow and looked back, is not fit for the kingdom of God. Why is that important? That means that you can't start something, you can't begin walking this race and not see it through till the end.

How do you do that? I can't see myself going back to Satan after walking with God. I don't know how people come out the church as if the world has something better. What does the world have that is going to last?"

A loud amen from Sister Smith allows him to catch his breath for one quick moment. He drinks some water quickly and continues with his message.

"So we have to hold onto the unchanging everlasting hand of God. I know that the church isn't perfect. I am here, so I know that it isn't perfect. But, I also understand that we are striving for completeness in Christ. Paul said it best, 'I press toward the mark, toward the prize of the high calling in Christ Jesus.' That is our mark, brothers and sisters!"

Congregation claps and the mood is uplifted by his words.

"Are you pressing toward that mark? Is your hand firmly placed upon the plow and are you looking forward? Satan wants us to keep our minds on yesterday. See, yesterday is just that, yesterday. Satan knows that the longer he has you focused on where you were, you can never get to where God has predestined you to be. You can never have the purpose, or goals that God has for you if you can't get out of yesterday.

How this was supposed to work out. Or, how this was supposed go. It didn't go that way. So now get up and try something new. Because God is still there and He will always be there. He has a plan for you and by the time you get it, you will be ready for the plan. So focus on Him. Let the Lord be your Guide and you won't have to worry about the rest."

"Amen," The congregation responds.

He continued and went through several texts to illustrate the points that he was making.

"Jesus said that, 'I am the way, the truth and the light: No man cometh unto the Father but by me.' If we desire to get closer to the Father, we need to direct all of our attention to

Jesus. There is an old hymn that we used to sing that said, 'turn your eyes upon Jesus. Look full in His wonderful face. And the things of this world will grow strangely dim, in the light of his glory and grace.' We need to heed the words of this song."

He walks off the pulpit with his wireless headset attached to his ear like a rock star at a concert. The church, recently upgraded the sound equipment to include this new wireless microphone.

"I am going to be mindful of the fact that it is communion Sunday and I am going to close. But, I would be remiss if I did not allow someone the opportunity to get to know the greatest Man that ever lived. I am glad to know Him and be able to call Him my friend. His name is Jesus.

See, I believe in Jesus Christ. Not because I am a minister. No, I knew Him before then. Not because I was raised in the church. No, because I have made many mistakes. So, being raised in the church did not stop me from being raised in the streets as well. But, I came to know Him for myself. I had to walk with Him. I had to call on Him on those cold nights, when I didn't know which way to go! That is why I can testify and say that it is good to know Jesus.

Not because of what Sister Betty says. Not because of what Brother Jester says. Not even because of what my mother and father say. I had to have my own testimony. I had to have my own walk. And now that I know Him… I can't turn back. I can't go back. He has been too good to me.

So the doors of the church are open… He is welcoming you with open arms."

As he looked out into the congregation, he could tell that the Spirit was working on someone. In his mind he was thinking that he had done what the Lord had required of him. In the congregation, the faces of the people look as if God, Himself, had come down and touched them. There were tears: of joy, of pain and release, and of hope. And, there was someone that was coming forward to join the church.

Will began to give his best rendition of a song that he felt was so fitting for his message at this point.

"He touched. Ooh, he touched me," he sang sweetly.

As he began, the choir joined in and began to finish the rest. Then the congregation followed suit. What started out as one person joining the church, end up with two, then four. Then six. Then eight. Then twelve: Then it finally ended with seventeen. But the one that caught the Pastor's eye was the one that he, himself, wished would never have joined his church. That was Michael Ross, Stephanie's fiancé.

Of all the people to reach that day, of all the people to come up to join the church, he couldn't help but wonder, why him? Why today? Why right now? Especially, after finding out about the wedding and the engagement and everything that had just happened but a moment ago, why? He was just not quite ready for that.

He held his composure though. Because Pastor Wright understood that he was a man of God before he was man. When he walked into the church, that was who he was and is- a Pastor. Pastor William Fitzgerald Wright: Senior Pastor of First Baptist Church at West End. God's work is his focus.

As he comes forward he shakes Will's hand and they embrace. Then he takes a seat on the front pew with the rest who felt compelled to give their lives to Christ or needed special prayer.

"Because this is communion, and because the Holy Spirit has so compelled me, I am going to take those who are serious about becoming a part of this union; those who want to be linked up with the Source of all their strength; I am going to take you down to the watery grave today for baptism. Can I get an Amen?"

In response there was a thunderous Amen.

"I know I said that I wouldn't be long today, but I have to do what the Lord would have me to do. I will continue to do what the Lord asks me to do. Amen."

And the church said, "Amen."

"Now, I will address these the candidates for baptism." Pastor said as he returned to the pulpit.

By this time he had sweat rolling down his brown face onto the collar of his white oxford shirt to the point where the collar was completely wet.

"To the candidates for baptism, I commend you on your decision to join this church. I pray that we are able to be a ministry unto you as you grow in Christ and that you would be an asset to us in witnessing to others. Now in joining with God's house, we have some things that you must accept to become a part of our church. As we go over these precepts, please respond in the affirmative if you believe this to be true. Your response should be yes or yea, no or nay. Amen?"

And the candidates responded, "Amen."

"Do you believe that Jesus is the Son of the Living God and sits at the right hand of the Father: The first born from the dead, and the intercessor for our sins?"

And the candidates responded, "Yea."

"Do you believe that the word of God preaches the baptism by immersion and that this was a prerequisite for salvation as described by Jesus, Himself?"

And the candidates responded, "Yea."

"Finally, do you commit yourself to a new life in Christ, and in this church that you might be a witness and a testimony to His goodness and love?"

And the candidates responded, "Yea."

"Church, what is your pleasure?" Pastor Wright inquired.

"So moved."

"Is there a second?" Pastor Wright questioned.

"Second!" A sister in the balcony screams out, and with that the congregation votes.

"All in favor say I."

"I!" The church replies. The very sound shook the foundation of the church.

"This is a little bit of a surprise. I am glad that I can still trust in the Lord and He delivers. Like they always said, 'He doesn't come when you want Him, He comes right on time.'" The Pastor says after that thunderous response.

"Well, let's bury the old man and raise the new one," he says.

Pastor baptized 14 souls for the Lord. They had communion and said the closing benediction at about 2:00pm. Just enough time to not be completely late, but not enough time to say that he adjusted his sermon for the communion service. Another high time in Zion, but Pastor Wright knew that this was all the Lord's doing and none of his own.

He understood still that he had a lot of growing to do to be the man that God wanted him to be, But that would come in due time. Sooner than he actually thought or could ever know.

Chapter Three

"Kristian! Come on, it's time to go."

Will yelled lightly to his daughter who was still in the balcony talking to some boy. He didn't really know that boy or whose son he was, but he was processing the idea of running a background check on him.

"Daddy, why?" asked Kristian to her father with a look of disgust on her face.

"He was just a friend of mine. Why do have to be like that?"

"You don't even know that boy. How do you know that boy? You don't know him. He doesn't go to your school."

"He goes to your church and you don't even know him?" She questioned. "I thought you were a people Pastor. How can you be that when you don't even know your congregation?" She says with sass in her voice.

"Who do you think that you are talking to?" He replied sternly.

"I don't think that you know who you are talking to. You need to watch that mouth of yours before I have to watch it for you."

"Yes, daddy." She said with a more subdued tone.

"Anyway, we are about to go back to your grandparents' house, so if you have anything left up there you need to get it. I need you to introduce me to this guy too, because if you are going to be all up in each other's face like what I just saw I need to know who he is." He said authoritatively, as any protective father would.

"Yes, daddy." She replied again as she headed back to the balcony to get her stuff.

Will walked out the front door of the church shaking his head. His mother, Cecilia Wright, could see his perplexed look and asked the obvious question.

"Will, what is wrong with you?"

"Let me ask you something, Ma. Was I a handful when I was her age? I know I was, but was I as bad as her?"

She laughed.

"Are you serious, Son?" She asked.

"Yeah. She is so sassy. And she is kinda hardheaded and stubborn. I mean…"

His mother cut him short.

"She is your child! You are, were, and will be all those things and more. You were the most stubborn child I had ever seen!"

"Ok."

"And by the way, stop being so hard on her and let her be a girl that is fourteen and trying to figure out what it means to be a little girl growing into a woman." His mother scolded.

"A woman? She is still a little girl. She has a long time to go before she becomes a woman." He rebuked.

"Will, you know she has her cycle right?"

Will's eyes grow as wide as his eyelids would allow.

"What? What cycle?"

"Her period. Her menstrual cycle. Duh." His mother said with a look of utter amazement on her face.

"Please tell me that you knew that? Please say that you knew that, William Fitzgerald Wright?" She said in her mommy voice.

"I am just kidding. Of course I knew that. Who do you think gets the pads?" He responded.

"Well what you don't know is that she has had a boyfriend

already. She is growing up and you ain't no spring chicken yourself. You need to figure out how to identify with your daughter because we have been talking…"

"What has she been saying to you?" he asked firmly.

"Now, don't you get that tone with me! You better calm yourself, young man."

"Yes, ma'am," he said taking a little of the bass out of his voice.

"We will talk about this later, because she is comin' up right behind you," she said directing him with her eyes to look over his shoulder.

Kristian walked up to the car and noticed the expressions that were on her father and grandmother's face. She knew that they had been talking about her.

"Were y'all talking about me? She questioned with an attitude, smacking her lips.

"See, Ma, this is what I am talking about. All that attitude; I am about sick of you and that attitude." He said scolding her.

"Will, you calm down. This is not that serious so just calm down. Kristian, don't you see that there are two grown people in front of you talkin'?"

"Yes, ma'am."

"So you need not come up here talkin' to us like we are some of your friends. I expect better of you. And what I expect, I get. Do you understand me?"

"Yes, ma'am." She replied with a lower frowned face. Her question was really geared toward her father and because he had just attacked her earlier.

"Now both of you get in this car if you're coming to my house for dinner." She said as she proceeded to put her seatbelt on and turn the ignition.

If they didn't know that she was serious before then, they knew it at that moment.

Pastor's parents lived in the Adamsville neighborhood of Wilson Mill Rd. They had lived there for a long while. In their

36 years of marriage they had spent 30 of them in their house at 2647 Wilson Mill Rd. It was not a very big house. It was modest but it was always home for them and their son.

It had become a second home for his daughter as well. She got the love and attention of her grandmother that she so desperately needed. Her grandmother understood that as well and didn't mind it either. With William being the only child and her nieces and nephews all grown up she had a longing that was met when Kristian was born. Back then things were different but she has always loved her granddaughter. She once said, 'Hate the sin, love the sinner.' She was referring to the way that everything happened. But never Kristian; she was her joy.

The ride there was riddled with silence because of the apparent disagreement between daughter and father. Grandma was determined to break the silence and kill the drama between the two of them.

"So, is this going to be a trip of silence or is the family going to talk?" She asked sarcastically.

"If this is going to be a ten minute trip of silence then I will turn on some of my music that you know I love to play."

"Nooooo!" They both said at the same time with the same amount of concern.

"Daddy, I am not a baby anymore. I just wish that you would understand that. I am a teenager. I just want to be treated like a teenager. I have feelings and I want to do stuff."

"Stuff like what? I know you are not talking about what I think that you are talking about? What don't I let you do?" Pastor Wright asked, with a stern look on his face.

"Why does it always have to be about sex, Daddy? I am not even talking about that. I was talking about just going out. I am tired of you not allowing me to go anywhere. What is going to happen? I am old enough to take care of myself. I am."

"Really?" He questioned with a slight chuckle.

"Yes. I am 14 years old and I am practically grown," she returned.

In his mind he remembered saying the same thing when he was younger, that he was grown at thirteen years old. It was almost nostalgic to hear his own flesh and blood repeat something that he had said so many times over. In the same breath it was problematic, because if she would say the same things that he said then he knew that she would feel and act the same way that he would as well. That scared him more, sometimes, than the devil, himself.

"Can you pay a bill? If you are grown now, can you pay a bill? I just want to know because grown people pay bills." He said cynically.

"Ok. So I see that if I allow you two children to talk you will not resolve anything." His mother said playing referee.

"Kristian, your father feels that you are not ready to be dating and I agree with him on that. However, William I agree with Kristian that she should be allowed to go out. I believe that if there is a group date or group event that is going to take place you should let her go, as long as it is supervised by a parent that you can trust. Now, that means, that you, Kristian, if you want to go out you are going to have to ask your father. Not me, ok?"

"Yes, ma'am." Kristian replied.

"Will, it's time to let your daughter grow up. She is getting older and she is not five anymore. You need to get used to this because it is going to get worse. Also, you need to get the numbers of the parents at her school and at church if you are going to let her go out, ok?

"Yes, ma'am." He replied.

By that time, they had made it to the house. William's father, Charles, was at home already finishing up the dinner that had been started that morning by Will's mom. The aroma that permeated from the seams of the house, was sweet of sweet potatoes, and fried and baked chicken. The second whiff smelled of collard greens, split peas and macaroni and cheese.

With all the food that he smelled, Will began to wonder if this meal was just for him and his daughter, or was there something that his mother forgot to tell him.

"Ma?"

"Yes, Will?" She answered back as they proceeded to walk to the front door.

"Is there something that you need to tell me about this dinner before we go in?"

"Well, there will be a few people from the church here to eat with us. Just a couple of friends that we decided to share our home and food with today."

"Uh huh. Do I know any of these people from our church?" He replied as his eyes expressed his suspicion.

"Well, lets see. There is Sister Betty."

"Ok."

"Sister Charmaine and her new baby."

"Uh huh."

"And I think Sister Walters is coming."

"Ok."

"I think we also invited Lil Junior."

"Why, ma? Why?" He asked.

He knew she was up to something. He had smelled the food, and he knew some of the cars that were there looked too familiar to be just strangers.

That information changed this dinner from relaxing, to a hostile environment in 10 seconds flat. Now, Will had to deal with the annoying chess game of words that happened whenever they are at the dinner table together.

"Ma, you really need to talk to me before you go inviting people to the house for Sunday dinner. I need to know these things so I can have an idea of what I am getting myself into."

"I know, Son, but we got on your daughter and I just forgot to tell you. I am sorry if this dampens your mood but I just couldn't invite around him when he is standing right there in the conversation. That would be rude. Besides, you are both preachers. Don't you think that whatever differences that you both have should be resolved and a truce be made between you?"

"Yeah. Yeah. You are right, but as soon as we sit down for dinner he begins with the inquisition. I am just tired of him trying to prove that he can be a better Pastor than me. His father made that decision, not me. I had nothing to do with it. I was just being the person that I am."

She understood the challenge, but believed in her son.

"I understand that, Will. But I also understand that you have to be a bigger man and change the way that you two operate. This jealousy or whatever it is won't end until you make the change for him."

"Why should I? I can handle it. I hope that he can." Will said with a smirk of cunning.

The table was set and the food was already ready as they walk in. Charles, Will's dad, was wearing the 'Kiss the Cook' apron that he was given for his birthday a long time ago. He had that old Wright charm going on as he was just putting the final touches on his world famous spicy blackened turkey stew. Famous for its bite, of course, with a name like that.

Will strutted about the living room with the same down home swagger that he moves about the church with. Always engaging, and always interested. There were no more than about 15 people from the church there in total, not including him, his daughter and his parents.

Finally, they sat down to eat. Of course, prayer is needed before dining, so Will's dad asked him to pray.

"Yeah, Will pray." Lil Junior responded.

"Let us pray. Father we thank you for this food prepared before us. We ask, oh Lord, that as we are seated to eat this food that you would forgive us of our sins and cleanse us of our unrighteousness. Now, bless this food, bless the hands that prepared it and allow us always to be truly thankful. In Jesus' name we pray. Amen."

As they lifted up their heads, Lil Junior said another prayer.

"And Lord let us please remember that all things come from you and that you have provided us with this, in Jesus' name amen."

And they all said amen, albeit, with a puzzled look on their faces.

As they proceeded to pass the food around the table, Will got up and excused himself from the table for a moment and went into the kitchen.

"Mama, can I see you in the kitchen for a moment?" He said, trying not to have a tone but doing a horrible job at doing it.

She got up and headed into the kitchen.

"What is it?"

"You see what I am talking about right? This is what I was saying was going to happen. He has already started."

"Will, don't get so caught up in that. Just let it go. I am going back to the table."

She walked back to the table. In short order, Will followed thereafter. Then conversations continued, and of course there were the occasional swipes at him about his sermon and the like, but Will just ignored it. He just let it go like his mother had asked him to. She did begin to notice what Will had been talking about.

After about three or more times seeing him make constant stabs at her son she had had enough. It was time for a mother to be a mother and step in on her son's behalf.

"I have had enough." She said.

Most people were puzzled, but Sister Betty had picked up on what was going on. She just watched to see how this new and exciting piece of the gossip puzzle was going to play out.

"Ma, I got this. Don't say anything to him. I will handle this myself." Said Will to his mother.

Will then got up from the table and walked toward the door.

"Pastor Stovall, can I speak to you outside please?"

"I am not finished with my dinner. Can't it wait until after I finish." He replied with a devilish grin on his face.

He knew what he was doing and he felt like he did it well. This was another opportunity for a character that he considered flawed to be placed out in the open. The character was Will's.

"Pastor Stovall, I believe that if your food gets cold, my mother won't mind putting it in the microwave to heat it up. I think that should remedy that problem, however as far as what I need to talk to you about, that is something that needs to take place right now."

"Ok… Since it can't wait."

Lil Junior got up from the table and slowly dragged himself outside to see what it was that he had such an urgency to talk with him about. As if he didn't already know.

"Lil Junior, I am not going to let you continue with this little game that you're playing at dinner today. It is embarrassing and I don't like it. IF you have a problem with me, get it out into the open and let's deal with it. I am tired of this." He said wagging his finger within inches of Lil Junior's face.

Now, Lil Junior has never been punkish. And, he didn't take too kindly to someone wagging a finger in his face. Lil Junior may have been his nickname but at six feet two inches tall, weighing in at 280 pounds, Lil was not what, he was. So, Will's five feet ten inch frame with just 210 pounds on it would be easy work for him.

"Listen Will, I am tired of watching you think that you are the one who runs this church. The church members and the constituency run this. I am a part of the board just like you and I am here to tell you that I don't think you are doing what's best for First Baptist. I think it is about 'Will the star' shining."

"You know what? I am so glad that you are not the only member of this church." Will said pacing back and forward.

"Because if you were, there is no telling what direction this church would be going in."

"What is that supposed to mean?" Lil Junior yelled vehemently.

Will took a few steps back just in case things got out of hand. He knew that what he was about to say might just be a little insulting so he used common sense to make his case.

"Let's just say, as I have said before, your father knew what he was doing. He did the right thing. Get over it. He wanted his church to grow and it has. The Lord has blessed. Don't you think that's good?"

"I could have done better."

"No. You couldn't have. See, you just don't get it. You don't have the right type of spirit. You are sitting here talking about 'Will the star' like I am trying to promote myself. This isn't even about me. I am just trying to do the will of the Father. You are the one trying to promote yourself. It is so about you. That is why you aren't the Senior Pastor, because you still don't get it."

"Well, fuck you!" Lil Junior said as he spat at his feet and began to walk towards him.

"You know what, Lil Junior? I am not going to fight you because I don't have to. You are still fighting with yourself and your decisions. But, I will promise you this right here. If you do not leave this property in the next five minutes, it will be the worst mistake of your 45 year life."

Lil Junior got within inches of Will's face and looked him in his eyes. He could see for the first time since he had known Will that he was not about to back down and that he was not afraid of him nor intimidated. In fact, when he looked into his eyes he saw that he was actually waiting for him to give him a reason.

Lil Junior also had realized that he had an audience. It would not prove to be what was best for his career or for his plans to be the Senior Pastor, if he got into a fight at the house of the Senior Pastor's mother after she so graciously invited him. All of these factors go against his plan.

"I will see you at the board meeting." He said, slightly bumping his shoulder into him as he turned around to head to his car.

"I will make sure I bring your plate." Will yelled smugly as he watched him walk to his car. Will wouldn't let his back be turned until Lil Junior got in his car. He didn't trust the situation nor did he trust Lil Junior.

As expected, Lil Junior skidded out of the driveway like some madman on his way to complete a death wish. As Will turned around to head back into the house, he noticed his audience in the living room window where they had been the whole time. His mother was proud that he had not allowed his pride and his manhood to get in the way of his faith and his responsibility to God. Sister Betty saw otherwise.

"I don't care that Lil Junior is my son, Will should have beat his ass." Sister Betty said.

"Sister Betty!" Will's mom said with shock.

There was a hush after that. Everyone was looking at Sister Betty.

"Well, it's the truth. I can only speak the truth, right? The Lord knows, I am so sick and tired of him being so spoiled and so brat-ish. He needs to be a man and change his attitude. I told him a long time ago, that attitude of his was going to get him nowhere, and get him there fast."

"I understand, Sister Betty." Will's mom said.

"If it wasn't for his father he probably wouldn't have done anything with his life. He was lazy then and he is lazy now. There is no such thing as entitlement. He needs to learn that. That is his problem. He thinks at 45, that we owe him something. We don't own him a doggone thang!" Sister Betty said.

Chapter Four

The house began to empty about a quarter till five. Plenty of people were getting plates wrapped in aluminum foil to take home to be eaten later. There were plenty of long conversations before the final goodbyes for the evening. For the others, they would be seen again at the business meeting to rehash some of the church problems, concerns and most importantly, the money.

This board meeting would be different, though. In light of the events of the evening, there would no doubt be talk of the potential fight between the two prominent Pastors. If not on the main stage, it would definitely be an underlying theme. For Will after what just happened, he would like to sit Lil Junior down. He knew that probably wouldn't fly with Pastor Stovall, Lil Junior's father, and he was going to have to talk to him before he could bring it before the board. He knew that he had to act fast though because with Lil Junior, the story spinning had already begun. Half the board was already in his corner. With the relationships they had with him, they would always be sympathetic to his cause. And, that being known, reiterated in Wills' mind what he already knew. Time was not on his side.

"Mom, I am so glad that Kristian was not at the adult table and was in her room for all of this mess that took place out here." He said, as he finished clearing the plates from the table.

"You know, Will, I kinda wish she did get to see all of this." She responded.

Will was dumbfounded. 'Why would my mother want my daughter to see this?' he thought.

"It would give her another perspective on what it means to be a man... and not only that, it would let her know the kind of character that you have. She needs to know that you are a man about your word. You aren't a hypocrite. That you actually practice what you preach, and in doing so you don't have to be soft about it."

As she finished her point, Will pondered to himself, why does she always have to have such good points? He proceeded to go and see what Kristian was up to in her make shift bedroom.

He opened the door to find her on the phone, as usual. It was as if the phone was surgically attached to her left ear. She was on the phone so much that an ear print of wax was left on the phone after she got off.

"Kristian, I need to talk to you so get off the phone." Will said in his irritated deep booming daddy voice.

Kristian apparently hadn't learned from earlier. She continued her conversation as if she didn't hear her father even though the person on the phone heard him as clear a day.

"Kristian, I am not going to ask you again, so please do it now." He said issuing his second and final warning.

"Ok, Dad. Give me a minute." She responded, fanning her hand dismissively.

"I have already given you enough time. Get off the phone. Right now!" He said, getting more and more frustrated with each passing second.

"Ok, girl, my dad is trippin' so I am going to have to let you go. I will talk to you later. Bye." Kristian said with attitude to the girlfriend she was on the phone with.

"What is it?" She sighed.

"I am going to ignore that because I don't have time for

arguing with you, little girl. I came in here to let you know that I am leaving and I will be back to pick you up after the board meeting. Ok?"

"Yeah, Dad, I got it. You are going to the board meeting and I will be spending the rest of my Sunday afternoon with Granma and Granpa. I understand that once again I will be trapped here with nothing to do but watch TV."

"Ok. I don't have time so I am going to let you get away with that, but you are really pushing it. I will talk to you later and we really do need to talk." Will said.

He gave her a quick kiss on her cheek and said goodbye to his mom and dad on his way out the door.

He didn't drive so Will took his mother's car to the church for the meeting. His mom's 1999 Camry was nice but he was used to his car. Beggars can't be choosers though, so he drove it on off to the church anyway. He couldn't get his mind off all of the things that had transpired that day. Stephanie, and that situation. Lil Junior and his wack personality. Stephanie soon to be husband getting baptized, where did that come from? Finally, his daughter and her little attitude, which he knew that he was going to have to adjust. Just so much for one to have to deal with in one day, he said to himself.

As he drove up into the church, Will scanned the church parking lot. It almost seemed as if everyone was there a little early. He noticed that Al's car was already there as was Lil Junior's car. Great, he thought. Will knew that Lil Junior would have already given Al, and anyone that would listen, his rendition of the events of the evening. And that would only prove to make his stance harder to move on.

Will headed to his study to get his mind ready for the board meeting. Board meetings were no walk in the park. You saw the dark side of a person's character at board meetings. The language was awful. They didn't care who you were or how long you had been in church or anything. They just wanted what they wanted and said what they needed to say to get it.

Board meetings reminded him that Christians weren't perfect, just saved.

Will sat down at his desk and lowered his head in an attempt to get a word in to the Lord. Every time there was a board meeting Will would say a prayer before he went down to the fellowship hall to talk with the board. Under normal circumstances, Will's eye was very even keel. Board meetings weighed down on him like two dumbbells on each shoulder. So he needed that extra prayer, just to make it through.

"Lord, I am not perfect, just saved. Remind me of that at this board meeting so that I can say and do the things that show others that this church board does not think it is better than its congregation. In Jesus' name I pray, amen."

He lifted his head from his prayer and in that same moment, in walked Al.

"Al, what's going on?" Pastor asked. He was glad to see Al's friendly face before he strolled down into the lion's den.

"You know your boy caught me before I could even get a chance to talk to you, right?" Al replied.

"Yeah, I know. I know. I am sure that he couldn't wait to give you his version of how the events of this afternoon occurred." Pastor Wright said with sarcasm written all over it.

"Yeah, and you know that I didn't believe a word of it. I know that you weren't the one who started it, which is what he said. I know that he was being his usual stupid self. He needs to get a life and leave you alone."

"I know, but what can I say? He has it out for me and I haven't even had a chance to talk to his dad yet." Will stated.

"I think he may have beaten you to that too." Al suggested.

"Why do you say that?"

"Because I think I saw Pastor Stovall Sr.'s truck out there when I got here and I have been here for about an hour."

Will looked down at the floor, and tried to remember how long it had been since Will told Lil Junior to get out.

"It's been about an hour since I told him to leave my mother's house, so I am guessing he has been up here all this time."

Will hopped up from behind his desk and headed past Al for the door.

"Let's go on and head down then. I will deal with it, however it comes."

The board consisted of twenty people in positions in the church. There was the head deacon and his assistant head deacon; the board of Pastors, which was four in all; the head usher, head deaconess and her assistant; treasurer and her assistant; minister of music; hostess, singles ministry, marriage ministry, children's ministry; Sunday school superintendent, and head of communications for the church. There was also the church secretary and church clerk, plus you had the historian for the church who kept the records of the changes that the church had made in the last 30 years.

The historian had no voting power at the meetings and neither did the church clerk. The secretary, however, could vote even though she was a paid worker for the church. She kind of worked for the Pastor to a degree, but she seemed to vote opposite him on most things.

The founding Pastor, Reverend Stovall, Sr. represented the senior citizens and their ministry. He counted as vote number Twenty-one. If it were ever split down the middle his vote or the vote of the Presiding Pastor, which was Will, would be the deciding vote. Let the games begin.

As Will took his seat in the middle of the horseshoe setup, board meeting came to order. As he sat, he stood back up. His spirit just wasn't right within him.

"Before we start this meeting, I would like to begin with a word of prayer. Let us pray. Father God, we thank you for being with us this day. We ask, oh Lord, that you would forgive us of our sins and cleanse us of our unrighteousness. We acknowledge, Lord, that we are not perfect, but we are saved. Help us to remember this when we consider the situation of others that may have issues that we are going to try to help them with. Please bless us all and keep us in your favor. In Jesus' name I pray, let the people of God say, Amen."

Will was intent on making this a very short board meeting. "I am letting you know, now, that I really want this board meeting to be focused. So, let's limit the talking and get right down to business. If it isn't about church business then it has no business in this meeting, ok?"

Silence from board.

"Ok. What is first on the agenda?" He asked.

The secretary went through the minutes from the last board meeting.

"At our last board meeting we review the stipend that has been given to the minister of music, we discussed it, but we never came up with a plan to increase, hold, decrease, or suspend. We also discussed the leftover proceeds from the building fund that had not been transferred to any other account. Since the church renovations had been paid off and the church is paid for in full, it was suggested that the remaining funds be transferred to the poor people's fund to up the coffers for that. We also discussed what would be our church's policy for teen pregnancy since we have had about seven teenagers come up pregnant in the last year, some of which have been very involved in the church. The record shows that the board had initially sought to censor them for one year, which in turn, meant that they would not be able to do anything in the church for one year. The dissenting concern was that this would lead them away from the church and would cause greater concern for these young people's future. The issue was tabled until the next board meeting. We also discussed end of year activities and the annual church budget. That is all that I have for the minutes."

"Board, what is your pleasure with regards to the minutes." Will asked.

"So moved."

"It has been moved upon. Is there a second to the board's decision?"

"Seconded," replied the First Elder.

"All in favor say I?" Pastor beckoned.

"I," the board stated.

"The minutes have been approved, and now we can go to the next item on the agenda."

The secretary looks through the notes.

"The old business is in regards to the church's response to the phenomenon of teenage pregnancy."

Pastor stood up and began to pace.

"I am a Pastor that has been ostracized by this very issue. You know that my daughter was born outside of the confines of marriage. I also understand that we have to do something to set a precedence that we do not condone this type of behavior. Also, that we will not continue to promote the talents of people that willfully sin and not only hurt their future but their present. It is not my desire to have any member of our church to leave because they feel like we were not there for them, but in turn, our God has a standard. We are all to attempt and be attempting to grow in His goodness not to be willfully sinning."

As the Pastor finished his speech, he thought to himself of his own sins and how he was dealing with the fact that he is doing the same things that those kids are doing. He felt the stamp of hypocrite on his forehead.

He pondered intensely, 'what can my answer be? I am addicted to sex? I have sex with a different woman every Saturday before I get up on Sunday to speak about what 'thus saith the Lord?' Is that what I am supposed to say?'

As he sat down he could feel his heart flutter a little bit. Palpitations. A tell tale sign that he was convicted by his own sin enough to dwell on it… for a little too long.

"At what point do we become hypocrites? We have sinned and we continue to sin. Are we going to put these girls on trial and make examples of them and not make examples of ourselves?" Sister Walters squawked, invading his mind as he thought the same thing. She had a daughter that had a child herself out of wedlock. All the talk of this so-called measure to show that the church will not tolerate loose behavior was striking a nerve with her.

"Sister Walters, what would you have us to do?" Pastor Wright asked.

"Pastor, you are not above this issue, ask yourself that question. How would you want to be treated if this was you all over again?" She asked with a sentiment of rebuke.

"What is the purpose of the church? We are to be a haven for people who are seeking to grow in Christ. We must show mercy and error to the side of mercy, but we must be mindful of the type of precedence that we set. I do not believe that the image we want to display to our children is that it is ok to be unwed and pregnant and up in the choir loft singing or directing the choir." Pastor returned. In so many words he was talking to her and everyone could tell. She did not take that lying down.

"Maybe if we would make the men as responsible as the women then we wouldn't have so many cases of unwed teen mothers out here. Pastor, by the way, you never married your child's mother, did you? Pastor... Did you?"

He could feel heat in his chest as every fiber of his manhood flared up like a fireworks display. He knew that he was being tested, not only as a Pastor, but as a person. Incensed, but attempting to be mature, Will approached the subject realizing that it was a slippery slope.

"Sister Walters, I understand that you are upset. I know that this is a subject that is very sensitive to you and your situation. I understand because I am a single parent, and I have a daughter that is growing up. Now, would my daughter have to adhere to the same scrutiny as everyone else's child with regards to this issue? Yes. I would make sure that she would be. I am not looking to create some type of witch-hunt committee to take down every teenager that makes the mistake of getting pregnant out of wedlock. But, I am looking to let every teenager in this church know, that we are not going to promote or cultivate that type of behavior at this church. We have standards that we must adhere to. We do forgive and move forward, but we must let it be known that we believe in God's word. The church and the children will respect us more in the future."

"Pastor, I understand all that, but you act like your baby is better than my daughter because she hasn't gotten pregnant."

"Sister Walters, can you just let this go?" Pastor Al interjects.

"I am so tired of hearing this. We are being fair. If anyone's child has a baby out of wedlock they can't lead out and be a part of any auxiliary for a time. All in favor say 'I'."

The I's rang out unanimously. Pastor Al looked at Pastor Wright as to say, 'I got your back on this one.' Still, Pastor Wright knew in his heart that she was right. What if Kristian got pregnant? What would he do and what would he say? What could he say? After all, she herself is the product of that same type of environment. He has always thought of himself as being different. In actuality, there were so many things in common between those two situations.

"Secretary, what is the next item on the agenda?" Pastor Wright asked.

Then they proceeded to discuss budget issues and the like. They went over some of the budgets for the auxiliaries and the fact that some were to be cut and some were to be saved. The usual questions were asked. How is this going to help in soul winning? Why is this program even necessary for the church? Can't you use your own money for this? Et cetera.

So they talked and talked and talked and after a while the Pastor called the meeting.

"If we have not completed anything now, we will complete

it at our next board meeting which is to be held the day before the next business meeting," he said.

All the stares turned slowly toward him as if he had just killed Jesus himself.

"I understand that you don't like my methods, but respect them. We will reconvene then."

As they began standing and murmuring under their breath, he began to pray.

"Father, I know that you have the power to change hearts and minds. Lord we pray that what we have decided upon tonight, we help others find out Who Christ is. So Lord, bless our church, and the decisions that we have made. Let them not be a burden, but a blessing. In Jesus' name I pray. Amen.

Pastor Wright made his way quickly to Pastor Stovall, Sr. He was intent on trying to talk to him before board meeting but because everyone decided to get there before time he had no time. So he decided he would make time before time ran out.

"Pastor Stovall, how are you doing?" Pastor Wright asked, with slight hesitation.

"I am well, son. How are you?" Pastor Stovall responded.

"I am blessed. I am blessed. Sir, I need to talk to you for a minute. Can we go to the study real quick? I have something that is on my heart and I need to talk to you about it before I make a decision. I want to know what you think."

Pastor Stovall could see that it was clearly a weighty issue. Nothing like what color the new church carpet should be or how much should he spend on a robe. Nope; nothing easy.

"If you want to speak to me about something heavy we need to go ahead on up there." Pastor Stovall said breathy.

As was it a burden to Pastor William Wright, the anticipation of it was a burden to Pastor Stovall. He didn't even know what it was about but just the thought of it was enough to make for a very long night. Pastor Stovall was enjoying the idea of not having to run a church. He just came and sat on pulpit every week. He and his wife, Sister Betty, could go to Sunday dinners at everyone's house and not really have to worry about meeting with the board and congregation. Sometimes, like today, they could go to different Sunday dinners and not even have to be around each other. After all, they had been married long enough to not be worried about cheating or the like. That, of course, was for the young folks to deal with.

As they made their way upstairs, the members of the board continued to discuss things downstairs. They discussed not as a committee, but in little conversations amongst various people. Church folk being church folk. This person talked to that person, and that person and the like. The head deacon was talking to Pastor Al about what happened earlier. Sister Betty was talking to Sister Walters about her daughter, Sherelle, and her new baby.

However the conversation that Pastor William Wright needed to know about was taking place right there while he was gone. That was the conversation that Lil Junior was having with Pastor Davis. If you were just watching them from a distance, you could see the familiar positioning of a sinister plot as it began to come together.

"You heard about what happened today, right?" Lil Junior asked Jimmy.

"You mean between you and Will?" Jimmy asked.

"Yeah."

"Well the word on the street is…"

"Forget the word on the street!" Lil Junior cut him short.

"Your Pastor has a streak in him. He is too arrogant for his own good. I should be in charge of this church and you and I both know it. I am the son of the founding Pastor and I am a minister. Why would you allow a stranger to run a church that you and your family built?"

"Lil Junior, I feel ya. I don't understand that either. But, you gotta admit this though, he has grown this church out."

"I could have done better. Ok. I could have done better. He is just a wannabe Bishop Jakes. He thinks that he can turn this church into a mega church or something like that. He doesn't have a clear vision. He is too young to understand. I really don't think he's that smart, really."

"I was with you until you said he wasn't that smart. I don't think that he is dumb. I mean he has brought seven hundred members in, in the last four years. I mean this church is busting at the seams and it has never been this full. Ever. Your dad can't even say that he has done that."

Jimmy touched a nerve on that last statement.

"Oh so now he is better than the founder of this church?" Lil Junior inquired.

"No, that is not what I meant. I was just say..."

"You were just saying that you believe that he is a better Pastor than my father?" Lil Junior interjected.

"Do you believe that Pastor William Wright is a better Pastor than my father?"

This question was a question of loyalty. To whom are you loyal to? That was the real question for Pastor Davis. He knew that he was loyal to the Stovalls but he was just trying to tell the truth. At that point the truth didn't matter anymore and what was important was saving face. He was learning a hard lesson all over again. All is fair in love and church politics.

"Will is a good Pastor, but your father founded and built this church with his bare hands. William...Will, could never be the man or the Pastor that your father is or was." Pastor Davis said.

"Very well put." Lil Junior responded.

So they continued their discussion on the way that things were and how messed up the church was and how Lil Junior should be Pastor. Lil Junior decided that his story was the right one even though he left out the part about him acting as if he was going to swing on the Pastor for no reason. Lil Junior was smart though. He knew that Pastor Jimmy was one of the biggest male gossips in the church. It was as if you were talking to the whole congregation when you were talking to him. He knew that by Wednesday night's prayer meeting, everyone would know his side of the story. Even if the side that they knew was as wrong as wrong could be.

Pastor Stovall and Pastor Wright got to the Pastor's study and began discussing the problem that needed to be discussed so earnestly.

"Pastor..." Pastor Wright started.

"You still won't call me Cleve will you?" Pastor Stovall asked cutting him short.

"I just don't feel comfortable with that. I know that you're my... I mean, I am the senior Pastor now, but I don't feel comfortable calling you by your first name. I mean you are still my Pastor." He returned.

"Will, I understand but at some point you are going to have to treat me like just a man. I am not God, nor do I claim to be above reproach. I still sin too. So work on that, son." Pastor Stovall said.

"I will."

"So, Will, what is the big issue? Let's just dive in because I think I know what it is already." Pastor Stovall said with a raised eye.

"Sir, it is your son. I can't take it much longer. He is a thorn in my side and I don't think that he is helping our church to grow as much as he is creating dissension within the house of God." Pastor Wright said.

"So you want to oust him, do you?" Pastor Stovall asks with purpose.

"Yes and no." A pensive Pastor Wright responds.

"What does that mean? Either you do or you don't." says Pastor Stovall.

"Well, it would make my life so much easier if I didn't have to deal with the drama that he brings. I would like him gone and I would like the fact that he was out of my hair and not trying to overthrow and overrule what I have done here. So, I guess with that said I do." Pastor Wright states.

"You have the right to do what you will, Will. I just think that he has helped you in ways that you don't know of. A lot of people would have left if he was gone. They would have left because they didn't see the family in the church anymore. They would have left because they didn't know you well enough. Not because they didn't think that you were a good Pastor. But, because people know him and they know me, they like the fact that our family built this church and is still in some ways a running part of it. So you have to understand, that he has helped you that way."

"Pastor Stovall, I understand all of that. What I want you to understand is that he is not helping to keep peace within this church. I hear a lot of things through the grapevine and I don't even like to listen to gossip. The one thing that I hear more than anything else is the fact that he is after my job. If he was bringing in a whole lot of church members with him then I wouldn't have as much of a problem, but that is not what he is doing. He is, in turn, causing a rebellion that I can't live with. This church can't live with that."

"You are free to do what you want, son. I just think that you will lose out in the long run. Plus, he is my son and I know he is a butthole. But, I believe that he is an asset that you are going to throw away."

Will stood up slowly. He looked sternly at his mentor, his second father, and he did something that he had never done before. He went against the founding Pastor's judgment.

"Sir, I am going to oust him. He will not sit on my pulpit again. I will give Pastor Davis his position. I would rather lose all the members of the church and start over from scratch, than to continue to put up with him trying to undermine my authority as the Pastor and shepherd of this flock. My congregation comes first. He is not good for the congregation and that is all that I have to say about that."

"Well, we will see if you can get that through the board." Pastor Stovall blasted back.

"Sir, I guess we will see." Pastor Wright said as to end the conversation.

A slightly irritated Pastor Stovall got up and walked out of his study. No words. No closing arguments. As angry as Pastor Stovall was, he knew that it was time to fully let this grown man, that he gave the reigns of his church to, run the church. And he knew in his heart, that Pastor Wright was right about Lil Junior. He was out to get him; he had been since Pastor Wright got there. None of that mattered though. Lil Junior is the Stovalls' son. And no matter what people say about it, blood is thicker than water.

The parking lot emptied and Will stuck around a little while just to try to clear his thoughts. For it to only have been one day, it felt like twenty. Stephanie, her fiancé, the dinner, the board meeting; just one thing after another. Just another Sunday, he thought. Just another Sunday...

As he sat there contemplating all of the day's events, his phone rang. It was his mother.

"Are you done yet? We need to know if we should take her to your house or keep her here." she said.

"Go ahead and keep her there. I don't know what time I am going to leave here. I got a lot on my mind right now. I will get her in the morning when she gets ready for school." Will said.

"Ok, Will. I just want you to remember that she needs you too." His mother said.

"I know, ma. I know." Will says with a subdued heart.

"Is she asleep?" He asks.

"You know she isn't. She is still on that phone. I will make sure that she is in the bed before 11:30." His mother responded.

"Ma, I know I don't say it enough, but I do love you and daddy for all that you guys have done for me over the years. I know that I haven't always been the best child, father and Pastor, for that matter. But no matter what, you guys have always supported me and my stuff. I thank you for that and I hope that you will continue to support me and..."

"Will, shut up," she said.

"You are so long winded. We have and will continue to support our son. We love you. We will always love you. So you don't have to go any further with that. Just handle what you need to handle. We will help you. I am just saying though. You need to get your priorities in order when it comes to your little one. She needs to be your first. Ok, Son?"

"Yes, ma'am."

"Call us when you get home, ok?"

"Ok."

"Son, I love you."

"I love you to, Ma."

"Bye."

"Bye."

Will held the phone to his ear for a moment. As he hung up, he realized that it was already eight o'clock. Time was never on his side. He thought that he was the last one in the church but it became a reality that he was not. Sister Smith was waiting for him at the door, teary eyed and weeping.

He walked over to the door and opened it to let her in because he could hear her sniffles from inside.

"What is going on? Are you hurt, are you ok?" Will asked.

"Well, Pastor, I hate to be a bother. But I need you to pray for me." Sister Smith said through the sniffles and the tears.

"I am just dealing with a lot and I want to be faithful to God, but at the same time I have these desires and I can't seem to get over them."

He could see right through it. He knew that she was trying to bait him. He knew it. What he wanted to know at that point, was if his insight was truly correct.

"What desires are you dealing with?" He inquired.

"I have impure desires... Sexual desires."

And those words rolled off her tongue much more seductively than the ones before them. She was attempting to make her play for the Pastor's affection. Not for a lifetime but definitely for a night. But the Pastor was not falling for the blatant and overt act of seduction. He knew that she was not a person that he could ever go there with. She had desperation written on her face and the fact that she was willing to go to those lengths to get his attention led him to believe that she would go to even greater lengths to bring him down in the end. He would have no part of that.

"Ok. Sister, I am going to have ask you to come back when there are other people at the church because I believe that this conversation and just the look of things could lead others to believe that something is going on between us. I understand your situation but I want you to understand mine."

"No, Pastor, I need help and only you can help me with this." She responded.

He knew at that point that he was in a predicament. Here he was in his office with a woman and there was no one left at the church. In fact, she wasn't even at the board meeting so how in the world did she get in? She must have come in right before everyone left, he thought. So, now he had to get out of his office, get her out of his office, and get home without her following him. He also could not let anything happen in his office because he, himself, had the same problem as her.

He was smart, though. Instead of sitting next to her, he stood away from her and he knew that if she came within a few feet of her he would have to leave the office and go out to the car. He was not going to get caught up so it could be the church news tomorrow.

"Pastor, I just need you to help me with my condition, right now." She said.

"Sister, all I can do is pray for you. I have a daughter that is waiting for me at home and I need to get there right away. So, we can pray and you can come back and reschedule during regular hours and we will pray over you. I will have Pastor Al pray with you and he will help you get through this as well as the rest of the deacon staff."

"Pastor, that is what I need to talk to you about. I went to him first. I had sex with him a couple of times and he has been trying to sleep with me some more but I wouldn't let him. He said if we did it, it would probably help to get it out of my system. One last time before I went down to the watery grave. So I did. But, then one time turned to two and two to four. Then the next thing I know he was calling me on my phone. I don't even remember how he got my number. This has been going on for about a month now and I just want to be free of these desires. I don't want to ruin his marriage. I know that you are not married, so..."

"So, you thought that you would come in here and try to seduce me?" Pastor Wright asked.

"I was told by somebody that you were a different kind of Pastor. You know, that you would take care of the flock if need be." She said with innuendo laced all in that statement.

"And, if you don't mind my asking, who told you that?" He asked, befuddled by that last statement.

"It's just a little rumor that I heard floating around the single women of the church. Apparently, someone has had a taste of you and they enjoyed it. So, I just wanted you to help me get over this thing that I have." She said as she got up and walked over towards him as a cat about to pounce her prey.

Will headed for the door to let her out.

"You shouldn't believe everything that you hear. More importantly, you shouldn't be so willing to move on a rumor. Goodnight, Ms. Smith." He said motioning her out the door.

"As much as I don't like rejection, I understand. Just do me one favor."

"And what is that?" He asked.

"Don't tell Pastor Williams that I told you." She asked.

"I won't tell him, if you do me one favor."

"Anything." She said quickly as she came in close to him in the doorway.

"Don't tell another soul what you heard about me. I don't want people believing lies." He said.

"Consider it done." She said as she walked out with a swagger that only a woman with her assets could do.

Now, this was no ordinary woman that Will just turned down. She was a very beautiful woman. She had it going on. From the crown of her 5 foot 6 inch head to the soles of her fully pedicured feet, she was a phenomenal woman. Her measurements of 36c-26-36 were nothing to be played with, which is why he knew he had to get her out of his office; the temptation. He could feel the lust within him as it began to well up. If it wasn't the smell that got his mojo going, it was the way that her golden brown skin looked in the light. Or maybe it was the way she licked her lips before she spoke. At one point he could hardly hear what she was saying because he was so focused on her legs in that skirt. He had thought the whole time that the devil will send you what you like, especially when you don't need it. And she was everything that he liked.

When she said what she said about Pastor Al Williams, all of that lust in him went out the window. This was his boy; his man. How could he allow this chick to put him in a predicament such as this one? And, on top of all that, he was married. He had in house booty. He and his wife should have been doing the dang thang all the time, unless she had closed up shop on him, which was a possibility because women do that a lot. All of these things raised questions for him, and he knew that for at least that night they wouldn't be answered. After all, Al was at home with his family.

He tried not to think about it but judgment began to enter his mind like a loud brash unwelcomed guest. Loud, because he knew that if this was true then all the self righteous, holier than thou talk of earlier that morning would make him the greater hypocrite of the two. Al knew all about Will's sins, but this? This was something that he was keeping to himself, Will thought.

If this is a true testament to the friendship that we have, then Will guessed that he was the only one that was being honest on that front.

Will closed up the office and made sure that he locked up for the night. He had had enough of the drama for the day. He prayed before he left the office and called it a night. He would have driven the car back to his house but because he already had his car at home he just left it at the church and would deal with it and his daughter in the morning. So many thoughts and so little time. He tried to process everything as the walk went on. He knew that the Bible verse had proven to be true: 'Take no thought for tomorrow because tomorrow will take care of itself.' There was enough in that day to be concerned with.

Chapter Five

Entry Two.

Why do I do, what I do? I know that will be a question. The bigger question to myself has always been how do I stop doing what I do?

I do what I do because, just like everyone else, I like it. I like sex. I love sex. I love making love to a woman. I love to hear her moan to every stroke. I love the smell of her body when it is wet with sweat from making love. I love to look at her face when I hit her spot and she winces in pleasure. I love to hear her pant when my tongue licks her clit just right. I don't want to delve into it too much but I think the point is made.

People love sex. Hell people love sin. They love sin because it feels good. It is all about the flesh. I try to stop, though. I know that this is a willful sin. I am addicted to it. I have been for so long that I have to get it when I want it. From whoever I want it from. If not from them then from the next one until then next one becomes the next one.

Sixty partners later and I have nothing to show for it. That really is very scary because I do want to get married one day. I cannot see a woman coming to the church and saying that I gave her something. Then the idea of me as Pastor getting something? NO way. I can't see me burn while sitting in the pulpit trying to preach a sermon regarding how God views sin, and the consequences of adultery. That would be a funny sight. I can see me up there twisting and turning trying to deal with the burn while I preach.

Plus, I use a condom every time. I will not do it without one. That just won't happen. I know that more than anything, getting another woman pregnant outside of wedlock is not the way to go for someone that is thirty-six years old and a Pastor. I have enough going against me without adding another to the mix.

I have slept with some of the women in my church but like I said they have pretty much kept it on the low. I know that has been hard for them, because women love to talk. I am surprised that I have never run into a crazy one who would put my business on blast like that. There was that one girl that wanted to, but I was able to get her to see things from my point of view. I think that was Latisha Clark. She doesn't go to First Baptist anymore. I think it was for the best. She thought so too.

She was on a mission to kinda ruin me. She wanted to tell everyone that we had sex and that I was out there like that. I knew something was wrong with her when she told me that she was ready to be the Pastor's wife when we had only had sex once. She told me she loved me right in the middle. Right in the middle of the first time we had sex! I mean I didn't even really chase this girl. I don't chase, they just come to me. I make one statement and that is usually enough, but I mean with her? She was just juicing to give me the drawers.

After about a week it was like I couldn't get rid of her. She would be there after church. She would call my mother's house. She was trying to get to know my daughter like a friend at church. She was just going overboard. When she contacted my daughter, I had had enough. It was done. I spoke to her regarding that. When we spoke that was enough. She was upset, and her heart was set on doing me in. Fortunate for me, though, I knew what she was going to do, so I had a lawyer friend send her a letter letting her know that if she went public,

I would sue. I think that was enough for her. After about two weeks she left.

Do I feel regret for this incident? Yes. Of course I do. I don't want to be known for being a person that is insensitive to women or anything like that. But I must admit that I was. I couldn't be sensitive to that because she was trying to take me down and I didn't want that to happen. I couldn't let that happen. I mean, this is my livelihood. This is how I make my living. So I don't even know how else it could have gone.

Besides that, I have my enemies and I know who they are. They would be licking their chops if it had gotten out like that. I think that incident might have more than a little effect on the other women who probably would have come out about everything. There are still a few that roll their eyes at me when they see me outside of the pulpit. And I have heard a few little things that they say under their breath about me but, nothing major and nothing that has been brought to the board.

Speaking of my enemies, I am so ready to get rid of Lil Junior. He is a thorn in my side. I am sick and tired of having to deal with the constant his second-guessing what I do. He is not my boss. God is my Boss. He is just another minister who is angry about the way things have gone regarding his ministry. If he wanted to still be the head Pastor he should have kept his church. He couldn't, though. He ran it into the ground and that is the reason that his father wouldn't allow him to be the Senior Pastor of First Baptist. I know that and he knows that. He feels like he can do better than me but his track record has shown that he is not in any position to second guess me; let alone think that he could run First Baptist better than me.

The Bible speaks of allowing God to fight your battles for you, and I believe that to be true. He is supposed to fight your battles for you. But I also believe that we play a major role in that with our attitude. I am not exempt from this. I believe that the problem that I have is with patience. I can be patient with most of my congregation. I can be patient with my mother.

But when it comes to Pastors, I have a problem with them not being who they profess themselves to be. I know that I am a hypocrite with this judgment that I am making. But I have to say what I feel.

Anyway, I know that my life is far from perfect. I am being judged each day and I am hoping that one day I will be able to overcome my own shortcomings in order to be the person, preacher, Pastor, and parent that God wants me to be. In Jesus' name I pray, Amen.

Chapter Six

The time was 5am and it was also the end of the third day of no rest for the Pastor. The thought of being judged by a hypocrite bothered Will enough. The thought that the hypocrite was his friend bothered Will all the more. Al was supposed to be his best friend. The one who was supposed to lead Will to the right answers. The one to whom he presented all of his problems with women and expected a solution. That is the kind of friend that Al was supposed to be. Not the kind who was cheating on his wife and then pretending to be holier than thou. Not the kind who was trying to put Will in a bad situation. Not that kind of friend. More than Stephanie getting married; more than her fiancé getting baptized; more than any of that other stuff- this was bothering him to the point of not being able to sleep.

There was also another issue that was on his mind: the fact that he had not seen his journal in a few days. No worries on that front though, because it had to be at church in his office, he thought. But there was always that nagging feeling that there may some truth in that thought. Like the Holy Spirit had revealed a morsel of truth for him to acknowledge, but pride, prejudice and a whole lot of doubt got in the way.

Will had enough though, of the sleep problem. He made up his mind that it was time to deal with the issue. The problem was always timing. How do you get Al to yourself without including his wife and his family into the mix? You don't want to be the cause of a happy home breaking up. Right is right and wrong is wrong, he thought. You have to be mindful.

Ring! Ring! The phone goes off. Surprisingly, it was not the cell phone but the home phone that was ringing at this God forsaken hour. The still of the morning taken away by the cry of a phone's ringing did not startle Will at all. He felt like it was going to ring anyway. But the voice that he would hear after hello, would be one that would shock him at that point.

"Hello, this is Pastor Wright." Will said.

"Pastor Wright, this is Officer Collins with the Fulton County police department. I was given your number by a Minister Alvin Williams. He told me to call you and let you know of his whereabouts and the like."

Will looked at the phone as if he was on Punk'd or some other prank television show. He knew that he was not talking to the police about Al being locked up. He just knew that was not what he was talking to him about.

"Officer, is it possible for you to tell me what this is about?" Will asked with worry in his voice.

"I am not at liberty to discuss this matter with you over the phone, but you can speak to the minister regarding this. He is sitting right here next to me." The officer said.

"Place him on the phone please, sir."

The officer passed the phone to the ear of a crying Pastor Al. You could audibly hear the frantic sobs of a man caught in something that he deeply regretted.

"Will, I am sorry." He spoke mangling the words in the midst of his sniffles and tears.

"I am so sorry. I need you to come get me, man. I need you. Come get me, man!"

Will couldn't even say a word. He just hung up the phone.

He knew that he was going to have a large amount of difficulty keeping this a secret. When he considered that his daughter was in the other room, she would have heard all the commotion if he had even reacted the way that he wanted to. What does a Pastor say to another Pastor who is caught up in some mess that the first Pastor doesn't really know anything about?

Will got up and dragged his lethargic body to the bathroom. He proceeded to fill the tub to the brim with water. This was his ritual for a day that he felt was going to be filled with strife. He plunged his head in the water, his symbol for the plunging that he was about to go through during the day. As much as he hated being right, he was.

He wiped his face with a slow careful hand. He was in no hurry because he already knew that Al wasn't going anywhere. He didn't really have anyone else to call. Will knew that Al didn't want his wife to know about this. He knew that whatever it was, his wife was going to kill him if she found out. 'Let him sit for a minute', he thought. Will had determined to spring the jailbird but he wouldn't do so with haste. After all, Al had gotten himself into this mess. Why not let the hypocrite deal with his own mess for a while?

Will feeling compelled by the Spirit, or by his own anger, said a prayer to calm himself, "Lord, I do not know what today will bring. I don't even really know what is in store for me now. I do know that you are God and you have kept me in all that I have been through. I pray that you will be with me as I go to see about Al. I pray that he hasn't done anything stupid. I pray that I am able to be level headed about this. Please don't let me judge him but please let him be mindful of his decisions and help me to be mindful of mine. In Jesus' name I pray, Amen."

Father time shifted the clock hands from 5 to 6am. It was time for Kristian to wake up and get ready for school. Will was reminded of this when the alarm began to ring. Time does not slow for anyone, he thought.

"Kristian, it's time to get up. Need to get it moving up there." He said as he finished making his bed. She didn't respond but the creaking sound of the hardwood floors let him know that she was moving at least. His ear followed the sound from room to room upstairs. It sounded as if she had made her way from the bedroom to the bathroom. He could hear the faint whisks of water going down the drain. She was in the bathroom. Will was beginning to remind himself of his mother. Those eyes in the back of her head.

"Kristian, do you hear me?" he asked loudly.

"Daddy, I am up. I know you hear me." She said sounding groggy and lethargic.

He left her alone for the moment. She has never been a morning person, he thought. He kind of realized and remembered that her mother never was either. That was another quality that she received inherently from her mother without ever knowing her.

Time grew short as he dropped Kristian off at school. By then, 6am had become 8:30am and Will had ignored many a phone call from Sharon, Al's Wife. As he pulled up to the school he noticed his phone vibrating again as it had done the whole trip there.

"Daddy, why aren't you answering your phone?" Kristian asked.

"Well, there is something that I have to deal with but I can't deal with it now. So once I can get to it I will call them back." He said in the comforting 'daddy makes everything better' voice.

"Is this about you and some woman?" She asked, as if she already knew the answer.

"Kristian, have a good day at school, ok?" He replied, ignoring her question.

"Ok. Love you, Daddy."

"Love you too, Kristian."

She shut the door behind her and he watched her walk to the main entrance to the school. He knew that after this, it was time to deal with another Pastor's issues. Fortunately it was not just another Pastor but it was his boy. His best friend.

Will had already put together the money that he needed to get him out. He just didn't want to have to call his wife without knowing what to say. He searched his mind but he couldn't find words that would fit. And the words that he'd use had to be factual, but he still didn't have all of the facts.

And even what was known would be incriminating to Sharon. She knew that he hadn't been home all night. She knew that was not what her husband normally does. She also knew that if he was going to be in any kind of situation, William, her husband's friend and confidant, was going to know what was going on.

Then on the flip side of things if you don't call anyone back, they are going to start to wonder what is going on with the Pastor. Which lead to William, Mister Senior Pastor, having to explain his whereabouts. That would lead to an even bigger headache, Will pondered. Decisions. Decisions.

William drove away from the school slowly looking at his phone. He noticed that he had 15 missed calls. Dang, he thought. As he reviewed his call log the number was the same for twelve out of the fifteen. It was Sharon's cell phone number. He knew what she wanted but he didn't want to lie to her. After all, she knows him and he knows her. She wasn't going to take any junk from him especially if it smelled like bull. She knew William well enough to know when he had bull coming out his mouth, so he was going to have to tread carefully when he made that call.

The more he looked at that number the faster he drove to Rice Street to see about getting that fool out of jail. The closer he got to the jail, the more upset he got about the whole situation. He was trying not to judge but he knew in his heart of hearts that this was some mess that could have been avoided. All he could see was tarnished images and long lasting repercussions. This was his appointed second in command. He was the Pastor when the Pastor wasn't there. Everyone would know tomorrow that he was there today. Still, all the questions. What the heck was going on with him and Sharon anyway? With that thought, she was calling him again on the phone. Once again he refused to answer his phone, yet he was ever so careful not to press the ignore button and let it ring through naturally.

As he arrived at the Fulton County Jail, he knew that the sight of clergy didn't matter to the inmates. He also knew that he wanted to keep this visit as quiet as he could. Though he had been there before with his prison ministry department many times, never before had he gone to get a Pastor. He asked one of the officers about the process for bailing out an inmate. The officer let him know that he would have to check with Information so that he could find out if the inmate even had bail and how much it would be. William was smart enough to know that it would be about one thousand dollars. He brought fifteen hundred dollars, just in case.

The lady at the inmate information desk let him know what the charges were and what the bail was.

"Mister Williams is charged with soliciting a prostitute for indecent purposes. His bail is set at fifteen hundred dollars." The clerk said.

"Are you sure that you have the right person?" William asks.

"He is the only one in our system. We have only one Alvin Williams in our computer. They have him as booked in at about 4am."

So that is what this is all about. Sex. Even for him it was about sex. He is such a hypocrite. These are just some of the thoughts that cloud the mind of William as he hands the lady a check.

"It will take about forty five minutes for him to be processed out." She said. Just enough time for William to figure out how to proceed.

Still trying to figure out what to say and how to say it to Sharon vexed Will. He knew that she was going to really need to talk to her husband and not to him. But she isn't going to want to hear that. She was going to want to know what was going on so she could crucify him. This was a time when she would have just cause. After all, Will thought, he was placing his family and his livelihood in a situation for a prostitute.

The phone rang again. It was Sharon again. Now that he had some of his own questions answered, he could answer some of hers.

"Hello, Sharon." William answers.

"I don't even need to know where he is. I want you to tell him something when you see him," she said struggling to hold it together.

"You tell him wherever he is, he can stay there. He doesn't need to come home. He can just stay wherever he is. Just tell him to stay there because that is where he belongs."

"Sharon, it's not what you think it is."

"Is it involving another woman?"

"Well…yes, but…"

"Does it involve sex?"

"Sort of, but not really."

"Then it is what I think. You are always trying to defend him. You are no better than him, yourself. When are you going to settle down and get married? I know how you are. He has told me about what you do and I know that birds of a feather flock…"

"Hold on, now. Wait a minute. Don't put this mess on me! This is between you and your husband. Not me. And whatever he told you, you might want to consider the source. He is the one that is caught up in this mess that he is caught up in. I have nothing to do with this. Besides that, I have been the one this whole time that has supported the relationship that you and he have. Why would you put this off on me?"

Sharon and William were silent for about a minute. She gathered herself and he, himself.

"William, I am sorry. I know that you love the both of us. I know that you have been an excellent friend for him and me.

I just don't know, though. I think that he looks at your life and sometimes he wants that back. It's like he wishes for what you have as if I am not good enough."

"That is where you are wrong, Sharon. He always talks about how happy he is that he has you and the kids. How much he is glad that he doesn't have to deal with all of the issues that I have to go through."

"Well, that is not what I get at home. I get him looking as if he doesn't want to be here. Like we are holding him hostage, against his will. I think sometimes that he doesn't find me attractive."

"Sharon, you are beautiful and he appreciates you. If he doesn't then he is only half the man that I thought he was. I know that he loves you with an everlasting love. These simple problems that you guys are dealing with will come to an end, I promise. God loves marriage and He made the two of you for each other. Don't worry about it, ok?"

"Is he with you right now?"

William didn't want to lie, but if telling a lie would save Al's marriage then he was going to tell it for the greater good.

"Yes, he is close by."

"Tell him that when he gets home, we need to have a long talk. So, he might as well get his mind ready. Either we talk today, or we will talk in front of a judge." She said with all the attitude that only a black woman could muster.

"I will make sure that I tell him that immediately." William said exhaling.

"Alright then, Will, send my husband home, ok?"

"Ok, Sharon."

"Bye, Will."

"Bye, Sharon."

That dreaded call had ended. William's breathing had been elevated and his blood pressure had been high, but now with the call over, he could feel his heart rate return to normal. Not happy about it all, but he believed that he saved a marriage, or at least help slow down the fallout. And that was good enough for him.

Time seemed to move much slower in that place than it did in the regular world. It was as if fifteen minutes were fifteen hours so Will proceeded to try and take a nap while he waited. So many thoughts were swirling through his head. So many questions that needed to be answered and were going to be once he walked out of that door.

10:45am: The doors finally open and Al walked out. His light brown skinned face looking as if it was in need of a shave and a wash. He looked regular with his golf shirt and jeans but his demeanor expressed his overall displeasure with the situation. At that point his gratitude was about to be tested.

"William, thank you. Thank you, thank you, thank you. You don't know how..."

"Al, I don't want to hear it right now. Let's just get out of here." He said as he signed the last of the release paperwork for his friend.

"You know that you are due back for a court appearance one month from today? You do know that, right?" He asked, scoffing at him as he would a child.

"You don't have to talk to me like that, dude, I know. I mean, thanks for everything but you don't have to act that way." Al responded.

"Did you not just get out of jail? Man, what is your problem? You can't humble yourself at all?" Will asked with an angry and elevated tone.

The air became thick at that very moment. Al had to take a step back and think about who he was and where he was and how it had all gone down. He was getting angry with his best friend, who in turn had every right to be mad. He had to ask himself the question: would I be mad if this was me?

Al didn't say another word until they had gotten in the car. After that last outburst by William, he realized that he was at fault and that he needed to apologize for even coming at Will the way that he did. Still the air had a thick feeling to it and tension was still there.

William, on the other hand, was still steaming from the statements made at the jail. He knew that Al could feel the air of tension but he didn't care. After all, if he had the gall to come at him the way that he did then he deserved to be mad. On top of that, there was the fact that William had saved this man's marriage and this was the type of treatment that he would get for it? Will just couldn't believe that. So he asked him the questions that had been keeping him up at night. The questions that he needed to get off his chest. He asked him about Sister Smith.

"What the hell is going on with you and Sister Smith?" Will yelled.

"What is going on in your fucking head, dude? A prostitute? You were going to sleep with a prostitute? What the fuck? Are you sick? Have you lost your fucking mind? You know Sharon is pissed. And then you have the nerve, the blatant audacity, to even think of getting an attitude with me? Who the fuck do you think you are?" William roared at him as he drove.

Al had never seen him this angry. Never heard him cuss or even holler to this degree. For a moment he even felt scared.

William felt scared too. He had never been so angry at a man, or a woman, for that matter. He felt like he could have literally choked Al because he was throwing away all of his blessings. Blessings that William wished he could have.

"I mean I had to practically lie to your wife about this. I had to lie and I don't lie for anyone. Not even for my own mother. You are going to fix this, and you better figure out how pretty fast." He continued.

Al just sat there for a minute and didn't say anything, like a child that knows that they are in trouble and speaking at that moment would have only made things worse. Knowing that his wife was angry, made the drive to that location more and more uncomfortable.

"Will, I am sorry, dude. I know that I fucked up and all."

"Dude, watch your mouth." Will interrupted.

"I mean, I know I messed up and all, but I still love my wife and I want it to work with us."

"It will Al, and I am not worried about that as much as I am about you and Sister Smith. What happened there?" Will persisted.

"How do you know about that?" Al asked.

"Don't worry about all that. I am asking the questions here. So, can you please answer my question?"

"We had sex." Al shortly stated.

"And?" Will asked.

"And we had sex again."

"And? Will asked again.

"And it was good. Look, she asked me about helping her through her issues with sex. I said that I would. But, man come on that girl is fine. You know and I know it. Plus, she was throwing it at me. Dude, I mean throwing it at me. Coming into the office at church and telling me that she had been thinking about me all day. Telling me that she didn't have any panties on and that she was wet. Stuff like that. Dude, I haven't had sex with my wife in almost a year."

"What?" Will asked.

"Yeah. No sex. No head. No nothing for the last eleven months, so I was suffering. I mean, I know I am not supposed to step out. You and I both know that. We know it better than anyone. But I mean you understand, don't you?"

Will wanted to say that he did but he couldn't. He didn't understand because he had never been married. He had never had a relationship that lasted long enough or that was involved enough to say that he could possible know what his brother, his friend, was going through. The closest thing to that with him was Miss Stephanie.

As they pulled up to Al's house, Will finished with his final words of wisdom.

"I can't say that I understand. I haven't had that experience yet. I don't know that I ever will. I know one thing, though. I didn't tell Sharon where you were, so you need to come up with a good lie. She is waiting for you at the house so you need to make sure that she is happy when the conversation is over.

"Ok." Al sighed.

"And one more thing, stay away from Ms. Smith. You have a wife. She needs to be all that you need. Make sure that I don't hear about this again, ok?"

"Ok."

Al got out and headed towards the door. As he pulled away, Will could hear his boy get reamed as he was walking in. Will said to himself with a chuckle, 'sometimes it is good to be single'.

Chapter Seven

The day went by faster after dropping off Al. He felt a sense of relief in finally knowing the why's and the who's of the whole incident. He kept thinking to himself about what had happened and how he would feel if he were in a similar situation. Being married and not being able to make love to your wife? Not having your wife want you in the way that you wanted her, for that long a time? Will couldn't say to himself that he would have done anything differently. The thought tended to be that he would have probably done worse.

The day ended with many calls by Al to tell him the outcome that was ongoing. She slapped him several times because she couldn't believe what he had told her. He said that he was glad the kids were at school because all of that was something that they had never seen and didn't need to see. She called him selfish. He called her selfish. They were both right. The good thing about it was that they agreed to go to counseling. Al suggested Will. Of course his wife objected to that from the start. Will agreed with Sharon. Bad idea. He knew that he was too connected to be objective and they needed an objective person to help their marriage; someone that they both would be able to trust and not feel like there was an unfair bias.

Stephanie entered his mind for the first time in a few days. The fact that her fiancé was joining the church was not much of a bother anymore. However, the funny thought for him was the fact that it could have been him and her. Stephanie didn't want to have sex anymore and he knew why. Still, it seemed that she would be the kind that would withhold sex if she felt like it would make him change his mind about anything. Once he thought about it, he knew he would probably do the same thing. Call it being a dog but Will knew his needs and that was one of them. If he didn't get it at home, he would get it elsewhere.

Two weeks passed, and things had returned to normal. The usual and mundane to most, but the usual for Will always involved a little variety. This week's variety began with Kristian's going out with friends on a Saturday night. Will, being the father that he was, had a few objections. But, what could he say to his mother and father whom Kristian had wrapped around her finger? She got her way and ended up going out. So, he figured he would get his prowl on, as well, by heading over to his favorite spot on a Saturday night, the Apache Café. He may have missed a week but he was at it again and Saturdays were always his best days for finding what he needed. And Saturday was upon us.

"What do you really want?"

Words from the mouth of a woman that he didn't know; they were the words that he wanted to hear. She was as fresh as the morning air but had all the things that he had grown to love about women. She was as fine as they come. She was forward enough, yet coy enough, to be the thing of the hour. Dark brown eyes that twinkled with intrigue. Her eyes were speaking volumes to him. But her body had spoken more. As she spoke he could only see how suck-able her shiny pouty lips were. As she leaned in closer to hear his questions his eye only noticed how erect and pronounceable her nipples were through her low cut top. When she got up to go the restroom before they left, his eyes couldn't help but notice how doable her round voluptuous ass was. His mind went there every time. Every week. This one was Tamara. She was the one that was going to change things, though. He had no idea but she was the one. The one that would take him and break him.

See, although in his mind he had just met her, she had known him for a while, for a long while. She had been a member at his church for about five years. He had baptized her but he didn't even remember that. Because she was a 'balcony' Christian, he never shook her hand after church. You know the kind. They sneak in for the sermon, and sneak out before the benediction.

She had been watching him for years and finding out what she wanted to know about him for months. She knew he had a daughter. She even knew his schedule: She knew that Mondays were for visiting. Tuesdays were for meeting with members that wanted his counsel. Wednesdays were for preparing for Prayer Meeting before Prayer Meeting. Thursdays were for Pastor's Counsel. Fridays were for his daughter and their time to go out. But Saturdays, oh Saturdays! That was her time. She knew what she would have to do and she had watched him enough to know what he liked.

She had seen him with Stephanie in the past. She even knew to an extent, how they broke up. She knew about Tiffany, AKA 'the little whore that could'.

Rumor has it that Tiffany got pregnant by the Pastor, but that was just a rumor. She was actually pregnant by someone else in the church that she was having sex with while she was sleeping with the Pastor. Fortunately for the Pastor, his church loves him because there were so many people that knew about that situation. But they also knew that Tiffany was a whore that would screw anybody. He was wise enough to have her leave the church and if she didn't, the scrutiny would come down on her because of her indiscretions, as well as the fact that she tried to blackmail and frame the Pastor in a certain light.

She knew that he had a thing for women like her. She had always known it. But since he had not really noticed her in church, she figured that she would meet him when he was out on the hunt. He never knew that anyone would be watching him the way that she was. He would soon find out that what you do in the dark is always being watched in the light.

As she returned back to her seat at the Apache Café, it was as if she was moving in slow motion. His mind could only think: flawless, with every step. How was it that he could be at this place with a woman like this? On top of all that, she was interested in him? He had slept with many women, but none like her. None like her. She was the Moon to his Sun. As star struck as he was he had to make his move because he knew that this was just going to be a sex thing. That is all that he was looking for on a Saturday night. A sex thing... No more. No less.

The more he looked at her, though, the more some of her feature became familiar to him. He was thinking that it was a case of déjà vu or something, but he tried to get it out of his mind. As the musicians played their riveting sounds of jazz, and salsa he motioned to her from the door. It was getting too loud to have a decent conversation so he knew that in order for his night to be complete, he had to get to a quieter location before proceeding to his place for the finale. So they packed it up and headed out the door.

"Did you bring a coat?" He asked.

"Yes, but I left it in my car. I figured it would be hot in this place, and I was right."

"Well, how do you want to do this?"

"Do what?" She asked, playing coy.

"You know- finish this conversation."

"Well, it is getting late, and I am a little tipsy. Can we just call this a night and a first date?" she asked.

"We can, or…" He said with a mischievous stare. She knew what was on his mind. She gave him the same stare back.

"We could finish this conversation at my house."

"I don't know about that. You might try to do more than talk to me." She said with a playful laugh.

"I promise I won't bite; at least not hard."

"I don't care if you bite; as long as it is in the right places."

"Trust me, I won't hurt you without pleasing you in the process."

With that said she strolled to her car to follow him to his house. It's not as if she didn't already know where he lived. She had been by the house before, not as a visitor but nevertheless she had been there. She pretended to follow as if she didn't know, but she knew.

In his mind the idea of her as just another conquest had changed. She had become much more in just a few hours. The idea of just sexing her up was starting to become a faux pas. She was worth much more than that, he began to think. That thought began to scare him. He knew that he still had the stigma of Stephanie and all. Plus, he didn't know her from Adam. So the idea of making her something special didn't make sense. He had already tried the whole relationship thing anyway with Stephanie and he saw how that turned out. The focus had to be on just getting that need fulfilled. Nothing more… Nothing less...

He turned down his lights on his car from full beams to just the fog lights as to not wake the neighbors. He had already had such an interesting week, that he didn't need anything else to add to it in the closing hours of it. She followed his lead and turned her lights down as well. Smart girl, he thought.

His anticipation of this encounter was unlike most before. She had him and she didn't know it but he did. His mind or his heart would not let him let the thought of her go. She was so beautiful, and damn, she was sexy. But there was something else there that itched him enough to keep him affixed in a way that he hadn't felt in a long time. Something there that he just couldn't shake loose. Something that kept stirring in his spirit that he couldn't break away from. The lust had subsided in him for this woman because of the feeling that he couldn't get off his chest. I mean what would you do? So he walked over to her car and talked to her after they parked out front.

"Look, I know I said that we were going to just talk, but really all I wanted, initially, to do was get you in my bed." He said bluntly.

"I am not happy to admit that but I can't even explain it, but I had to be honest with you. But I can't do that now. There is something about you and I don't know what it is but it's something that is causing me to like you more than I should. Honestly this should just be a sex thang. That is what I like, and that is what I am used to."

"Well...I don't even know how to respond to that." She said blushing. She didn't know how to take it. She knew that she wanted to make love to him. She could feel that from her core. But, she wanted it to be love making, and not just sex. She had been longing for this opportunity, but not so much as to lose herself to an urge that would make her just one of the ones on his list. She also realized something. She had the upper hand. Because if he could admit that to her, then she had a little piece of him that he didn't just give away.

"Look, I know that I have probably shot myself in the foot with regards to us. Honestly, if I were you I wouldn't date me or have anything else to do with me either, especially after that." He said humbly.

He took a minute and grabbed her hand and lowered his voice to a more deep tone.

"But, I would love another opportunity to show you, the type of man that I really am. Can I get that opportunity?"

In her mind she laughed. He was really trying hard she thought. But she didn't want to make this too easy for him. After all, she knew him so much better than he knew her. She knew about all the ladies and everything. She decided to play along.

"Just call me and we can see what happens from there. Ok?"

"Ok."

He gave her a hug, and expected that there would be a possible good night kiss. He leaned in for the kiss and her hand went up to cover his mouth.

"Good night, William." She responded. You will not charm you way into my drawers tonight, she said with her eyes.

He looked at her and thought to himself, 'Damn. Damn. Damn. I just messed that up. If I could have just kept my mouth shut.' But, what was he to do? Will's conscience was working on him. Even he thought that God had finally said that enough was enough. Still, he was as horny as ever and his ritual was not to be broken.

For every man that has ever been a player, and for men that don't even want to admit being one, there was always a backup girl. You know the one that you call when all of the others have moved on with their respective lives and you know that there is no chance in Hades that you can get back with them. There is always the backup. She can be the ghetto girl that you hook up with once or twice a year for that time. Or it could be the one that you keep close enough for her to feel like you are with her but far enough away to know that she doesn't really matter that much.

His backup was always Tiffany. She didn't mind it much either because she would fit him into her schedule and he would do the same. If she had a man, he knew his place. Likewise, if he had a girl she knew her place. But, the lines did blur when she thought he was the father of her child. She actually would have kept the baby if he was. But she knew, and a test told her as well, that he couldn't possibly have been the father of her child. It was that situation, that whole thing right there, that ended it with him and Stephanie.

But the urge to merge had always led him to find warmth in the arms of the opposite sex. That urge had not ended because of a moral objection with regards to Tamara. Tiffany had everything that he wanted for that moment.

She was outfitted with a five feet five inch frame. A nice tight ghetto booty with just enough up front to hold on to. She was freaky enough to have tried almost anything once, but had just enough Christianity in her not to completely stay out there. She had her vices too, though. She loved sex just as much as Will did. She loved being pleased by him but he was not the only suitor.

He knew that as well, especially after the whole pregnancy thing. That pissed him off to no end. He knew it was his fault more than anyone. His problem with how it went down was the fact that she brought it to him first. Like she just knew it was his. He thought that wasn't possible considering that he was using condoms every time. So that made him even more suspicious of her. So instead of one condom, two became the norm.

They did what they do well together. They became one for the moment. It was their night again, and they made it last. Position after position and orgasm after orgasm. Finally they exhausted themselves with their exploits. They collapsed their sweat glistening bodies down on her cherry wood sleigh bed, high off the scent of their own pheromones and friction. Happy in pleasure, and joyous in lust; yet the euphoria of sex and satisfaction was only temporal. The reality of life settled in much more quickly than either of them wanted it to.

Will began to remember the fact that he had to preach in about four hours. There he was with 'the mistress'. That was the nickname that he gave her. He had dated so many and been in a relationship with some of them, but she had always been there as the mistress. Never the wife but always the mistress he said to himself.

Tamara was still on his mind. She had become a fixation just that quick. Even after having as good a time as he did with Tiffany he still was focused on Tamara. Still couldn't believe how honest he was with her about what he wanted. Then it dawned on him. That is how he should be all the time. At that moment he realized more that his sensibilities had become numb to his exploits. It was no more about the person as it was about the act. 'That which is flesh is flesh,' he thought. 'That which is spirit is spirit.

Chapter Eight

Entry Twenty Six:

If the end was now, what would I say to God about what I have done? How would I act when he presented me with my sins? I don't know. I do know that I am trying to overcome all of them. I must admit that I do enjoy sinning. I think that is the problem with most of us, we enjoy it too much. I mean I have asked God some questions and He gave me the answer to them. Like why make sex feel good? If he didn't make it feel good then who would do it?

Think about it like this. If it was a chore then nobody would have sex. If it hurt then who would want to get pregnant. None of us, men nor women, would be happy with the idea of having to endure pain in order to have a child. So the act had to be something that would be pleasurable to us so that we would be fruitful and multiply. Of course, now it is more recreational for me, but I must admit that I love the feeling. That is why it is so hard to stop.

I am just beginning to think about all of the consequences for my actions. I am going to have to answer to Him for everything. All the women: Tanisha, Tawanna, Mia, Sandra, Stacey, Shrameka, Sanji, Rebecca the White girl, Lolita, Maceyanna, Marquita, Laqushina, Stephanie, Tiffany, Alexis, Julia, the White girl, Victoria, the stripper, Ronnell, the stripper,

Adrian, Ann, Shante, Mary, Kim, Yolanda, Sylvia, and Sylvia's cousin, Denise, Jasmine, Sherri Ann, Sheryl Lynn, The sisters that were White, Nisha, the crazy one, Nishe the sane one, Tisha, Rita, Robin, Nia, Vivian Lee, the darkest, prettiest girl that I have ever seen.

There are others, but the list goes on and on. I have given a lot of them what they wanted and they have moved on and gotten married and they are living happily ever after and all that. However, for some I didn't given them what they wanted and I knew that I was not giving them the thing that they desired most out of me. They wanted a relationship and I led them to believe that it was possible with me. That was not the case.

I knew up front, as I always know, whether it is just going to be a night thang or something more serious. In fact, I dare say that most people know what their plans are or what they would like to see with a person when they meet them. You have an idea about what is going to happen with a person when you meet them. You know if you are feeling someone after that initial conversation. If you are feeling them then guess what, you are going to be more open to a lot of things.

I made them feel like I was but I wasn't, so I am going to have to answer to God for that. Of course there is the whole fornication thing. But I believe that God is forgiving of that if I would marry one of the ones that I am fornicating with! That is the problem, I am in pieces. There is a piece of who I am that has been transferred to all of these women. A piece of me that I can't get back, and I want it back. They have moved on with their lives and have husbands, children and families and I am still alone.

I know I said before that I love being a bachelor, but at times it is a lonely world. I have my daughter, but she is getting up in age now. She is almost grown, herself. She spends a lot of time with her grandparents; that has always been the case. My mother keeps telling me to spend more time with her and I do, but she is becoming her own woman. It is just me now.

I sit and I watch from the pulpit. I see Stephanie and her man all hugged up and sometimes even kissing. Nothing over the top, just a light peck on the lips and then attention forward to listen to the choir or something. You know, I miss that. I miss being in love with her. Man, I miss being in love. Sometimes I think about it. You know, having that better half. Someone that has your back and is down for you til the end, that is what I want.

I hate to say this but I am very jealous of them. Stephanie and her fiancé, Michael. I am jealous of their relationship. I am happy for her but at the same time I wish that it was me. I know it could have been but it isn't me. I never had a chance to just sit in the congregation with her while we were together. There was so much of our relationship that was shrouded in secrecy as if I was having an affair or something. I didn't want the church to know because then the rumors would fly. It's not like the rumors weren't flying already. There will always be rumors, but there won't always be a Stephanie and Will. She is going to marry Michael and I am happy for her. I hope that she isn't being too quick but I am glad that she found what she needed in order to be who she wants to be.

So what am I going to do? I am going to stay black and live. I am going to be happy with being me. Guess what? I am the Pastor of a 1400 member church. I have a beautiful fourteen year old daughter that needs me to be here for her. I have a mother and father who love me and my daughter and support us with their love. I have a Pastor that is my mentor and my friend. I have my brother at arms, Al, who is going to be in the trenches with me always. I think I have a lot. And what ever I don't have and need, God will do the rest.

Chapter Nine

Pastor Jimmy Davis just wanted to keep his job. He didn't want any parts of a conspiracy. He had family and friends at First Baptist. The idea that he would be involved in something that would cause chaos turned his stomach. But, he had loyalty to Lil Junior and that was making this such a hard situation. All week he had been bombarded with conversations about how horrible Rev. William Wright was First Baptist. Things like, William is unfit to be the Head. Or, how could we let this Pastor with a bastard child be the leader of our church?

"Don't you think that you are taking it a little too far?" Jimmy said.

"He took it too far by becoming our Senior Pastor." Lil Junior said.

"Look, this is about the standard that we have as a church. I want you to know that he is not the type of person that we should have representing us to the world. We are God's children, and as one of those children I feel that he is not in keeping of our traditions and values."

"You are just jealous." Jimmy responded.

"Why would I be jealous of him? Who is he to me? I mean he is just a man. No more and no less." Lil Junior said smugly.

"He is the man that your dad, who by the way, founded this church, chose over you to be its next great Pastor. He has been just that too. He has been good to First Baptist. He has grown it from what it was to what is now."

"And what is that? A church that allows its congregation to wallow in their sins like a pig in slop?!" Lil Junior asked angrily.

"Lil Junior, I am your friend and I will forever be that. I just don't want any parts of this that you are trying to do. I mean this guy is an ok guy. Yes, he can be a little arrogant, for that matter we all can be, but when it comes down to the preaching he gets it done. You can't deny the numbers."

"So, what? I don't care about the numbers. I know that he is not right for this church. If I have to be the voice crying in the wilderness then I will be that voice and I will continue until my voice is heard."

Pastor Jimmy got up and began to pace. They were at Jimmy's house for about an hour at that point and Jimmy figured that this was going to be one of those issues that Lil Junior was not going to give in on.

"I am telling you, Jimmy, he is not perfect. He has his secrets and he has his lies, just like all of us."

"Then why go after someone that is just like you and I then? Why do you have to prove this?" Jimmy asked in frustration.

Then it came to Jimmy.

"Well, I have heard rumors over the years about him. That he was and has always been a lady's man on the low." Jimmy said in a low voice.

"Are you sure that is reliable?" Lil Junior asked intently.

"Well… I mean it was like a big rumor early on when he first showed up. However, with his continued crusades and with the church growing as it has, no one has even brought it up anymore. It's like he just became a saint or something in the course of four years, so those things seemed to disappear in the midst of all that stuff."

"See, that is what I am talking about. He ain't no saint." A vindicated Lil Junior resounded. This was an angle that he knew could be exploited so many ways. Now all he had to do was choose one.

"So, how can we work this?"

"We probably don't have to." Jimmy said.

Lil Junior was a little confused by that statement.

"Lil Junior, we don't need to do this because what ever he is doing in the dark will come to the light eventually. We need to let God fight our battles for us. If this is God's will then it will come to light anyway."

"I am a little confused with you right now, Jimmy." Lil Junior said holding his head.

"One minute you are giving me the juice on him, and the next you are telling me to let God fight my battles for me? Why give me the juice then if I am just going to let God fight my battles for me? I just don't get it. I don't understand how you can go from one extreme to another. You have put his stuff out there now. So I am going to find a way to get it out there further."

"You don't have to." Jimmy said again.

"Why not?" questioned Lil Junior.

"Because he brags about it in his diary."

"What? Men don't write in diaries." An amused Lil Junior responded.

"So, not only does he have a bastard child but he is also a gay Pastor?"

"No, there is nothing gay about him. I have read some of the stuff in there and trust me he is not gay. He gets around." Jimmy said.

"So, let me get this straight. You have known all along about this journal or diary or whatever, and you never mentioned it to me? Why would you hold out on me like that?"

"It's not like that. I mean, you have to understand. This guy really loves the Lord and he is working so hard for this church. But just like everybody he has some stuff that he is trying to get through. So he writes it down to help him get through it. I wasn't even supposed to know about it but I just happen to be getting something off his desk and I saw it wide open there. He had just written an entry and forgot to close and lock the thing. I mean, when I say he gets around, dude, trust me, he gets around. So, I just never said anything because it wasn't any of my business and it wasn't any of anybody's business to be honest about it."

The deviant side of the mind of Lil Junior went into overdrive. The goal had become very clear. In fact the goal had become crystal clear. The best revenge was going to be served in the words of the man who wrote them. Pastor Wright would undo himself with his own words. Any man bold enough to write his deeds on paper was bold enough to have to stand and account for them. The only question that remained in Lil Junior's mind was how do I get to the book? How do I get my hands on it?

"I already know what you are thinking." Jimmy said.

"You are trying to figure out how to get your hands on this man's book."

"Yes, I will admit, that was where I went." Lil Junior said smirking the whole time.

"I just don't understand why this so important to you. You could be helping to build up this church. Instead you are trying to tear it down."

"Jimmy, you are right. You don't understand. Your father didn't make the decision to choose someone else over you for a church that you have been a member of since you were a baby. You haven't had to see your father's joy when he looks at another man, who is not family, preach to a packed congregation. I mean, he treats him better than he treats his own son. Why should I not put him out there? I just want to show my father how wrong he has been. How much better it would have been if I was there."

"So, you think that you would have been better?" Jimmy asked.

"I know I would have." Lil Junior said with confidence.

"There is no question within me that I would and can do a better job than him. I am the man that God chose for this church. My father chose someone else but God is going to use me to make that decision right. I am going to make sure that I make that decision right, too."

"So what are we going to do about the whole diary thing?" Jimmy asked. He was curious about what this fool of a friend was thinking. He knew in his mind that Lil Junior was never meant to be the Pastor of that church. He wouldn't fit. He didn't have the mind of a Pastor. He was way too selfish and too self-absorbed to be anybody's Pastor for real. He wanted to know before something happened and it would be his fault for telling him.

Unfortunately for Jimmy though, Lil Junior knew that he would never go through with anything. He had already started devising his own plans for mischief and mayhem that involved the commandeering of that diary. He knew that he could not depend on Jimmy because Jimmy really did like the Pastor. Plus, just based on the fact that he had told him all of this stuff about the Pastor and all, he couldn't possibly tell him the truth. Jimmy would just have told the Pastor everything, the same way he told Lil Junior.

"Jimmy, I will let God work it out for now. But when I get a plan together I will let you know and we will commence with revealing who this man really is." Lil Junior said.

"Well, I am glad that you are so convinced. Because, I still see him as my Pastor and my friend. I mean I deal with things with my wife. I deal with my own issues. So I think he's a better man than me. At least he tries to deal with his issues." Jimmy said.

"Jimmy, I hear you. I hear you. Look, I am going to head on to the house, though. I think that I have had enough of discussing William Wright for one day. I am through with that. We will talk again at prayer meeting. I will get with you then."

"Ok, Lil Junior. Don't forget to get your hat in the front room closet."

"Ok, Jimmy, I am gone." Lil Junior said as he walked out the door.

He had made up in his mind that he was headed directly toward the church. He had a key after all. He knew where the diary was going to be most likely and to get into the Pastor's study was easy. There was a door that led from the Pastor's study to the treasurer's office. He had a key to the treasurer's office and they normally didn't lock that door they just closed it. With it being Monday and usually at that hour no one was at the church, he knew that he would be able to get his hands on that diary. Then he began to wonder the obvious. Why would the diary still be at the office when Pastor was not there? If he wrote what Jimmy said in there then it would have to be close to him at all times he thought to himself. It still made sense to him to check the office anyway so that is what he intended to do.

As he got to the church he noticed that there were no cars parked there that he could see. The lights in the parking lot did a very poor job of making anything visible. Even so, there still seemed to be no one there that would slow down his plan of breaking and entering. At that point it was either do or die.

He turned off the lights to the vehicle, and made his way up to the church inconspicuously. He parked his car in a spot that would be harder to see. Stuck his key into the side door of the church and unlocked it. The church alarm let him know that he had about fifteen seconds to unlock the password on it or it would call the cops.

He remembered it well so with no sweat off his brow he disarmed it. He moved right along to the next objective, the Pastor's study. As he walked down the hall without turning the lights on he heard voices in the distance. Young voices. Voices of teenagers that shouldn't be in the church at 11pm unattended, he thought. He made his way further down the hall to find out who it was and why they were in the church at that hour.

As he got closer he could hear that they were playing or something in that room. They were in the mother's room which had a bed and chairs so that the mothers could feed or let their children sleep while they continued to watch service. He slowly crept closer to hear what was going on. He felt like he knew those voices. He did.

Kristian and Shelby, he thought. How old is Shelby? Isn't he like 16 almost 17 years old? Didn't Pastor's daughter just turn 14? He pondered that briefly because he knew that was just more ammo for the arsenal that he was putting together. The goal however was to get to the diary, if it was there. Lil Junior needed to see for himself what type of goodies lay dormant in that book that Will was writing.

Lil Junior walked slowly back to the treasurer's office to open the door. He had to keep quiet because even though they weren't supposed to be in there, they were. He wasn't supposed to be there either. He opened the door and found the office in its usual fare. Slightly disorganized and slightly organized, depending on who you asked. He closed the door and tried opening the side door. At first no success, but Lil Junior is no quitter. He tried again and again until he was finally able to pull it open.

His first thought was to check the desk. Of course, that was not where it was. It wasn't in any of the drawers either. He checked the Pastor's restroom to see if maybe it was in there but to no avail. It wasn't in any of the most obvious places. So Lil Junior started tapping the walls to see if there was safe or something in them that he didn't know about. He wanted to make sure that he was thorough in his search before had to start looking at other locations.

Just as he was about to give up he looked down in front of the Pastor's desk. He noticed a quarter or something. He looked at it more closely and it was a quarter. As he stooped down to pick it up he saw the diary sitting next to the desk on the floor. Resting where it had been for the past six days because it fell out of the Pastor's bag and he didn't know it. Black leather with a clasp that held it closed. A form of security but not a very strong one, Lil Junior thought., especially considering what secrets lay inside. 'If this was mine,' he thought, 'there is no way that I would allow it to get into the hands of my enemies.'

Lil Junior knew he had gotten what he wanted but he didn't know whether to leave the kids the way that they were or to bother them and have them to call him out later on for being there late too. He figured he stood the best chance by just leaving the office in disarray and making them think that a break in occurred. The kids that were there weren't supposed to be, so things were really working out to his advantage. If push came to shove he could say that he saw Shelby's car at the church at that hour.

He never thought it would be so easy for him to just get what he wanted. If he had known about all of this before now he would have handled this a long time ago, he thought to himself. Now things were going to be different. He had all the ammunition that he needed in order to change the game for real. He was going to make it known to everyone what was really going on with the Pastor. That which was done in the dark would be brought to the light, and that light would bring him his time to shine.

Chapter Ten

Entry Number Thirty.

I am so sick and tired of Lil Junior and his mess. He doesn't know me and he will never understand the fact that he does not have what it takes to run this church. He wants to run it but he would run it in the ground if he did. I really am sick of him. If it wasn't for his father I would get rid of him. I get so tired of having to justify my actions to someone that isn't even worthy of justification.

On top of all that he is on my board of Pastors for this church. Why would I put someone that I blatantly don't trust on my board of Pastors? This man is causing me to lose my religion. I just don't like him. I know I am supposed to kill him with kindness. But, man please, I don't have a kind word for him. He is dirty. He does dirt and he will receive dirt in return in the end.

I am just tired of having to deal with him in meetings and at bible study. He is trying to upstage me as if this is a competition or something to that nature. There is no competing when you are the one in charge. Why compete? You don't have a say so. Just leave well enough alone. I am going to have to pray for myself and for him because he upsets my spirit so. I know that I allow him to and I understand who I am battling with but it still gets to me, every time.

I have been thinking a lot about the fact that my daughter is going to be turning 15 in like ten months. I know that is a long way away but I just have this hard time dealing with the fact that she is getting older. I think I believed that she would be younger for a lot longer and now the years just seem to roll by. I didn't believe what my mother used to tell me about how time flies. One day you are this again then you wake up and poof! Life has passed you by.

I am a believer now. She was so right about it all. I never would have thought that it would have moved so fast. I mean Tawanna has been dead for 14 years now almost. I know sometimes she wishes that her mother was here. I wish that she was here. I have a hard enough time dealing with my own issues and my relationship with Kristian has been strained at best. I mean I have had to deal with church issues and they always may seem to come first to her. I am sure that it does. But I love her with all of my heart and I hope that she understands that. I do all that I can for her and I hope that she feels that is the case. Being a young father ain't all that it's cracked up to be.

I still wish that it were easier for me to get married. I know that there are a lot of women who would love to be with me and have me as their husband but they really don't want me. Not that I am a celebrity but they want to be that Pastor's wife. You know, they want that first lady status. Not that it's all that wonderful to be. But they just want it. Some people get off on stuff like that. I know that I am not one of them. I just want to do God's will. I just want to make Him happy.

That is a hard calling when you have to fight with the flesh so commonly. That is what I try to do but I am having a hard time with it. I love what I love and it is hard to break habits that you have had for the last 13 years. I pray that the Lord will help me and deliver me from myself. In Jesus' name I pray, Amen.

Chapter Eleven

It had been about two weeks since meeting Ms. Tamara Green and Will had not heard as much as a hello from her. He was expecting her to call him but in the same breath he knew better. Why would she call after what he had said? If she did call she would have seemed desperate. He knew that and so did she. What kind of self respecting woman calls a man after he admitted that he was only looking at her initially like a piece of meat? So the only question that really remained was when would he call her?

He tried earlier to muster up the nerve to call at the end of the first week but couldn't. Every day thereafter was a reminder to him of how much of a punk he was. Here he was the Pastor of a relatively large church and he couldn't even pick up the phone and call this woman to let her know that he was thinking about her and wanted to see if she was interested in going out on a date. That was way too much for him to handle.

As he opened his eyes on another glorious Sunday morning he also realized that it had been two weeks since the last time he had slept with anyone. That was unusual, but he had figured that it was going to be like this. That is, if he was going to be honest about it, he would try being honest with himself. He knew that anyone at that point that he dealt with, outside of Tamara, was going to be a booty call. He also knew within himself that he wanted to see where they could go first before he looked for a booty call. So Sunday morning proved to be a Sunday unfamiliar, yet unmistakably good and bad at the same time.

The phone rang as it always did on a Sunday morning. Al was requesting that they make the morning run as usual. He just wanted to see if Will was at home or out and about. Nothing special to say this morning, Will thought.

Will prayed the prayer, and began with his breakfast, coffee and his call to his parents to check on his baby, Kristian.

"Ma, where is Kristian?" Will asked.

"She is in her room asleep. We need to talk about her, but remind me after church, ok?" His mother asked.

"What is going on, Ma? Is there something that I need to know about? If there is, can you tell me now? I would rather know now than to have to go into service with this on my mind."

"Are you preaching today?" She asked in an effort to defer.

"No, actually I am not preaching today. I have Al preaching today. I need to keep his mind occupied because of all the mess that he got himself in with that prostitute who was actually a cop."

"What?" She asked, surprised by that one.

"I couldn't believe it either. I was shocked when I went down to the jail and had to bail his behind out. He just doesn't get it either." Will said, with aggravation in his voice.

"He has a beautiful wife. Why would he want to throw all that away?" his mother asked.

"It's more complicated than that. I am just trying to do what I can to help their marriage. They have already started going to counseling and I hope that will help them to get to where they need to be. I think it's going to be a long time before things are right between them, though."

"How is Sharon taking all of this? Does she know about the prostitute?"

"Heck no!" William said abruptly.

"I wasn't going to be the one to have to tell her and I told Al that he better come up with a good lie because that was not going to go over very well if it came out. I reamed him, Ma, about the whole thing, because he had an attitude after he got out. I was like, 'do you have the gall to come at me with an attitude?' He got it together, though."

"Well, baby, I am going to have to go. I am glad that you are still trying to do what's right, regardless of who you are doing it for." She said.

"Ma?"

"Yes, Will."

"Don't dare think that I have forgotten about what you said. I am going to get with you after church so that I can find out what is going on with my dear old daughter." Will said sternly.

"You just need to remember that you were her age once and sometimes even now I still can't tell the difference between the two of you. You know I still hear things about you as well and it ain't pretty. You need to be careful where you lay. You hear me?" She said sternly.

Of course her statements automatically trump his so she had once again put her son in his place.

"Yes, ma'am." He said with a humbled voice.

"Love you, Ma."

"Love you too. Will, and we will see you at church."

"Bye."

"Bye."

He hung up the phone thinking of what she meant. You were her age once, what does that mean? He was conflicted because he thought about the fact that he and Tawanna had gotten pregnant at such a young age. Hell, but not that young, he said to himself. Now he had all types of pictures going through his head. The thoughts of having to raise his daughter's child while she finished school were not appealing to him. That was not the future that he had planned for himself or for her. She was messing up everything.

Then the thought of who the baby daddy could be. Shelby. Shelby! That was the name of that boy she was in the balcony with, Will thought. He snarled within himself at the idea. How would that look? A preacher who already had a child out of wedlock, having his child bear a child out of wedlock? That would really be great for the image of the church that you are Senior Pastor of. How could he Pastor a church when he couldn't even lead his own child to do right?

Since his mother had completely ruined his morning with news for him to ponder, the thought of calling Tamara was far removed from his mind. His focus was on talking with Al and asking him for his take on the whole situation. He knew that Al would jump the gun a little and that was what he had done. Jumped the gun, because she really hadn't said exactly what it was that she wanted to talk about. So, he had speculated everything.

Al had problems of his own, though, going on at his own house. It seemed as if the things that he had been trying were not working. He still was not having sex with his wife. She still didn't know about the prostitute but she still didn't trust him. They were sleeping in separate rooms and she was starting to set aside money for a divorce. He didn't know about the money, though. He knew everything else, and that was enough to make him uneasy.

He had tried everything that he could think of to get her to at least open her heart to him again. They were having date nights. He was giving gifts and calling her at work all the time. None of it seemed to worked. Annoyance seemed to be her reaction by most, if not all, of it. Sunday morning was the morning that he was going to leave and in his mind he wasn't going to be coming back.

"Sharon, I am getting ready to go and meet Will at Pascal's." He said as he loaded up the Ford Explorer with his things. He didn't get everything, but just enough to last for about a week.

He didn't want to alarm anyone but he needed to get ready for what was probably on the way.

He didn't know about the money that she was setting aside but he could just feel that it wasn't going to be right again. So he figured within himself that he would rather leave now than to be put out later.

"Al, could you come here for a minute?" Sharon asked.

She was no fool either. She knew something was up because he wouldn't normally announce that he was leaving to go meet Will at Pascal's. That was always a given for Sunday mornings. He would meet Will and then after they finished, he would come back and pick up the family. She wasn't a fool and she wasn't going to let him get off that easy. He was going to have to let her know what was going on before he could leave.

He made his way upstairs to find out what she wanted. The kids were still asleep and he didn't want to wake them but she probably already had when she yelled to ask him to come up before he left.

"Yeah, baby?" He asked her.

"Is there something going on?" She questioned.

"What do you mean?" He responded looking suspiciously.

"I am not dumb, Al. I know when you are up to something. This has the workings of you being up to something. What is going on?"

"Baby, I...I just don't think it is working out."

"So what, what are you trying to say?" She asked looking confused.

"You and I, I don't think it is working. I have tried everything that I know to try but you don't seem to want me or this anymore and who am I to blame you. I understand. I am not mad because I made the mistake. But I have been trying to work it out and it just seems to me that you don't really care about me anymore. So I am just going to move out until we can get things back together or until we can get this divorce done."

"I...Who...How did you know?" She asked with a look of amazement.

"I may seem a little lost to you, but I am not stupid either. I knew that you were thinking that because you have never treated me like you have been treating me. I can see the writing on the wall as well. I want what is best for you and for me. If this isn't going to work then I am willing to let you have your space while I get myself together and have my space. I didn't really want to talk about this until after church today, because I have to preach and I wanted that to be my focus for today. I don't get this opportunity very often, at least not in front of the whole congregation. So can we just leave it at this and discuss it later in the day?"

"Well...Yeah." She said.

She didn't wear the look of shock well. She didn't know what to do at that point. It was as if she had been dumped and didn't know how to respond to it. She was anticipating dropping the divorce papers on him. But, for him to move out on his own recognizance, well that was not what she expected at all. The idea of him being gone had been a good one before this point. Now that it had become a reality, she didn't feel so warm and fuzzy after all.

Al didn't enjoy that at all. He didn't have a feeling of accomplishment by saying what he said. He felt more than anything like the greatest of failures. He had failed his kids and her because of his desire. He wanted to make love to his wife. That was all that it was. Is that such a bad thing, he thought. Of course that was not the bad thing. The bad thing had always been the fact that he had sex with Sister Smith and he was trying to have sex with a prostitute that turned out to be a cop. That is what started all this mess and turned his life upside down.

As he walked out the door he could hear her sniffles through the gap of the door hinge. As much as he wanted to stay he had to go. Staying with things the way that they were was not going to make their home happy again. Even though leaving wouldn't make it better either.

This was the first time that Al was late for Pascal's. He had never been there after Will. There is a first time for everything.

"You are late, my friend." Will said to Al as he walked in.

"Yeah, yeah, I know. Had a lot on my mind and a lot to deal with before I left home."

"So, what's up? What's going on with you and the wifey?" Will inquired.

"You mean the ex-wife?" Al responded.

Will's mouth dropped. His heart rate increased. He couldn't believe what he had heard.

"What?!"

"You heard me. I think it's over, dude. It's over."

"No, no, no… See, it's not over. It's not over till I tell you that it's over. You need to go back to the house and talk to your wife so that you and she can make amends. You don't even know what you are doing right now do you?" Will asked vehemently.

"You are right. I don't know what I am doing. I don't know what to do. I love her, man, I do. I have tried to work it out. I have tried everything that the counselors have been telling us to do. But she is just not trying to cooperate. She is just not trying to give me another chance.

I know that I have to earn my way back in. But, dude, I am telling you. It seems like I will never do enough to make it right. She isn't really giving me any indication that she wants us to get back together. Everything that I do is just wrong. I am not getting a break at all. If I could just see that at some point she was happy then I would continue. I would feel like I had a chance. You know, that I had something to continue to fight for."

"What about the kids? Aren't they worth the fight?" Will added.

"Why do you think that I am still here? I love them as much as I love their mother. I haven't stopped loving her or them. I still love them with all of my heart and I want things to work out with all of us. But, dude, I am not going to be bitter and unhappy in my own home. I would rather be bitter and unhappy somewhere else if that is the way that I have to be."

Will felt like he had been hit by a one, two combo in a prize fight. Dazed and confused, but determined to give Al some advice to help him believe enough in his marriage to try to save it.

"Dude, I don't know what to tell you. But I do know this. There aren't many out there like Sharon. You are going to be very disappointed if you are looking for someone to replace her out here in the dating world that I live in. I promise you that. You need to do some real soul searching and think about what really matters. Because she is all that you have in the end. And that is much more than what I have, trust me."

The waitress interrupted them long enough to grab their orders. Silence on both sides of the table as these men thought long and hard about this grave situation that Al was faced with. Then Al posed a question.

"Will, answer me this: should I not want to have sex with my wife? Should I want to have sex with someone else?"

Will thought about that one. He was so right in everything that he had just said. The problem was that he decided to step out. That was the whole problem. That really was the root of the issue. He needed to let his wife know what he really wanted from her and be honest about that.

"Have you told her that you love her and that you just want to make love to her?" Will asked.

"I mean, I have tried telling her that through what I have done for her to try to rekindle the flame." Al responded.

"No, that is not what I asked you. Have you, in no uncertain terms, told her that you want to make love to her?" Will inquired again.

"Well, no. I haven't said that to her." Al answered.

"Ok. There is your problem. Problem solved." Will said.

"How, again, is that solving the problem?" Al asked with a confused look on his face.

"It's very simple. Your wife doesn't think that you find her attractive. She thinks that you want to be single. So she has been feeling like you don't love her and why would any woman make love to a man that doesn't really want them?

You need to let your wife know that you love her. You don't need to beat around the bush. You need to tell your wife that you love her. Plain and simple. 'Baby, I love you.' That is all it is going to take. You say you love her right?"

"As much as a man can love a woman." Al replied, confidently.

"Then just tell her. Make sure that she knows it is from the heart. Make no mistake about it. When she can see that you are telling the truth, you will be able to fix it." Will finished.

"So, what are you going to preach about today?" Will asked.

"The title of my sermon is 'Looking to Heaven for Earthly Answers'." He replied.

They began to discuss the text and the overall flow of Al's sermon. Will tried his best not to influence his sermon but to just encourage him in his preaching.

"Will, I know you have more experience than I do with this congregation, but I believe they will feel what I have to say."

"Al, I think that you are absolutely correct. I don't think that they will have a problem feeling you and what you have to say. In fact, you will do very well. I am glad to have a chance to watch for a change. I believe that you are a capable minister and an excellent preacher so I don't expect any problems."

"Uh huh." Al said giving him a deep stare like he smelled something fishy.

Al didn't believe a word of Will's answer. He smelled a rat and he was going to find that rat out.

"You are up to something. What is going on with you? I know that there is something going on?"

"I think I am going to see if I can find out about this girl that I met a couple of weeks ago. I can't get her off my mind." Will said with a playful smirk on his face.

"Dude, you got that 'I am stupid' face on. Who is this girl and what did she put on you?" Al asked.

"Well, her name is Tamara."

Al thought about it for a minute.

"Tamara…why does that name sound familiar?"

"I have only seen her a couple of times like maybe three."

Al's mind was jumbling all the images that he had of women in Atlanta. That name just seemed too familiar to him. Like he had seen her or met her somewhere.

"How does she look?" Al asked.

"She is high yella with long hair and no, you don't know her. She does look familiar to me, though." Will said, thinking about it himself.

"What a minute. You said she is light skinned right?" Al inquired.

"Yep." Will replied.

"Does she have legs for days?" Al questioned again.

"Yep." Will replied yet again.

"Dude, she goes to our church." Al said looking at him as if he had seen a ghost.

"I am telling you, dude. She is here every Sunday. You have even shaken her hand. Dude, she goes to our church. Her name is Tamara Green. She is fine as all get out. You have seen her before. You just don't see her that often so you have forgotten who she is."

"Naw, dude, that can't be her, I would remember a girl like this." Will utters back.

"You should remember this girl. I have mentioned her before and you didn't notice her. She has been going here for a while, man. She sits in the balcony and she leaves early. I am telling you that is her. I promise you if you make your way to the balcony before the benediction you will see her. That is the same girl. She is fine too. Boy is she fine!"

Will just sat there in amazement because he could remember her then. Al was right. She had been at church all that time and he never had made a move on her. How could he have missed such a beautiful diamond in the rough for that long? Well, things happen for a reason he thought. His time was now.

So time had marched forward and the normal Sunday discussion was at an end once again. Will was more anxious than ever to get to church, for obvious reasons, of course. That reason centered around the balcony and whether or not he would be able to see her. Now his intentions were to sit with the congregation like any normal parishioner would. That, of course, was not what would happen at all.

Will took his car back to the church. Since he didn't have to preach he didn't have to go over sermon notes. Nor try to clear his thoughts so that he could hear a voice from heaven. This time he could just go the church and be a part of Sunday school. But trouble lay at the door. As he walked in the Deacon Jester hit him with the news.

"Pastor, there has been a break in. Someone apparently ransacked your office looking for something." Deacon Jester said.

The Pastor walked into his office and it looked pretty much like he had left it. The only area that looked touched was the area that lead to the Treasury Office. That is where all the books and things were tossed around. He also didn't see any signs that a break in had occurred. No broken locks and it didn't look like they were really looking for money because no one said that the treasurers office had been ransacked. Someone was looking for something of his.

"Deacon Jester, tell me this, why is it that they didn't go into the treasurer's office?"

"That is what we have all been trying to figure out. It doesn't make any sense to us and it didn't seem like they were trying to vandalize the place either. We all thought it seemed really strange."

"It doesn't *seem* strange, Deacon Jester, it IS strange. I think that it was an inside job. It was sloppy and no alarms were tripped. No police and no broken glass. Whoever did this didn't break in, they just came in and didn't have a key to my office. Were the custodians on duty last night?"

"No, they come in on Friday nights. If there is anything left to be done on Saturday night then the deacons do it before we leave."

"When did the last deacon leave?"

"We were out of here by 8pm."

"So, basically between 8pm and 8:45am someone came into this church and into my office and did this?"

"As far as I know, yes. I know that I was the last deacon out. I also know that none of us came back after that."

"Ok thanks, Deacon Jester, you have helped a lot. I am just going to go through my things to see what is missing. We may need to call the police, but I will let you know. For insurance purposes."

"Ok. That is fine, but I did have one question."

"What is that?"

"Did you know that your daughter was here last night?"

William Fitzgerald Wright's face had never turned red before he was asked that question. It was as if everything in him had just been undone because he didn't know that his fourteen year old had been at the church unmonitored. He knew something was up because of what his mother had told him, and in so many words had failed to tell him. This was not a conversation that he wanted to have.

William turned around slowly and pulled it together for a moment. He had to make sure that this wasn't just a case of mistaken identity. But, considering the fact that he had been there for a while, Deacon Jester wasn't going to mistake her for anyone.

"Are you sure that it was my daughter?" He asked intently.

"Well, it looked like she had been crying and she was here

as I was leaving. She didn't look very happy. I was about to talk to her to see if she had a ride or just to find out why she was at the church but then your mother picked her up so I figured she was alright. Is she ok?"

Good question, Will thought. Even though it was a good question it made Will more angry. Angry because he didn't know. Angry because it wasn't like he had to be anywhere or do anything the night before. He wasn't out on the hunt, he was just at home, which is not that far from the church. That angered him more because instead of coming home, she went back to his parent's house.

"Yeah, she is fine. I don't think that she was crying, though, I think maybe she was having some issues with her contacts. She just started wearing them this year and she has had problems with them recently since they were a new pair and a different prescription." Will replied.

He had to lie. Anything else would have made him look incapable of handling his daughter. His pride and his hypocrisy wouldn't let him lead people to that belief. That was too much even for a man of the cloth to take. Especially for a man of the cloth who is supposed to have it together.

Al arrived to find Will in his office trying to place some of the things that had been on his shelf back into their rightful place. Al looked at Will working to do that and realized that he too was still in shock about it. He seemed as if he was ok, but Al could tell that something was amiss. There was that unnatural gleam in his eye that led him to that conclusion. But the more he looked, the more he realized that it had nothing to do with his office being ransacked. It was something altogether different.

"Will, wh-what is going on?" Al asked.

"Well, nothing, outside of the fact that my office was broken into and I don't know what happened to my daughter or why she was up here at the church alone and crying yesterday.

Outside of that, nothing is wrong." Will said with a straight face.

"Ok. Ok. So, when did all this happen again?" Al asked in amazement.

"Well, let's see. It had to have happened somewhere between 9pm and 9am this morning. Somewhere in between those hours, we think."

Al looked around the room to try to figure out who 'we' was.

"Who, again, is we?"

"The 'we' that I am referring to is Deacon Jester and myself."

Al was relieved. For a minute there he was beginning to believe that Will had snapped. But his answer let him know that there was still a little bit of sanity in that brain of his.

"Well, have you spoken to your daughter yet about everything?" He questioned.

"Nope, not yet. I will be speaking to my mother first, who lied to me this morning. She has a lot of explaining to do."

"Will, I don't want you to leave this office without having prayer with me, ok?"

"You know what, I don't think I can be sincere and pray right now, Al. I am so upset, d man. I just don't like the idea of my daughter not telling me what is going on with her. I am supposed to… I mean, I need to know about these things when they happen. I don't need any surprises, and I not know about it. I have enough surprises with this church."

"You are right about that. But come on, dude, you are always at this church. You do spend a lot of time away from her. Maybe she did want to tell you or maybe she would be afraid to. You guys have been butting heads as of late."

"True… True."

"Now, you remember being her age, don't you?" Al inquired.

"Yeah, I remember."

"Did you go to your parents and tell them the first time you had sex? For that matter, did you go to them when you got into some trouble?"

"Uh, no and no."

"That is what I thought. I didn't either. They had to find out on their own. Now, why in the world would your daughter be any different? They say the apple doesn't fall far from the tree."

"Yeah, I guess you are right. No, you are right. I don't know, Al. I just expected that our relationship would be different. I was expecting her to be closer to me."

"You were right to expect that Will. That is fine. But deal with the choices in your life. You chose to be a Preacher, a minister. You had to make some choices on what kind of minister you were going to be. You spend a lot of time out visiting the sick during the week. You also have a lot of meetings with constituents and the like. Then, on top of all of that, you do what you do on Saturdays. This is how it has been for the last four years. When you are away, who is Kristian with? Your mother. So you have to expect that she would be closer to the only woman that has been consistently in her life for all of it."

Will sat there quiet for a moment. In his mind he realized just how right Al was. As much as he had thought about it, he had never thought about it quite like that. What Al said just made so much sense. He was right about everything.

"Al, let's pray." Will exhaled.

"Father, we pray that whatever the situation may be, that your servant William Wright be able to have the serenity necessary to handle it within himself. We ask that you would bless his daughter, Kristian. We place whatever has happened to her in your hands for she is your daughter before she is William's daughter. We ask that you would allow his relationship with her to grow and prosper. Lord, if there is anything that is separating them, let it be removed and torn down, never to return again. Lord, we thank you for our past and our present. And we are praising you right now for the future that you are preparing for us. In Jesus' name we do pray. Amen."

Will felt better after that prayer. Al actually felt better, too.

The jitters that he had about his sermon went away. He felt like he could approach the pulpit with the power and authority of God. He was inspired. And he felt like he had helped his friend who had helped him recently. He also felt better about the power of God in his own marriage. He thought about what Will had said to him earlier and was going to take his advice as well. He was going to go to his wife and tell her that he loved her and that he wanted to make love to her. That is all that he ever really wanted.

Chapter Twelve

Tamara Green was sitting in her normal spot. She was at church on time as usual. She drove from Smyrna to church every Sunday to hear the Word and to see the man that was on her mind, Pastor Wright. Now, she had never been a church groupie or anything, but she did have this private thing going for a very public Pastor. And everything that she wanted was right in the palm of her hands and she didn't know quite how to take that. She realized within herself that she was in one of those be careful 'what you wish for' situations; because it might just happen.

Her problem was the fact he had revealed to her, a side that she really didn't think existed within him. She thought it was all hearsay. She thought that they were making that stuff up. For him to step to her the way that he did, oh, no, she thought. But still, she was conflicted. She still had a thing for him. She didn't know how to let that one go. On top of that, as much as she didn't like the way that he came off, She liked the way that he came off. A part of her was feeling it. She wanted him to come off that way. Maybe it was the alcohol or maybe it was just the umph on the inside of her, but knowing that he wanted her like that turned her on that night.

Of course she would never let him know that because she wouldn't want him to try that again. She did feel like if she had followed where he was leading, she would be where all the others were, and that was not going to be her plight. She refused to be a number in the list of numbers. She wasn't a virgin but she wasn't a slut either.

It's funny but she knew that he would be looking for her. She didn't know when but she knew that much. There was no way that he would allow that to be the end of their conversation. She also knew that he would figure out that she was a part of his church. She just didn't know when. She was about to find out when.

Will made his exit from his office to let Al settle in and get ready. He was supposed to be on pulpit in support but Al gave him a reprieve because he understood his situation. Plus, he wanted a critique that he wouldn't be able to have from the pulpit. He believed that Will would be better suited in the congregation anyway.

Will knew that he wouldn't be sitting with his family. He knew that he didn't even want to look at them yet. He had to get his mind off of everything and what better distraction than Tamara. Seeing her in the dark was a delight. She was fine in the thick of dark shadows and dim lights. He wanted to see her splendor in the fullness of a well lit church. That was not all that he wanted to see, but he kept his mind and his lust at bay. After all, he was in the house of God.

Lil Junior slithered into the Pastor's study to see if they had seen the mess that he left. Of course, he had to play the role of shock and awe.

"I can't believe someone would do such a thing." He said.

"Who had access to the church?"

"I don't know all who have access. The Pastor said that he believes it to be an inside job. It looks that way to me too." The treasurer responded.

He went into the Pastor's study and found the deacons and the Pastor's praying as they prepared to start service. He was late and, as always, didn't know how to make a humble appearance.

"Amen!" He said inappropriately.

"In closing, Lord please bless this service and every person that enters our sanctuary today. Please let your Spirit fall upon all of your people as we lift your praises on high. We thank you for today, yesterday and forever to come in Jesus' Name we pray. Amen."

"Amen." They concurred.

Lil Junior noticed that Al was robed. As tradition dictated, only the speaking Pastor was to wear a robe, so that would have to mean that Al was speaking. Now, who gave Al license to speak? Of course, he knew the answer to that one but it still irked his nerves.

"So, you are speaking today." He said with slight attitude.

"Yeah." Al returned with the same type of attitude.

Lil Junior looked at him with spite written on his face. Al looked back and recognized what was headed his way. He knew that Satan's imps would try to change the spirit in the sanctuary and in his heart. But, he was not going to fall for it.

"You know what, Lil Junior, I don't have time for this right now. I am going to do what God has determined for me to do today. If you are going to be on pulpit this morning then we are about to march in. If not then I pray that the message will touch you from the congregation."

He left it at that. Lil Junior didn't even have time to respond. It was time for service to start.

Will made his way up to the balcony and to the row where his future conquest awaited. She was sitting pretty in her clingy green dress with heels to match. The outfit fit her to a tee. Not too flashy, yet enough to be noticed. Not too revealing, but enough to intrigue. Everything to accentuate the positives, but never too much to reveal more than necessary, he thought. After all this is the church not the club and she knew the difference. That just added to his intrigue and his desire to get to know her better.

As he slid past about three people on the row he was greeted as a Pastor would be. The questions and answers; then more questions and prayer requests. A Pastor's work is never done, even when you aren't on pulpit he thought.

Finally he reached his goal, her. He saw that she had her purse sitting next to her as if she was saving a seat for someone. He didn't greet her but asked the inevitable question.

"Is this seat taken?"

"If it was, would it matter at this point?" She asked snappily.

He looked at her with slight shock on his face. She coyly smiled at him to let him know of her tease.

She moved her purse as to allow for a buffer between the two of them. She did not want to give the impression that they were together.

"I am surprised that you even knew it was me considering how long I have been going here and you never noticed me before." She said to him, looking forward as the choir began to sing.

"Who said that I didn't notice you?" He replied.

"Let's say that you did notice me. Why is it that you treated me as if you didn't know who I was? And if you did notice me, why did you try to treat me like I was one of the hoochies that you would deal with?" She asked. Her demeanor ever graceful, yet he could see that she was not budging on her point.

"Ok. I give. I give. You are right, I hadn't noticed you. But I realized the reason that I hadn't noticed you is because you were the balcony type."

She turned and looked at him on that statement.

"The balcony type?" She questioned.

"Yeah, you know... The sneak into church kind. The ones that never stay for a whole church service. That kind of church member." He said.

"Oh, really?" She responded.

"Yeah. Am I wrong?" He asked.

"You tell me."

"Well, let's see. You are a beautiful woman that apparently

likes going to the club. You don't get in until late and you have a tendency to sleep in late. So, you get to church late on the back end of that. You don't like to be crowded in downstairs, so, you sneak into the balcony. Since in your mind, no one really pays attention to the balcony, this is your place of refuge. On top of all that, you usually just dip out before the benediction and that way you beat the crowds and never even meet your church family or the Senior Pastor, for that matter."

"Wow. You just have me all figured out. I am just amazed at how absolutely incorrect an individual can be. That was so well crafted, though. Like you thought about it for such a long time. It deserves at least an A for effort."

"Ok, well, tell me then. Why have I never noticed you?" He asked playfully as the choir sang the second song for the service.

"Well, I will leave it to timing." She replied as she slowly turned forward again to listen to the choir.

"Timing? Why, timing?"

"Let's see. You were with Stephanie. I was with someone else. A lot of your time was spent in your other pursuits, and you know what I am talking about. I paid attention to you but you never noticed me. Yes, I did leave early a lot because I was involved in other things that made it difficult for me to stay for the whole service. I am a member of a sorority and I have soror events that I have to participate in. Meetings, et cetera, so I had to leave early a lot. On top of all that, I didn't know if I wanted to even make myself known to you, considering your reputation and all."

"What reputation is that?" He said waiting for the right words to come out of her mouth.

"It's not what you think. You are a driven Pastor, so they said that it would be hard trying to be a woman in love with you. That is what I wanted to be."

His heart stopped for a moment. For a moment he took her seriously, but in his mind he knew that she had to be joking.

"William, I love you." She said. Then she snickered. He looked at her for a moment sternly and then finally his frown turned upside down into a smile of acceptance.

"I got you with that one, didn't I?" she asked snickering through her question.

"Yeah, you got me alright. You got me." He said smiling slightly. He wasn't as amused as she appeared to be. He knew better than to believe her completely. Even if he did believe her, his heart wanted to believe that there was a certain level of truth in that statement. And as luck would have it, his intuition would be correct.

Tamara was smart enough not to stay too long on that subject. She didn't want to bring too much unwanted attention to something that he was not prepared to deal with. She did want to see what his reactions would be to that idea. Even as she laughed through the statements that followed, she was taking note. She was a calculating woman and she knew how to do her homework. No need in putting yourself out there when you know that the other person is not ready. Then there was the fact that they had not even gone out on a first date yet. So, that would be the next question to be asked.

Tamara turned and looked softly into Will's eyes.

"So, when are we going to go out on a date?" She asked.

Will was slow to answer that question.

"I will get back to you on that one. Pastor Williams is about to bring the message."

Chapter Thirteen

Pastor Alfred Williams stepped up to the pulpit podium with a sense of urgency and power. His conscience was cleared of all the things that had happened within the last few weeks. At this moment it was a conversation with God's people on God's behalf. And he was ready to speak.

He had prepared for this moment in his spirit. His wife and his relationship with her prickling his mind, yet his determination and resilience were the fire that burned. He knew about all the wrong that he had done, but purpose overcame past transgressions. A fire within him compelled him to speak the words of God with a power and authority as he had never done before.

Instead of the nervousness that once would befall him in the wake of his crusades, he was filled with a burning desire. A fire like none that he had ever felt before. Even though he had to deal with Little Junior moments before, none of that could change his focus or his desire to speak the Word of God.

"Good morning, First Baptist."

Congregation responded with a good morning in return.

"I am glad to be in the house of the Lord one more time, how about you?"

They clapped in response.

"I would first like to give honor to God Who is the head of my life and the ruler of my soul. I secondly would like to thank

Pastor Wright for this opportunity to break open the Bread of Life and preach to this church as the Lord would have me to. Now, turn in your Bibles to the book of Romans chapter eight verses thirty-two and thirty-three. When you have it, say amen."

He waited a moment as he continued to see and hear the turning of pages. Surreal it seemed to him. He had crusades and all but there was a different aura to the church on a Sunday morning. An aura that always made him feel alive.

"Again, that is the book of Romans chapter eight verses thirty-two and thirty-three. When you have it, say amen."

Congregation responded with an "amen".

"Take a deep breath, we are reading this together. 'For I am persuaded that neither life nor death nor angels nor principalities, nor things present nor things to come. Nor height nor depth nor any other creature shall be able to separate us from the love of God through Christ Jesus our Lord.' The title of my sermon is; For I am persuaded."

As Will listened attentively to him from the balcony, he could hear the passion in his voice from the very beginning. He knew that this was going to be one of those special occasions. When the Spirit was like fire shut up in the bones of a vessel named Alfred. Instead of continuing his romance pursuits, he realized that duty was calling.

"I am going to have to give up my seat after all. I need to get down stairs to the front row so I will have to get with you on that date thing another time. But if we are going to go out on a date then is it ok if I call you?"

She looked at him with a 'well, duh' kind of face.

"Were you expecting a special invitation?" she asked with spunk.

"Well, I don't have your number anymore. I mean, did you really expect me to call you after all that went down that night?" He asked.

"Yes, in fact, I did. You were the one that owed me an

apology. An apology, I expect to receive over dinner this week. So, when you call I expect it to be regarding our date this week."

She looked at him with a look that touched what she wanted to touch. She knew what she was doing and even though he knew it too, he couldn't resist being drawn in.

"Ok. I know what you are doing but I am going to play along. What is the number?"

"It's 404-683-4937."

He takes his cell phone out and adds her to his list.

"Make sure that my entry is different than all the rest. Because, trust me, I am going to be different." She said with sass rolling her neck playfully.

"You already are."

As Will made his way out the balcony to head down to the front row, Pastor Williams was getting warmed up. You could hear it in the way that he roared in his presentation. He was pounding his fist on the pulpit as he talked about how even though he had been through something that year, he was still in the fight.

"I have not thrown in the towel! I am still in this fight. I have been down. Satan thought he had me. The flesh thought it had me. But, God! I said, God, lifted me up!

So, I am persuaded that life will not stop me from serving Him. Death will not separate me from His love! Angels can't keep me from calling on Him. There is neither a king, nor a prince, president, governor, nor a mayor, that can separate me from Him! There is nothing today that can do it, nothing yesterday that could have done it, nothing tomorrow that will! There is nothing high enough and nothing deep enough to keep me from my Jesus!",

The congregation was stirred up as he preached. Sister Smith was crying and standing, waving her hands saying, 'Thank you, Jesus'. Sister Calhoun was shouting hallelujahs from the back.

"I refuse to be a washed up Christian! I will not be brought down to a powerless Christian that doesn't believe that the Word is worth the ink that it was printed with! I am sick and tired of sick and tired Christians!

God is sick and tired of powerless, prayerless, excuse-driven, backsliding, lazy, whoa-is-me, ungrounded, spiritless, loveless, cold hearted, wannabe holy roller, Christians that act like they haven't sinned but are constantly excusing their sins and judge other harshly for theirs. He can hardly stomach the big 'I' and little 'u' mentality that exists today. There is no big 'I' and little 'u', there is only Jesus who is the Top and the Bottom of it all.

So, I am persuaded that God will be my focus. I am persuaded that I will be a witness even when others aren't. I am persuaded that there will be joy in my life, despite what I am going through. That I won't be that gossiping Christian. That I won't be that backbiting Christian.

I am persuaded that I will trust in the Lord with all my heart and lean not to my own understanding. In all of my ways I will follow Him and He will direct my paths!"

The church was in an uproar at this point. Everyone from the balcony to the first pew was standing and clapping. His wife was crying. That broke his heart at that very moment, and he had to say something to get what he was feeling of his chest.

"You know, this year has been a hard one for me and my family. I haven't been the man that I needed to be for my wife. I haven't been the man that needed to be for my children, either. The devil tried to set a trap for me. I am not going to say exactly what has been going on, but I am going to tell you that I have learned that I will not be moved from the side that God exists on. I believe, no, in fact, I know, that God has a purpose for me and that purpose has nothing to do with the things that I was being drawn away by."

He began to stare intently at her as she cried looking back. She was holding their youngest son in her arms and the tears were like streams running down her face. His composure was broken and he could feel his eyes welling up with tears He wasn't afraid of crying because he knew that he had a reason to.

Small drops became larger ones. He just stood there for a minute and looked at her with those tears falling. Once she noticed his tears she started crying all the more. She couldn't believe that he was actually crying. It was as if it was just to let her know that it was not quite the end. She felt at that moment that maybe, just maybe there was chance for them. He felt the same way. He cleared his throat and then he began to speak.

"I think that God is in the mindframe of reconciliation. He wants to bring families back together. He wants to bring my family back together. I know that my wife loves me. I just want let her know now that I am sorry. Baby, I love you and I know that I have some things wrong in our past but tomorrow will not be like yesterday was."

He walked down from the pulpit and grabbed his wife and hugged her as tightly as he could. She hugged him back in the same fashion, sobbing on his shoulder at the same time. The whole church was peppered with clapping and shouts of hallelujah as they embraced.

At that time, Pastor Will stepped up and made the appeal.

"If there is anyone who is ready to be persuaded; if there is anyone that is going to give up the things of this world and if you are really ready to look at this world from a new light; then I am urging you to come on down and stand here with me. The doors of the church are open and God is waiting on you and He wants you to come to him and lay your burdens down."

As he continued to open the doors of the church, Pastor Williams continued to hug his wife and hold his son. He was just crying on her shoulder. She couldn't stop crying and holding him as well. Sister Kincaid held the children as they stood there.

Pastor Will, while he was holding the doors of the church

open, decided that they were also going to pray for the marriages of the church.

"I know that I may not seem as if I know what it's like to go through something in a relationship such as marriage. And you are right, I don't. But God has compelled me to ask all of those who are married to come to the altar. We are going to pray for the marriages of the church. We know that the devil is attacking the family. So we are going to pray for your families, that God might be the center and the Cornerstone of you household. He is reminding you that He has your best interest at heart. So, take him at His Word."

The front became filled with families, first, including Pastor Williams, his wife Sharon and their children. There were over fifty families in front of him. Pastor Will didn't really realize just how many families were dealing with issues until he made that call. He thought that maybe, just for a moment, that Al was the only one dealing with it. But the realization became so apparent when all of those families came rushing up to touch and agree for that prayer.

Pastor Will prayed and had Pastor Al Williams to pray as well. Will embraced Al before the prayer and spoke a word in his ear.

"I know that the Spirit really touched you up there. I am glad that God can still use you and I believe in you, man. You have just taken the step that God wanted you to. I knew that He had a purpose for everything. I want you to close this prayer out and then I am going to let you spend the rest of the time with your wife."

When he finished his prayer, and looked around, Al saw that there was not a dry eye in the church. Not a dry-eyed male nor female, though none of the males would ever admit it. That was one of the highest days in Zion ever; because Al just let the truth in his heart come forth in his message.

Will began to think in his mind about reconciliation. He saw how Al had been given a second chance at love with his wife. That led him back to a place that he would often go. It led him back to memories of Stephanie, and why they didn't work. She was, after all, the only woman with whom he had maintained a long lasting relationship even if he knew in his heart of hearts that she and he just weren't meant to be.

For the first time there was another person that he thought of, as well. Tamara. He thought deeply about her the same way that he thought about Stephanie. If thinking about Stephanie was a problem, then thinking about Tamara was the mother of all problems. She came with a certain degree of difficulty because she was in the church, and she knew Stephanie.

Then reasoning gave way to a very smart question. Why do I care about what Stephanie or anybody thinks? He began to focus on the fact that people talk, etc, but his mind just couldn't let go of the truth of the matter. Pastors have a right to date, be married and be happy. But that was still another thought for another day. Today was a day to remember. It was a time to think about how good God was. Let go and let God.

Chapter Fourteen

Kristian Wright was at church that day and she was crying as well. She was crying uncontrollably but she didn't want her father to see. She snuck out of the church during the call, in hopes that during the commotion her father wouldn't see her. But she had no such luck. He noticed the tears and the fact that she left. And as hard as it was to focus on that during the heartfelt appeal, that was what became the next thing that he focused on in his mind.

See, for a father that was also a Pastor, he hardly had time to focus on his daughter the way that he needed to. He felt guilty a lot for that because he knew that she resented him for that. After all she didn't ask to be brought into this world. She definitely didn't ask to be born to a father that was going to be a Pastor.

On top of that, she had seen so much in her life with him. Stephanie, and having to hear about that and how it ended. The jokes from other children about her father and the fact that she was a bastard child of a minister. These things were constant in his mind. Yet with all that in his mind, he was not prepared for the words that were about to come.

"Will, I told you that I needed to talk to you after church today. You do remember that, right?" Will's mother asked on the phone.

It was about 3:30, and an hour and a half had passed since

church had ended. She knew that there were a lot of people that were trying to join the church and to get prayer requests in. But, it had been long enough for that, she thought. She figured Will was stalling.

Will, on the other hand, was trying to figure out why it was so important for them to talk now considering that when he asked questions earlier she seemed to be evading his questions. Something must have changed between the time that he spoke to her that morning and him speaking to her then, he thought.

"Yes, I am on my way home. I just had to finish up something here at the office but I will be on my way."

The more she badgered him about his whereabouts the more the cryptic nature of the non-conversation irked him.

"Ma, I am curious. Why now are you in such a rush to talk? You seemed like talking was something that you didn't want to do earlier. So, what's up now? Is there something that I need to know about?"

Will's question brought on a moment of awkward silence. Then, finally she spoke.

"I am not going to tell you anything over the phone. I will just tell you this. You need to talk to your daughter!" She said. Then he heard a click.

Confusion was nothing new for Will but he had never seen his mother behave the way that she did then. At that moment Al walked into his office. He looked at Will's face as he was holding the phone and asked the obvious question.

"Will, what's up with you? Why are you looking like that?"

"Well, let see. I don't know, my mother just hung up on me and she keeps telling me that I need to talk to my daughter. Something is up, and I am going to find out what it is."

"Well, do you want me to roll over there with you?"

"Nah, man, you need to head home to your wife. This is my cross to bear."

"Yeah, and you helped me with mine. Now, I am going to

help you with yours. I will call my wife and I am sure that she will understand."

Al called his wife and spoke to her about what was going on. She told Al to tell Will that she said hello. He did.

"Dude, my wife thanks you for everything. She thinks that you are like a saint even though you are a whore." Al said laughing.

"Tell her that this saint/whore said thank you for your support." Will said with a smile and laugh.

As funny as that statement was, it couldn't suppress his concerns. He knew he had to get home to find out what was going on with his little girl.

Al jumped in the car with Will and they headed to Adamsville. The air was still with silence even though Al tried to liven things up. He turned on the radio and sang in broken chords with all the songs. Will smirked and eventually commented on what was on his mind.

"I think that my daughter either had sex, is pregnant or something to that effect." Will said with anger in his voice.

"Why? Why do you think that she would do that?"

"Rebellion... She is mad at me for being me, the Pastor of First Baptist. I know it's my fault but I believe that is what it is. I mean why else would my mother seem so upset about everything?"

"Well, let's see. Could it be the fact that you hardly see her? Could it be that you are always whoring around on Saturday nights and she has to spend so much time with your mother and father? Could it be that you are so able to be involved in the lives of other church members and not in her life? Could it..."

"I get the point." Will said cutting him short.

"I know that I haven't been the best father. But I think that I have been a good father considering what I have been through."

"And she has been a good daughter considering what she has been through." Al replied.

"I mean she doesn't have a mother and she has had to learn how to be the woman that she is becoming through your mother. Who has done an excellent job, by the way, but she is kinda out of touch with the current times. Don't you think?"

Will responded with a nod.

"Then, on top of that, you are not showing her what manhood is all about because she hardly sees you in action. When she does see you in action you are really just caught up in something with church or some woman. The only time she even has seen you in a good relationship for a long time was with Stephanie. How do you think it makes her feel to know that she is marrying some other dude, when she was like the closest thing that she had to a step mother?"

It always seemed different to hear the truth from someone else. It had a stinging effect. Will couldn't deny that it was the truth. And sometimes the truth hurts.

"You need to think about this from her point of view." Al concluded.

"I know, but that is the hard part. By the way, that was some excellent advice. Just remember this. It is easy to give advice, but it is hard to live by it. Your day is coming too, you know." Will said with a smile.

"Yeah, but by that time I will be so old I will just be too tired to worry about it." Al returned.

They finally pulled up to the house. Will parked and noticed that Stephanie's car was out front. He knew that license plate anywhere. 'Satisfy' is what it read.

"She always seems to be there for Kristian when she needs her, even now." Al said as they got out the car.

"Yeah, I know. Always there for her but never there for me."

"Remember who you are before you forget and revise history to make yourself feel better." Al said.

"You know Al, I really love you. You really know how to piss me off." Will said with a slight quick laugh and then a hard stare.

"Let's just be real. That is all I am saying."

They walked into the house and they could hear the muffled sound of women conversing about something. Then, there was also another sound. A sound that Will had not heard in a very long time. It was the sound of Kristian crying. And that sound always broke his heart.

He walked in quickly and asked the obvious question.

"What is wrong with you Kristian? What is going on?"

They all turned and looked at him in unison; Kristian, teary eyed. His mother on the verge of crying herself, and his question did nothing to assuage her contempt for him at that moment. Then, there was Stephanie. She looked at him with an attitude that pierced his very soul. She looked more disappointed with him than she had ever looked in as long as he had known her.

He asked the question again as if repetition would confer an answer quicker.

"What is going on? Krissy, why are you crying?"

His mother stood up and he knew that his answer would not be what he wanted to hear.

"You are the Pastor of this big church. You are the mighty mighty Senior Pastor that is growning a church till it is busting at the seams, but you don't spend anytime to try to understand or even protect your one true family; your only daughter!"

His mother said at the top of her lungs. Will had never seen his mother so angry with him before but deeply he knew with good reason. Everyone was right about how William Wright had been so wrong in the way that he was treating his daughter. He played dumb to save face though.

"What are you talking about? What is going on, Ma?"

"Why is it that you do not know what is going on in your daughter's life? That is a bigger question. Huh? Why is it that she can depend on others to be there for her and not you? Why is it that you are praying to God every Sunday and you are not even spending any, I mean any, time with your daughter? Is this what God wants? Is this how it should be for a family that is leading a church?"

With that said Will yelled as loud has he could.

"Enough!"

With that the air stilled and their faces declared that this wasn't going to be an easy evening.

"I did not come over here to go to war with my mother, nor my ex! I came over here to talk to my daughter. So, I would kindly appreciate it if everyone, including my mother, would kindly give me that opportunity please!"

Stephanie then stood up and spoke.

"Do you really think that she wanted to talk to you about anything? That is your problem, Will you can't see through your own ego? We called this meeting because she needs to tell you something and she wanted us to be here with her to say it to you."

Will had had enough of the phantom secret that his daughter was suppose to be telling him. Everyone was alluding to it, yet no one was coming out and saying what it was.

"What is this secret? What? What is it? I am tired of this game. Is she pregnant? Just tell me, is that it? I don't think that I can take too much more of this. So just tell me. Is she pregnant?"

"Yes, Daddy, I am." Kristian stood up slowly and said. She had tears streaming down her face. Her words trembled as she spoke them. You could see that she was so afraid. She didn't know what he was going to do or how he was going to react. Yet, more than anything, she was just afraid of the future.

At that moment his face dropped. It was as if all of his fears, all of the fears that he had conjured up within himself, had just materialized in an instant. And there was nothing that he could do to change that fact. But there was so much that this meant to him. First, that meant that his daughter had lost her virginity. Secondly, it meant that she had had sex without a condom or the little negro that had sex with her, he thought. His chest tightened on the thought of all of this.

Kristian was waiting for him to say something though. She wanted him to just hug her and tell her that everything was going to be ok. But anything at that point would be better than what she saw on his face. His look spoke of disappointment, apprehension and fear. None of which brought comfort to the mind of a 14 year old who was new to the cruelty and disappointment that life could bring.

And the look in his eyes was vexing to her. It wasn't a disappointment like when she made that one bad grade on her report card. Nor like the time that she stole a dollar from her grandmother and got caught. No, this was the disappointment that only a father could have in his daughter. It was as if he was ashamed.

"Why are you looking at me like that?" She asked as tears ran down her face soaking her chin until the collar of her shirt had become wet from them.

"You hate me, don't you? Daddy, you hate me, don't you?"

Still, not a word uttered by him. Will just looked at her. He couldn't help it but he just saw her in a totally different light at that moment, and his face reflected it. He started remember how he had promised her grandmother that he would take care of her if she just let him keep her. How she would be so much better with her dad. How it would just make more sense for everyone. Then, bam! He has a teen age daughter that is having a baby at the age of 14. Not only was she four years younger than he and Tawanna, but she was also his daughter. The Pastor's kid. He couldn't even process that.

He turned around and walked out the door. Not a word or a syllable. As the door closed everyone was sitting there looking at it as if he was coming back and that was a joke…but he didn't. And even as that ended, this day was far from over.

Chapter Fifteen

The room remained filled with silence and the only sound that resonated was the occasional car driving down the street. Shock oversimplified the moment as no one in that room expected the outcome to be so disheartening. No one could believe that Will had just walked out without saying anything. Al looked at Will's mother. Will's Mother looked at Kristian whose tears were still flowing during this whole ordeal. Kristian looked at Stephanie. And Stephanie looked at Al.

"Well we don't really know if she is pregnant Al." Will's mother said.

"What?!" Al replied with a puzzled look on his face.

"Yeah, she has missed her period, so there is a possibility. But this girl won't go and get a test done. She has been so scared that she didn't even know how to approach the whole pregnancy test thing."

Al just looked at all of them.

"How did you expect him to take this? Did you think that he wouldn't get upset?"

"This is what we expected. This is what we were expecting to happen because he jumps the gun too quickly." Stephanie said with a straight face.

"He needed to know that his daughter was so scared and so upset about having had sex and everything that she couldn't even go back to church after today. She wasn't going to come back. She needed to talk to him about this, but she knew that he wouldn't be understanding or try to even talk about it. And look at what he did. Does he seem in any way understanding?"

"Because you hit him in the head with a lie!" Al rebuffed Stephanie.

"Would you expect him to be hunky-dory about his daughter's future? I wouldn't be. I would be pissed off."

Al walked over to Kristian to talk with her.

"Kristian, your father loves you. He wants what's best for you. You are one of his greatest concerns."

A teary eyed Kristian looked at her Godfather without a blink.

"The only thing that he cares about is me embarrassing him as a Pastor. He doesn't care about me. If he did he would still be here. He wouldn't just leave me like this! He wouldn't!"

The more she spoke the more her voice trembled with emotion.

"I need him. He is my daddy! He is all that I have! My mommy left me, why would he leave me too!"

Al could not come up with words to help soothe an ache as old as that one. He didn't even know that the longing in her was still there for her mother. After all, it had been so long since Tawanna's name had come up that he had almost forgotten that she was even around. Time makes you forget, he thought. But, love, like what Kristian had for a mother that she had no memory of, love makes you remember.

Will got to his car and sat there as his emotions stirred up inside him like some thrill ride at Six Flags. He didn't stick the keys in the ignition. He didn't even close his car door. He just sat there trying his best to get control over his emotions. He knew that his leaving may not have been the best thing for him to do. But he also knew that the words that he had to say would not have been any better. He could not talk to his daughter in a way that would be damaging to her emotionally. As much as it pained him, he understood that she would not fair any better if he was to kick her while she was down.

As angry as he was, he just felt so much more like it was his fault. He had failed. He felt like this was his punishment for all of the women that he had slept with and never cared. This was definitely something that he cared about. He knew that there would be consequences for his actions. But in his wildest dreams he never thought that those consequences would be associated with his daughter. That was his purpose for keeping her away. When he would do his dirt, he didn't want her to come in contact with his dirty ways.

"So, where is he, Al? Where did my coward of a son go? Where did the big Senior Pastor go off to?" Will's mother taunted.

She was the most ashamed even though her attitude showed more anger at her son than shame.

"He could even be man enough to talk to his own daughter about something that they should have talked about so long ago. I can't believe this. I just can't believe this."

Al looked at all of them. They looked despondent. Not one of them had prayed or asked God about anything. In fact neither had he.

"Mrs. Wright, I think it is funny now but none of us have prayed about any of this. Not me. Not you. Not your son. So I am going to ask you all a very simple question and I want you to answer it with yes or no ok?"

They all nodded in the affirmative.

"Ok. Do you believe that Jesus has the power to change things?"

Again they all nodded in the affirmative.

"Ok. Then we are all going to join hands and we are going to pray about it."

"I don't want to pray about it. I want my son to be a man about it." Will's mother rebuked.

"I want to pray about it." Will's daughter said still teary

eyed but a lot more calm. She seemed eager when prayer was brought to table. And that was all that Al needed to hear.

"Kristian, if you want to pray about this, then we will pray, ok?" Al asked.

"Ok."

"As for the rest of you, if you don't want to join in praying for the Lord to help us work things out for the best then you can just be quiet while we take our requests to the God of our creation. Thank you."

As reluctant as she was, Will's mother still joined in for the prayer. She knew in her heart that this was the right thing to do for everyone. She had seen enough of God working miracles in her life to know that Al was right from the start. Sometimes anger can blind you from the truth.

As Al began to pray, Will got out of the car. He prayed before he got out of the car as a means to prepare himself for the rest of the conversation that he was about to have. He knew that his daughter needed him more than ever now. He would not allow his anger, pride, or his disappointment to get in the way of him being there for his daughter.

"Father, it is in the name of Jesus that we pray for this family. We believe that you have a way of working things out for the good of them that love you. It is at this time, Lord, that because we do love you that we are bringing our petitions to you."

As Will walked in he could hear Al praying his heart out. He just stood at the door and watched and listened to his friend pray for his family.

"Lord, we need you like we never have before. We need you to bless Kristian. We need to know what your will is for her life. We don't know Lord, if she is pregnant or not, but you know Lord. So we are going to depend on your will to guide us. Lord, she is going to take a pregnancy test today and we are going to be here for her either way. But Lord, we are praying that you will be guide her into the right direction. If she is pregnant then, Lord, help her to be a good mother. Don't let her give up on life because of the bad decisions of yesterday. Help her to make good decisions for tomorrow so that her testimony will be made perfect in your sight.

And Lord, if she isn't pregnant, let her go and sin no more. Let this be the only warning that she needs in order to stop having sex before marriage. With all the things that are out there now that are seeking to destroy us, we don't want something like this to become the end of her life, not just the challenge to her future.

Lord, we thank you for all that you have done in our past. We thank you right now for what you are doing in our present. And we thank you in advance for the future that you have prepared for all of us. In Jesus' name I pray. Amen."

As they opened there eyes, Kristian looked and saw her father standing there. He looked ashamed at his actions but she knew that it was time for them to have a long talk. She was just so glad that he had come back to the house. Even as she was praying something in her believed that he would be there when she opened her eyes and as sure as the sun was setting, he was.

Will's mother was not as loving or appreciative as his daughter was to see him. She almost felt like it was his situation all over again. Those same feelings came back from fifteen years ago that she had not let go of. She had to check herself even after the prayer. She could feel it and she knew that it wasn't his fault. It was everything else.

Stephanie, on the other hand, felt like she had done her duty. After all, she wasn't supposed to be there anyway. She was engaged to another man and she didn't have to deal with all this drama with him. But she did love Will's daughter. So much so, there wasn't even a question about whether or not she was coming to see about Kristian. It was just going to happen.

In all of this, though, she felt that tug that she had hoped was completely gone. That pulled her towards Will, that connection that she had had with him in times past. She felt it again. That was one of her greatest fears; that she would feel it again and be drawn back into that web. As slight as the tug was, she still could feel it and it pissed her off.

All she could think about was that he's this cheatin' ass holy-roller Pastor, that has the most beautiful daughter in the world and he can't get his love life straight. Not even for her. Then she put in two years of her life with him for nothing more than heartache and pain and a possible pregnancy by one of his hoochies that he would sleep with. And she is still one of the hoochies that he sleeps with now.

"Will, can I talk to you for a minute before you talk to her?" Stephanie asked as she began to gather her things to leave.

"Sure Step… what's up?" He asked.

They walked toward the kitchen to get some privacy because she needed to be candid.

"Look, you need to know that she really loves you. She respects your opinion and looks up to you more than anyone. You are like the apple of her eye. Don't break her heart like you do all of your girlfriends, ok?"

"Why…"

Will attempts to speak but Stephanie cuts him off.

"Just don't break her heart. She is just a little girl. Be careful with what you say. She wants to know that everything is going to be ok. That is all that she wants to know. You need to let her know that. I don't care what you say, you let her know that she is going to be fine no matter what. And that you will be there to support her and that you won't turn your back on her. Remember she lost a mother. You lost a lover but she lost a lot more."

Stephanie left those words on his ears and walked back into the living room to get her stuff and headed towards the door. Will walked right behind her and headed out the door with her.

"Will, you are coming right back, right?" Al asked, trying to figure out where he was going.

"Yeah, I am just walking Stephanie to her car." Will replied closing the door behind him.

"Well, I guess prayer really does change things because he is back to handle the business he should have handled before he walked out." Will's mother said out of nowhere.

As Stephanie got to her car Will grabbed her hand before she could get in.

"What is all this?" Will asked.

"All of what, Will?"

"Why answer a question with a question?"

"Will, I don't know what you are talking about?"

Will looked deep into her light brown eyes thinking that he would be able to read her. But all he perceived was her lack of enthusiasm for the conversation that they were having.

"You know exactly what I am talking about. I have known you too long for me not to be able to read you. What is going on with you?"

"Will, let me ask you a question. Does it really matter? Does it? I am getting married in a few months and that is that. So, it doesn't matter. Ok. It doesn't matter."

"Well, why act on the emotions of it?"

"Will, I wasn't. I was so messed up by the fact that you left your daughter in that house by herself to deal with the fact that she might be pregnant. Then I started to see the pattern. You know how to leave your women but you don't know how to stay. Learn how to stay Will!"

She snatched her hand away from him as she got into her car. She took off as fast as she could, leaving him with that thought to ponder. And ponder it he did.

As he watched her car leave, those words reverberated in his head over and over again. They became like the vibration of church bells after the initial ringing. They continued to strike and shake his heart with their pitch and tone. But not enough to take his mind off of the fact that she was still in love with him in some way, yet not enough to be his.

Will walked slowly back to the house. He knew that this could be a turning point that could be mismanaged. He knew that God was working in him and with him and through him and maybe even against him for his own good. Hypocrisy was the word that had been in his mind for a while. He had become everything that he didn't want to be. He had become a hypocrite.

Will forgot that his daughter was born out of wedlock and that he was the father. Sympathy and years had clouded his mind from the fact that he almost didn't get to finish high school, let alone college because of the need to support a family. If it had not been for the fact that Tawanna passed away he would have had to truly be a man and be the head of a household barely old enough to have children, himself.

"Hypocrisy." Will said as he walk back into his parents house.

"What?" Al asked.

"Nothing… I just need to talk to my daughter. I need to let her know that I am going to be here for her regardless. I am not going to be happy about any of this but I am not going to crucify or kill anybody for something I did myself some fifteen years ago. I was young once and I am old now and I know that you can make mistakes in life. I have made enough of them. So, I am just going to let her know that I love her and I that I am always going to be proud of her even when she makes decisions that I don't agree with."

As Kristian heard every word, her face lit up with appreciation. She had for so long thought that he didn't care but she could hear the sincerity in his voice. She knew then, that she had misjudged a lot of what she thought to be receiving from her father. He was a father that was stern but for good reason and he was explaining it to her.

"Daddy, I love you."

"Kristian, I love you too. I am sorry about..."

"Daddy, no more. You have said enough. I am ready to go and get the pregnancy test. I am ready."

Kristian wiped her face and smiled. She gave him a hug that only a daughter can give a father. Love was wrapped up in it. It had been so long for them that it felt like she was a little girl again. She hadn't hugged him in a long time.

"So, am I going to the drug store to get this test for you or what?" Will asked his daughter.

"No, Daddy you don't have to. We already have one here we just haven't taken the test yet."

Those words sounded like music to his ears. Not the sweetest music, because he still didn't like the fact that they had to do what they were about to do, but music nevertheless.

"So, let's do it then, Kristian."

"I don't really think that is something that a little girl should have to do in the presence of you men. So, here is what will happen. Will, you and Al take a walk or go somewhere and talk or do something. Let me handle my grandchild like I have been all these years. Ok?"

Mrs. Wright had said what a nervous father and Godfather had hoped to hear: their way out of the situation.

"Krissie, we are still going to talk; I haven't forgotten."

Kristian was glad that he said that.

"Ok." She said.

They walked out the door and she and her grandmother went to the restroom to handle the issue at hand.

"Nana, I was thinking that I am going to go it alone on this one."

Kristian said as they headed to the restroom with the pregnancy test in hand.

"Are you sure you know what you are doing?" Grandma asked nervously.

"Yeah, I guess. I am old enough to get myself into this mess then I am old enough to deal with the consequences. But Nana, don't leave ok?"

Mrs. Wright, as staunch and as rough as she had been, understood. With tears in her own eyes she said what she knew would be true as long as she lived.

"I will never leave you. We're family. For better or worse, we will be here no matter what."

Chapter Sixteen

Lil Junior finally had an opportunity to sit down and read. His life had filled itself with an unusually enormous workload of evangelistic efforts. He had church ministries that he was over that were also keeping him very busy. But he finally had a chance to really sit down and read what he had been waiting to read. The diary of Pastor William Fitzgerald Wright.

The very idea of this diary buttered Lil Junior's biscuit. He ate it up. It was just the type of revenge that he enjoyed. It was as if God, not Satan, had set everything in order for him. To him, he knew that all of the secrets of a man that he hated would be written in that book. It was just so tantalizing to him he could barely stand it.

The problem was that he had to be discreet about it. Although he wasn't married anymore, he did have a roommate that went to church with him. That made it a little difficult to leave the book lying around. And the only other times that he had that he could read the book was when he was on the road. But for this one week he had his house to himself. And that would allow him time to carefully and meticulously study the words of his self-proclaimed nemesis.

He sat down with a bottle of Sutter Home Moscato at his study table with the book. He fashions the desk lamp properly so that ample light shines on the pages. He had planned for this particular event to be exhaustive. He made his coffee and tea for good measure. He knew that this would probably be his only opportunity to read it from front to back and he wanted to make sure that all the notes and the information was written down so that he could use it for later.

It was very clear that at this point the thought of what is good for the church was far from the mind of Cleveland Stovall, Junior. He didn't care anymore about the wishes or desires of his father. Nor did he care about the concerns or reservations of his mother. He didn't even care about the faith and hopes of his congregation. No his concerns were not even with how God viewed what he was doing. No, Lil Junior, in his own mind, is doing what is best for everyone, including Lil Junior. That is, he was proving that Pastor Wright was not the right man for the job.

Lil Junior had built a pretty good case up in his mind for not working with Pastor Wright. He was the only thing that was standing in the way of his redemption and his reign in the highest office at First Baptist. Pastor Wright also occupied the affection of his father's heart, which was something that for years he had sought to gain back.

So, for Cleveland, this had been a battle that was dear to his heart. He knew that he shouldn't have to do this but he also knew that he was right. He had to be…His life depended on it.

As he opened the black leather covered book, it looked as any Bible would look. The cover was smooth soft leather that felt great to the touch of hand. The pages, though used, still appeared stiff and sturdy to the fingers as Lil Junior thumbed through. He could clearly tell that the book had been a prized possession and was not going to be something that wasn't missed. This thought electrified his senses all the more.

As the first page was a warning to anyone that read this book:

And God will judge them according to their works
Both great and small, male and female, bond and free.

To all who read, know that I am human too
Therefore judge not that ye be not judged for with what judgment ye
Judge ye shall be judged; and with what measure
ye mete it shall be measured to you again

Lil Junior laughed audibly at the warning. The only thought that entered Lil Junior's mind at that point was how pretentious a person Pastor William Wright was. As for the warning, he didn't care if God said it Himself at this point. He was thirsty for blood and he had blood in the palm of his hands, at his disposal. 'Moving right along', he thought.

The first entry was about Will and Stephanie. The lovebird stuff that he could have lived without, but there was something in there that was of great interest. It seems as if Pastor noticed that Lil Junior does not like him, he thought. This was no big surprise given that Lil Junior made it no secret that he was not one of his most favorite people. But there was something that did shock him; just how much of his past that Pastor Wright knew about.

As he read the next excerpt his blood boiled within him.

Cleveland Stovall Jr. is the oldest of all of us. He is the eldest son
of the Pastor and the only one that has been helping his father
with this church since he founded it. He is also the one that the
majority of the members thought would be taking his father's
place. When his father picked me, he walked off the pulpit.

He left for a while, the church that is, and started his own
church. Even took some of our churches members with him
when he started his church. Now, mind you, that I was only 29
when I became Senior Pastor. He was 42 years old and had been
with his father at this church since he was 19 and in college.

The reason his father told the board of ministers that he did not give him the church as Senior Pastor was because he had an attitude problem and that is not something that a Pastor needs to have. He said that he loved his son dearly but he did not see in him what he saw in me- the temperament, patience and the passion for people, which his son lacked. So, as a Pastor he just did feel like he would be good fit.

But the fact that he saw all of those things in me infuriated his son. I had never seen him so angry. His eyes were not angry with his father though, which is how I would have thought they would have been. His eyes were pointedly angry with me. I am not the one that caused this but forever in his mind I will be the one that did.

See, he has this belief that I stole the affections of his father but it was never that way. I just wanted to be the best preacher that I could be, and I knew that I would learn a lot from his father. He never tried to do that. He believed that his father was a relic. He was a Pastor of the civil rights movement with a civil rights style of preaching. I understood that the man just knew how to reach people. He would tell us that the way to be loved and the way for a church to grow is to reach people. The more you reach them and show them that you are approachable, the more they will become followers of you and will help you reach others. So, I was a fan of his father and he was not. That is not my fault, per se. I believe that he just thought that blood was thicker than water.

The end result has been good and his father was right for what he did. With me and Al, we have two services every Sunday. We never had that before. Our church has grown from roughly 570 members to over 1400 members since I became Senior Pastor. His father taught me what I needed to know. People are the key. Make them believe in the mission of the church, and get the community involved in the church. Make it about the community of people that the church surrounds. He taught me so much. I understood him better than his own son did.

Lil Juniors eyes welled up with anger.

'Who the fuck does he think that he is?' Lil Junior thought.

His anger was unfounded in the words that were said. In truth the diary was right about it all. Lil Junior had thought of his father as a relic of the civil rights past. In his mind, gone were the days of marching together for the common cause of the people. The new way was prosperity and that was the ministry that he wanted to preach. But his father knew that people wanted still to believe that the church could make a difference in the community. Not for the purposes of prosperity for all, but for purpose of uniting a community under the banner of God.

He tried to move on but Lil Junior could not. He wished that the truth was not so blatantly before him in black and white, but it was. He didn't want to believe what he was reading but he knew it to be true and he was there when it was said. The problem with it was that it was something that he had thought to himself in private with pain, only to have it brought back to him in Will's diary, in shame.

This pricking to Lil Junior's heart only added to the resentment that had already settled in. But nothing could remove something that he was not willing to forget. And his goal, even more so at that moment had not changed. He was going to have his church come hell or high water or hell again. Pastor Wright and no army would stop that. Not even his father could stop that.

One hour of reading had been enough for one day but not enough for him to feel like he should stop. After thinking things through he knew that his time was limited and that if he was going to be able to use this tool against his adversary then he would need to be quick about it and have enough ammo to wipe him out. So he had to get past himself in order to move on in this diary. Moving on…

Entry Number 38:

Sometimes it feels like I am in this by myself. It can be hard when you don't really feel like you have the support of your family and friends the way that you support them. They seem to have to keep their distance because the fact that you are this 'big time' Pastor and they don't want to do this or that around you because you are supposed to be this way or that way. I am just a man that is trying to become who God wants me to become and be connected the way that He wants me to be connected. Nothing more, nothing less.

Entry Number 78:

I believe that I am going to have a problem with finding love. I need to know that a woman is with me for the right reasons and not the wrong ones. I need to know that she can believe in me when I can't even believe in myself. I know that I can be a little unconventional in my ways and I am a little needy, anyway. But, I need to know that she is there for me and can understand that I am always going to need her to be that backbone, that grounding for me. To keep me real, focused and honest with myself and with everyone else.

It is a hard life for me to live right now because I have to shoulder everyone's problems, myself. She would have to be my sounding board and shoulder my problems and I would be willing to do the same for her. As long as she has my hand in her hand and the same, we would be ok.

Reading more and more of the diary undermined Lil Junior's purpose. The more that he read, the more that he understood him. The more that he understood him, the more he hated himself for hating him. Cleveland Stovall, Junior wanted to believe within himself that William Fitzgerald Wright was all bad. That every fiber of who he was as a minister was a staged farce. That he was this thug that had come into First Baptist with a purpose and a mission that was stealing and cheating the church out of its goal and its purpose. He just knew that having his diary would show that to be true. But it was far from that.

As he continued to read Will's life story in his own words he realized that this was a man that was as unsure of himself, as Lil Junior had ever been. He had his doubts about his ability to be a good father. He had his concerns about being the Pastor of such a large congregation. He had his beliefs about whether or not he would ever see the light of day in a marriage. The more he read the more human he became, hell, the more likeable to Lil Junior. And that bothered him.

As long as Lil Junior could keep him separate in his mind he could hate him forever. But now he was seeing him for who he really was. Naked truth and a naked understanding of Will, a man that he had hated for so long, only to find out that he was just like him, blew his mind.

He kept asking himself; "how do I stay angry with someone that I can relate to?" As much as he believed that he deserved to be the Senior Pastor he just couldn't get past how much he could relate to his fears. Maybe it was the fact that Will had articulated everything that he had been feeling for all those years but his mind dwelled there for a moment. That is until the list came up.

The list was what Lil Junior had been waiting for. The list was the one thing that could destroy Pastor Wright and change the leadership at First Baptist. And the list was in the Diary.

Tanisha, Tawanna, Mia, Sandra, Stacey, Shrameka, Sanji, Rebecca, the White girl, Lolita, Maceyanna, Marquita, Laqushina, Stephanie, Tiffany, Alexis, Julia, the White girl, Victoria, the stripper, Ronnell the stripper, Adrian, Ann, Shante, Mary, Kim, Yolanda, Sylvia, and Sylvia's cousin, Denise, Jasmine, Sherri Ann, Sheryl Lynn, the sisters that were White, Nisha, the crazy one, Nishe the sane one, Tisha, Rita, Robin, Nia, Vivian Lee, the darkest, prettiest girl that I have ever seen, Sharlanda, Nevada, Kendia, Kendra, Michelle, Sasha, Yasmine, Eulene, Yvonne, Kimberly, LaQuashina, Evelyn, Penelope a White girl, Mesha, Jennifer, and Shandra.

When he looked at the list his eyes glowed with excitement. Pushed to the back of his mind was the fact that he could relate to him. That thought was no longer an option. Pushed to the forefront came the power of this new found information to crucify his adversary. He knew that he had what he needed now. Everything about the list was juicy enough to make it easy for him to manipulate the situation. But how would he use it? He could simply just blackmail him into stepping down. Or he could just out him. Or he could do both. 'Decisions… Decisions…', he thought. It was like being a kid in the candy store. You have all of this candy in front of you. What are you going to eat first?

He didn't finish the diary that night. He chose to revel in his find. Knowing that he had Will, his enemy, in the palm of his hand, made Lil Junior's dreams more pleasurable as he slept that night. And even if his dreams weren't pleasurable, his plans were enough to keep him sound asleep for at least one night.

Pastor Wright was going to be having a more sound sleep, himself. Maybe for just this one night but at least the idea of his daughter being pregnant was no longer a possibility. The pregnancy test had confirmed that she wasn't. He had prayed that prayer and believed that God would not put more on his little one than she or he could bear. After all, if Kristian became pregnant it would have been his responsibility to take care of the child. Like father like mother.

But more importantly than that, it would have severely limited his daughter's potential. A potential that he had hoped would only be limited by her imagination. She wanted to be a lawyer and she had the determination and the gift of gab so the only thing she needed to do was to get into a good school and finish. He was going to be there for her every step of the way. That was his goal and he planned on accomplishing that in her.

Yet still, Will had questions about everything even after that fact. Like who was the possible baby daddy? Was it the guy in the balcony? Was it someone at school that she dealt with? Would this be enough to make her change her actions?

It was a hard thought because it meant that Will, as a father, had to image his daughter having sex at the age of fourteen. It was hard for him to be rational when thinking of his teenage daughter in that respect. Everything in him wanted to go and beat some teenage boy to a pulp, which was still a good idea, so he thought. But a better idea was to find out who it was that was sleeping with his daughter. That was something that he needed to know.

All the doors were closed in his house and the cold and quiet of the night had nestled itself in. He and Kristian decided that she should stay at her grandparents for the night just because that was where she had been already. He needed this opportunity to rest his mind and she needed the same. His empty home had never been more appealing then it was at that moment.

He had already let his daughter know that he still wanted to have a talk with her. He knew that having a talk that day would not have been good for either of them. She had cried enough and he had been angry enough. The conclusion to the matter for that day was the fact that she wasn't pregnant. That was good enough...for that day. Tomorrow would be another chapter and another story that would be handled in its own time.

Tamara on the other hand had been left in the corner of his mind. He just remembered that he was supposed to get back to her regarding the whole date thing. With everything that had taken place, his mind had just been focused on so many other things that the idea of the date had just been last on his list. He still wanted to do it, unfortunately she was the last person to know.

His mind floated to the fact that he had not heard from her all day. He went to check his phone to see if he had any missed calls from the woman that he was hoping would be a new interest. He found that he did. She called five times. His mind was so focused on the ongoing drama in his life at the time that he didn't even realize that his phone had been vibrating with messages for about four hours.

He glanced at the message and call-list on his phone and noticed that he had 15 missed calls. 'A Pastor's work is never done', he murmured to himself. He decided to check to see who had called.

"Hey, it's me. I called to see if we were still going to try to go out today. I was hoping that it would be but tomorrow would be ok as well. Anyway I really enjoyed our conversation and I hope that we can do that again and maybe get to know each other a little better. Anyway, you have my number. Hit me up…"

Her voice rang cool and calming to his overstressed ears. He was glad to hear a voice that was not in any way associated with the mess of the evening. As much as she was a distraction she was a welcome one indeed for the night had been long. He had only enough time in the rest of this day to check his messages and go to bed. Remembering that he had made it through that night like all the ones before it. As trying as it had been he had another opportunity to get it right. And that was his prayer. To move forward, getting it right.

Chapter Seventeen

The following Sunday, Al and Will met at their usually place at their usual time. The place, of course, was Pascal's and the time was 7:30am. Kristian stayed with her grandparents and Will was actually on his best behavior. No bed warmers for this particular time. He figured that he should truly do what he had determined to do in himself. That was to sleep.

He had been so busy being the Pastor, the bachelor and lover, and the father for so long, that he hadn't allotted enough time for sleep. So when you don't allot for it, it allots for you. He made a decision that sleep was just better than everything. But even in resting, his mind would not allow him to. He had to find out a few things. Number one, who was the young or old man that was having sex with his daughter?

Every time that thought entered his mind his temperature rose a degree or two. He didn't know how to handle the feeling that kept growing and growing in the pit of his chest. He had a little girl, his little girl, that was having sex with someone that may be her age or older. Wasn't she too young to be having sex? He asked himself that question so often but the problem was that fact that he too had been sexually active early himself.

But he was an older man and a different man now than he was then. That was his way of trying to rationalize the reason for being harder on her than he ever was on himself. But his mind would not let that be the end of his thought. He was reminded of the fact that his whoredom had not stopped even to the current day. So would he choose to be a hypocrite and be harsh about something that he was doing himself? Or be real with himself and his daughter and reveal that he too had a problem with the flesh and that he was working through it and had been working through it for a while?

Al was great, though. He and his wife Sharon were working through their problems with a lot of energy. The couple had found a reliable babysitter. They were going out more often and spending more time in prayer together. They had even taking an opportunity to sign up for a marriage ministry retreat just for the two of them.

Al had made up in his mind that he would not go to bed angry with his wife anymore. His motto had become 'we can work through anything;. Sharon realized that all her husband really wanted was some affection and she was ready to give it to him now. Gone were the acts of malice in the bedroom. She was no longer the Nazi between the sheets when it came time for lovemaking. She was open and wanted to please her husband in every way.

Now that part was a little puzzling to Al because she was doing all the things that he had wanted her to do. The sex with his wife was great. She was giving him oral. He, of course, as always, would please her in the same way. She was open to new positions and they were trying the hard ones. His wife, once prudish, was now educating herself with 'The Joy of Sex' and 'Kama Sutra'. She had no problem with all of the new tricks of their sex life. But in Al's mind, what was it that changed to make her into this new person?

Al was not complaining. But his mind could not help but wonder if she was cheating on him. He knew that she had been upset by some of the things that he had done. He knew that the whole prostitute fiasco was still somewhere fresh in her mind, and that if she did cheat, he deserved it. But what he couldn't understand is, if she was cheating, then why was the sex with him so good?

Conventional wisdom said that if someone had been sleeping with another man or woman, the husband or wife would be able to tell because the other party would become disinterested in sex. That thought didn't set quite right for Al because he had more sex with his wife in the past month than they had in the past 3 years.

Sharon, on the other hand, had just come to the true realization that she loved her husband. She just wasn't very sure before, and with good reason. He was a dog before they got married. She knew of all the women that he had gotten down with over the years and how he and Will would hang out and do their thang. And then there was the infamous "List".

The List was the collection of lovers that had been compiled by the both of them from high school through, at least for Al, they got married. Al's list numbered thirty-four. It included every woman that he had ever slept with and whether or not they were good. As for Will, his list had not stopped. It currently numbered about fifty women and counting.

Al was required by Sharon to destroy the list when they got married. In fact, he was so bold that he called everyone on the list and let them know that he was getting married. He wasn't quite able to reach everybody because some of the numbers had been changed over the years. That was one of his bachelor party activities. The burning of the book, but of course, the calling of the numbers came first.

Sharon fell back in love with her husband when she saw him on the pulpit preaching and letting her know before everyone that he loved her more than he ever did. She loved him for apologizing and meaning it; for being willing to seek counseling for their marriage and for not giving up. She was glad that she had married him. And that happiness in her and the love that had been rekindled in her was making her horny.

They say that women have a stronger sex drive than men.

Take that into account and couple it with the fact that she had been holding out for about a year, and even then was only having it once a month. So she had been hard pressed for quite some time. To be back in love opened the floodgates, which let her be able to be the sexual being that she was. Of course, in opening the floodgates she never let Al know what he was about to have to deal with.

So Al was puzzled. He couldn't figure it out. He didn't want to just ask her about it because he felt like that would be rocking the boat. He thought to himself, if I say too much about this, I won't ever have sex like this again. Yet still he couldn't help but wonder about things. It was too much for him to take considering how he had been and was at the time.

"Dude, do you think that my wife is cheating on me?"

Al sipped his coffee and looked at Will with mischief in his eyes after asking that loaded question out nowhere. There had been a moment of quiet between the two of them at that point anyway. Will was still thinking about everything. That question almost made him spit his coffee out of his mouth.

"What?"

A shocked Will asked, immediately placing his coffee down.

"I was just wondering, do you think that my wife is cheating on me?"

Will looked at Al with an 'I am with stupid' look.

"I don't know, man, I was just wondering. Things have just been too perfect lately. I just don't understand how we can go from being one way to being another so quickly. If that was the case then why didn't it happen this way before?"

"Al, I understand what you are saying. I do. But, look at it from a spiritual standpoint. You prayed about it, right?"

Al nodded in the affirmative.

"So, that means that you believed that God was going to move on that prayer, right?"

Al again nodded yes.

"So, God made good on His answering of your prayers. What is the problem, then?"

Al was about to respond but then Will came quickly with another statement.

"What is the problem, negro? From what you are telling me, the sex is better than it has been. Then on top of that, y'all are having it more often that you have in years. She is doing all the things that you like and more. Plus, she is satisfying you orally. And that is something that she never did, even if you did her. It sounds to me like you don't know what you want."

"Dude, it's not like that."

"Yes, it is, dude. Your wife went from being cold in the bedroom, to being a Spanish firecracker and you are complaining. She is doing things to make you want her more and she is happy about doing them. She doesn't mind trying something new. Is the oral good?"

Al nods again confirming his approval as he sipped his coffee.

"Then, she is giving good head to her husband. With all of that going on in your favor, you want to ask is your wife cheating on you. Give me a break. Be real, dude. To me it sounds like you are getting what you asked for and you are scared of it."

Al looked at him for a minute. Will looked back and slowly lifts his coffee up for an audible slurp.

"Will, I am not afraid of my wife."

"You are right. You are not afraid of her. You are afraid of what you asked for. You wanted to have sex with your wife. You wanted to be more intimate with your wife. You wanted her to want you. She is and does now, everything that you wanted her to. You guys are happier than you have ever been and you are still complaining. Don't you think that is a little scary acting?"

Al didn't respond. Will just looked at him for a minute.

"I'm just sayin,"

Will cleared his throat and went on to finish his point.

"If it was me, I might be scared, but she would never know. I would enjoy my wife until I couldn't enjoy her any more. On top of that, have you even talked to her about it?"

"No, Will, I haven't. I am scared to. I don't want her to stop and place me back on punishment. I am very happy with the sex that I am getting and I am glad that things are working out for us. The part that I am having problems with is the fact that...she is just so good now.

I mean, before it was just ok. I liked it but it was just ok. But now... dude, she be putting her thang down.

9:30 had made its way to the timepiece on Will's arm. Will noticed the time and began to finish his coffee.

"Al... according to the Word, marriage is honorable and the bed undefiled. Bang your wife and enjoy it. Be happy that your sex life has returned."

They got up from their table and left their tip. As they walked from the table, Al asked Will a question that he was not prepared to answer.

"Will, have you ever slept with a married woman?"

When the question came out, it was a bother. Will thought to himself how to answer that question. If he were to be honest it would be yes. And he felt he could be honest with Al. But he didn't want to even put that out there with his best friend. That was an answer that was best suited for his diary.

"No. That is one line that I won't cross." Will replied.

"I have."

Will just looked at him. Al's answer just made his feel bad for lying and worse for making himself seem holier than thou.

"Please say it was not a church member. Please say that it was not someone from our church. Please say that. Please. Pretty please."

Al was being honest and open about it.

"I have had an affair with Tylese."

Will had a panic face on. Shock and awe came to mind. He

could barely breathe. It was as if someone had stood on his chest and stopped him from breathing.

"You are sleeping with Tyrone's wife? Deacon Tyrone's wife. That is who you are sleeping around with? Our friend, Tyrone? The one who goes above and beyond when it comes to serving the church? That Tyrone?"

Al couldn't even look at Will.

"Ok. Ok. Tell me this then. Has this continued since you and your wife started to get more intimate?"

Al looked down as they walked to their cars. He was pretending that he didn't hear the question.

"Ok, Al, I am going to repeat the question. Are you still fucking a deacon's wife in our church?" Will asked in an almost yelling tone.

"Because if you are, I need to know that. I have been giving them marital counseling. Your dumb ass is messing up still. A deacon in our church! An active deacon in our church! What are you thinking?"

"I know dude, I know." Al said with tears in his eyes. Will was already overwhelmed by all of the church drama and Al's added philandering was not making his life any easier.

"Ok. Ok. I get it now. You want to take the guilt off. You want to feel guilt free. I am not going to help you with that. Sharon is a good woman. She will be a better woman to a man that loves her and won't be cheating on her every chance he gets. Keep on, you are going to fuck around and lose your wife and I won't be able to keep you as a Pastor. Keep it up!"

"Will, I am sorry."

"Sorry didn't fuck the deacon's wife. Sorry is not the one that is still caught up in mess when your wife is showing you everything that you have asked for. What is wrong with you? Then you want to come at me, asking me is she cheating. If she isn't, she should be."

Al was silent. Everything that Will said was true. With each word he felt smaller and smaller.

"You need to fix it, dude. I am not getting myself mixed up in your mess. I have enough of my own. In fact, I am not going to do the counseling anymore. You will be doing that on your own. And if they get a divorce, if they even think about getting a divorce, her blood and the blood of their marriage and yours is on your hands."

Al just looked at him.

"I just want for once there to be a Sunday morning, when I am not going to church and preaching with something on my mind like this. I just want to preach the acceptable Word of the Lord."

Al thought about it for a minute.

"I am going to remind you of something because I think that you have forgotten. You are a whore yourself. You have had so many women at the crib this year it makes no sense. Do you remember what Jesus said in Matthew about judging? I think it was 'judge not that ye be not judged and with what judgment ye judge ye shall be judged'.

You need to take stock of your own stuff. You are no better than I am. You just haven't married a woman, but you are married to the cloth."

Then there was the pinch. Will felt it because he knew that Al was right.

"You are right. I am just as bad. I am sorry about what I said." Will said as his mind wondered back to all of the indiscretions that he had made in just the past two months alone. But it did not moot his point as it pertained to Al and his relationship with his wife or the deacon's wife for that matter. And Al knew that Will's words meant action was necessary.

"No, I needed to hear that. I also needed to know that they are going through marriage counseling. I am going to leave it alone." Al stated.

"Sharon loves you, dude. You love Sharon. Make that enough before you don't have that anymore." Will said as he gave Al a hug and got into his car. Al got into his car headed back to his house to get the wife and kids for service.

It was a typical Sunday service. Slightly mundane because of what had just been exposed. Al knew that his friend was right about everything. He had been right about his relationships in the past. He was right about Sharon and everything. He was even right for chastising him for having an affair with Deacon Tyrone Walter's wife. His problem was that he was addicted to the thrill of it all. But, his friend helped him see that this was a dead end road that he was traveling on at break neck speed. Everything that he ever wanted with his wife was at his fingertips and he still couldn't let the side action go. He knew that he had to make a decision. He just didn't know how to do it.

William, Senior Pastor of First Baptist Church was better in his own mind. Al had set him in the right frame of mind too. You are not sinless. So, for Will, all the service was about reflecting on how things were, and looking forward to making them better than they were.

Yes, service was ok. But what was even better was the fact that the Word of God was making its rounds in the hearts of these two Pastors.

Chapter Eighteen

"I am taking it to my father!"

Lil Junior yelled at his mother for not backing him. He had come over to talk with the elder Stovall about his plans and what he knew. Lil Junior knowing that they would not be pleased with his decision to take such a divisive course of action.

"Why can't you support me on this one, ma? I am trying to right a wrong that Dad made when he chose to make that man our Senior Pastor."

Sister Betty cut her eyes at her son incensed by his tone. She knew the conniving ways of her son all too well. She also knew of his unnatural hatred for William, not because he had done any one thing. But, because he represented everything that he was not; that was the real problem. Lil Junior hated Will for being better at ministry than he was.

As she looked at him, she saw that this was just another opportunity for him to go against his father. It was always about a son wanting to outdo his father. She knew that he just wanted to be accepted by his father, who, of course, had always accepted him. Senior just didn't believe that his son was ready to run his church.

"I am not supporting you because this is not what is best for the church. You know and I know that Pastor Wright is the best thing that has happened to this church since your father. He has studied what your dad has done over the past forty years and has emulated it to great success. You don't even like your father's methods. You don't like his preaching style. You don't like his outreach. Why would you take that to your father and then have him be moved against everything that he has done for the church that he loves?"

Lil Junior rolled his eyes at his mother in disapproval.

"You are just as bad as him. You love that church more than you love me!"

Sister Betty was not in the least bit moved by his melodrama.

"Boy, you are so... I don't understand how you say the things that you say. You don't have to listen to me. But you need to listen to somebody because your envy is going to do more harm, for you and for a whole lot of people, than it will good."

Sister Betty walked out the room disgusted with his attitude and ashamed to call him her son. Lil Junior didn't care. He was listening to everything that she said, but he heard none of it. His mind was made up. He had all the evidence that he needed. His plans were coming together but he needed to see what his father would do or say.

For Lil Junior, this was the greatest vindication that a man could ever have. He had long doubted his father's choice. He had long been at odds with his father's decision-making abilities. No one would support him in that thought because his dad was the man that built that church with his bare hands from the ground up. So he could do no wrong. Now was his opportunity not only to show the world that his father was wrong, but also to out the person that he despised. No greater opportunity had ever presented itself for Lil Junior.

But, Lil Junior had another problem. He couldn't do what he should have done because he was so caught up in his thoughts of revenge. He had to go and tell his parents like the little kid that still lived in him. He had to get their approval first. As much as he disliked his father, in his mind he knew that his father had sustained him. He was the reason that Lil Junior even had made it as far as he had.

Lil Junior was not the best child when he was younger. Being a Pastor's son was not an easy life. There was always the constant teasing that took place. The constant razzing about how soft a Pastor's son is. How much of a goodie-goodie he was. So he was in trouble a lot.

He dropped out of high school at sixteen and went to live with his uncle in Chicago for a while. That was not the best move for Junior. The change of scenery was supposed to make him a better man, but living in Chicago in the 1980's was a bad choice for someone who already had a knack for finding trouble. His uncle sent him back after about a year.

When he returned from Chicago, he told his father that he wanted to preach. His father sent him to Carver Bible College. It was there that he found his calling to be a minister and to preach the gospel. This made the elder Stovall a very happy man.

He had always hoped that his son would be a minister like him. He had always wanted to mold his son into the kind of minister that would be able to take over his church. So, from then on, Lil Junior would help with the church functions and fill in the gap where needed.

The problem was that Lil Junior did not want to be molded. He wanted to run things his way. See, for Lil Junior, he already had an idea of how things were going to go now that he was a minister in God's house. He figured that he would be promoted soon and would start working himself into the finances of the church. In his mind the big business of the church interested him more than the people of the church ever did.

Plus, he wanted that spotlight. He wanted to be seen. He wanted to be on the front row in the center aisle of anything that was church related. Didn't matter how or who saw him, he had to be the center of attention.

His father had watched him long enough in the early years

to understand that he was not ready then. Senior believed that over the years his son would be able to see in him the type of Pastor he needed to be in order to grow a church. That he would see the integrity in his father. His son would see Cleveland's slowness to anger and his true desire to serve; but Senior never saw the turn, the change in his son. It never came.

However, Lil Junior did help the church grow over the years. He was there from 1984 till 2004 first as a deacon then as a youth Pastor. He stayed a youth Pastor for about eight years until he was moved from that position to the position of evangelist. He would always do well as an evangelist because it played to his best side. He had the ways of a storefront preacher. His testimonies and insights on what was going on with people at that time were good. He understood people.

The problem with understanding people was that you have to relate to them. He understood and because he did so he tried to manipulate them. Things would just come out over time. He was caught up in some money problems with one of the church members. He convinced this one sister to give him some money to invest and she never saw the money again.

All of these things led to the sore relationship that he had with his father. Couple those things with the fact that his father told him that he did not see him at that moment as Senior Pastor material. That and his pick for the Senior Pastor position was a very young and inexperienced Pastor that was on fire for the Lord. He always felt as though he had made the wrong choice and that his father was doing that just to spite him. Yet with all that he has said, the church has grown by leaps and bounds.

So with all the ammunition that he had, his purpose was to prove to his father that his decision was wrong. He finally had the weapon that was irrefutable and could not be misconstrued or taken out of context. William's own words in print. His moment had come to shine, and he was not going to let his father take that away.

He made his way to his father's study in their house in Hampton Oaks. It was as much their house as it was Lil Junior's because that is where they had been only for a year and they were in and out of town because of the Pastor's speaking engagements. Lil Junior knew that the conversation would be a hard battle so he figured that he would come out swinging.

"You were always wrong, you know that, don't you?" Lil Junior said standing in the doorway to the study with a smirk on his face. He was reveling in his anticipation of victory.

"I found him out. I knew there was just something not right about him."

"Junior, let me ask you something. Why are you coming over here with all this noise in my house?" asked Cleveland Stovall, Senior.

"Is there something that you want? Did you even speak before you came in with all this noise?"

"Dad, I am… I am sorry. But I needed to tell you something of the utmost urgency."

"Ok, I don't need all that. All those big words don't do anything for me. You could have just left it at I need to talk to you about something that is important. I know important."

"Well, Dad… Ok. That is what I meant to say…"

"Well, Son, what do you need to talk to me about?"

His father still caused him to be unnerved when he spoke to him. Yet he persevered to get to his point.

"Well… Speak up, Son!"

"William is not fit to lead our congregation. He does not have the moral character necessary to lead this congregation."

"Moral character? What are you talking about, boy? Are you still chasing that dream? Why can't you be happy where you are?"

Lil Junior didn't like that question.

"Because…When I know that you have made a mistake I want to correct you on it, like the times that you have corrected me on mine. You made a mistake… correct it."

His father, the great Cleveland Stovall, Senior, looked deeply into the eyes of his only son. He could see the hurt, but he didn't quite understand it. He could see the frustration and the anger but because he knew what he had done for his son, he could not understand why there was so much of that type of stuff in him. He thought for a quick moment on these things and then he let him know what really was, and what was about to take place.

"Junior, listen... You have no idea what you are doing. I know that God has been good to me. He has been good to you too. Do you think that you coming to me with this is going to change the fact that he is the Senior Pastor?"

"Yes! It will because you are just the first person that I am taking to. I am taking it you first. Then I am taking it to the board. Then, if not the board, to the conference of Baptist ministers. I will bring it before the Southern Baptist Convention if I have to!"

Senior pitied Junior.

"Son, have I not given you enough? Have I not gone out of my way to make sure that you are taken care of, even when you really didn't want to take care of yourself? Haven't I?"

"Dad, maybe you did do the one thing that you should have."

That last sentence changed the attitude of Rev. Stovall, Sr. He knew that there was no getting through to him from that point forward. Now it would just be a battle of loyalty.

"I am not going to let you do this. I just want you to know that. I am prepared to go through whatever I need to go through in order to make sure that you are not the new Pastor."

Saying that only gave Junior a sense that he could possible get him ousted. Junior ate that up. He felt like he had won some of the battle.

"You know that I am right. You know, that is why you are trying to stop me from being the new Pastor. Why would you do that to your only son?"

"Because you are not fit!" Senior yelled.

The air hangs still for a moment. Then Senior spoke again.

"You are not fit. You don't love people like he does. You aren't concerned about the wellbeing of the congregation. You don't care about the direction of the community. You are interested in interacting with the choirs and helping them to achieve the potential that you see in them. You don't care! The only person you care about is yourself!

This guy that you hate so much, is a great minister. He is a man of his word and he cares about the people that he pastors. The only person that you have ever cared about is you. I have wanted to tell you this for a long time but that is your problem. You care about yourself and will do anything to make yourself look good. That is how you were when you were younger, that is how you are now. And I don't understand. I just don't understand."

Junior just sat there for a moment.

"So, I guess that is that, then." Junior smugly stated.

"Just know this, Dad. Whether you like it or not, a change is gonna come. Just be ready for it."

Lil Junior got up and stormed out of his father's house. Not so far removed from many other nights like this when he was a younger man. This time however, his haste and his fury would hold the quality of so many lives in the balance. And, as usual, his logic would concede defeat to his emotions again.

His father knew that this was not the end. No, his father knew that this was just the beginning. Just the tip of the iceberg for Lil Junior's relentless plan. A plan that was destined to fail even though Lil Junior couldn't see it right in front of him. He also knew that the more that he told Lil Junior that it wouldn't work is the more he would try to make it work. Determination ran deep in the Stovall family. His greatest frustration was the fact that for Lil Junior it was never for good and always for evil. Never for the right things and always for the wrong things, Pastor Stovall thought.

He sat in his study just to take the burden of pacing off his legs. These things pressed his heart like a brick in mud.

He knew that it was time to have a nice long chat with his protégé about his extra curricular activities. He also knew that there was about to be a storm brewing at his church so it was time for the troops to get ready to weather it. This is the time to see what Will is truly made of, Pastor Stovall thought.

He knew that the real issue was not the one that was about to be dealt with. No, the issue that was about to be dealt with was the issue of a minister having sex when he is not married. And as grand an issue that was, it was not the issue that he wanted to be on the minds of a congregation that was growing in the faith. William Fitzgerald Wright was an asset for First Baptist Church. How does one prevent him from becoming a liability? This was the question that rang out loud and true in the mind of an old preacher.

"How do I deal with this? I am supposed to be retired. This is something that a young man should deal with." Pastor Stovall said as he sipped from the cup of coffee that Sister Betty brought for him.

"I mean I am trying to deal with my son versus my son in the ministry. Both of them are in the ministry and they are both my flesh."

"True, but you have to do what is best for them and for the ministry." Sister Betty responded sipping her tea.

"What would that be? I'm an old man. I don't have time to be caught in these kinds of squabbles."

Sister Betty stared at her husband of 45 years and knew that he would realize that his answer was insufficient at best. She knew that she could expect better from even a man as old as him. He knew what that look meant. His response would indicate this.

"You don't have to look at me like that, I understand what I need to do. I am going to talk to Will about everything. I know."

"And?" His loving wife probed.

"And, I will try to help him with this situation to get through it. But it is purely up to him to make it happen. He has to want to move in another direction before a change can take place."

"Well how did you get over your mess?" His wife asked as she coyly reminded him of his cheating ways in the early part of their marriage.

"Wha? Well what do you mean?" He asked, playing dumb.

"Don't act like you don't know what I am talking about? You know what I am talking about. Don't play dumb, Cle." Sister Betty said with a hint of irritation in her voice.

"Do I have to remind you of the fact that you haven't always been saintly?" She asked with that irritation growing stronger.

"No, you don't have to remind me. I, I know that I have had a similar problem in the past."

"How did you overcome your issue, seeing that you are over it now, aren't you?" She questioned him probing and, in some ways warning him, to be careful of what his answer would be.

"It was family that kept me from doing it again. A loving wife and son and the idea of what that was worth to me is what kept me from getting caught up anymore." He said as if he had rehearsed it a million times before only to say it a million times more.

"Good answer." Sister Betty responded. She was glad even at her age to know that the answer had not changed.

"So, that is what you need to tell him."

"The problem with William is that he doesn't have the type of family or commitment that I had at his age. So, how can I tell him that?"

Betty got quiet. Her face tightened as she thought of what to say to her husband to help him in this endeavor. Then, out of nowhere, it hit her.

"Let him know that his church is his family, and to continue in the way that he did would be like denying the church and his church family that depended on his wisdom and guidance."

Cleveland Stovall thought and realized that he couldn't have said it better himself.

"That is why I married you Betty. You really are the brains of this outfit."

Sister Betty smiled with approval.

With that said the dilemma was settled. However, the situation was far from over. It had always been said that when it rains it pours. Will was enjoying what was the palm of his success, yet the failure that seemed so distant had made itself known on the horizon and it was growing closer. As Will's mother would always say, that which was done in the dark would come to the light.

Chapter Nineteen

"Old men have young eyes you know. We see what you see. We know better than you do, you know. And we would do it better too if it weren't for such old bones and a worn out pecker." Pastor Stovall, Senior said with a slight chuckle. He was glad that he was able to have the talk that he wanted to have with Pastor Wright, aka Will. He needed this time to make sure that his hand-picked successor understood that he was concerned about the things that had been said by his son. He also knew that things were going to get a lot worse for the both of them. Knowing what he knew, he needed to talk to Will before things got out of hand.

To Will, however, this conversation seemed out of place and a bit unnecessary. Will was already dealing with the fact that his daughter was having sex, which was the last thing that he ever wanted to deal with in his life. There were the other issues that he needed to be checked within himself. Also there was the fact still that he had unresolved issues with Ms. Stephanie. She was still the biggest thought in his mind, even though his mind had moved to another, namely Tamara.

No flame there, though, because there had not been enough time spent between the two of them. Tamara was busy doing what she did and Will, being that he was a Pastor, was doing what he was called to do. As much as he needed her to be there, his focus would not allow her the opportunity to be. So much so that she had begun to wonder if there was still a spark there on his end.

"Will, I know that I am going on and on about what probably seems like nothing to you. But really, I am trying to tell you something. And what I am trying to say is important."

Will became attentive and sat up to make sure that he was ready to hear what Pastor Stovall was about to tell him.

"Go ahead, Pastor, I am ready."

Pastor Stovall cleared his voice and began to say what he needed to say.

"I have never been one to mince words. You know that I will say what I feel. But, I am smart enough to know what not to say at what time and who to say what to."

Pastor Stovall paused and took a breath. His expression was enough for Will to be concerned. It began to unnerve him because it seemed like this was way more than what he had expected this conversation to be about. In his mind he just thought that the Pastor was just beating around the bush because he didn't have anything better to do. The longer Pastor Stovall paused, the more it became apparent that there was a real problem.

"I know about you and the women. I know about it all. I know that you have a problem with too many of them and it is going to have to stop now."

Will closed his eyes and didn't say a word. He emptied his lungs of air and then breathed in deeply. He almost felt like he had been hit by at truck. He didn't have a clue that it had gotten out there like that but he knew that it was building. After all the stuff that had been going on with his life, he hadn't even thought about the fact that his business, his own dirty little secret, could have been found out.

"I didn't want to have to address this. I have avoided it in the past. I know that we all have our vices and our issues that we have to work through. I had a similar one, myself. But, this is no longer just a personal issue. It is about to get a lot more public and I am trying to help you by letting you know that you have to shut it down now and for good."

William looked up with determined eyes and asked, "Who knows?"

"That is not important, Will. The important thing is…"

Before Pastor Stovall could finish his sentence, Will cut him short.

"I need to know who knows, and I need to know it now!"

Wills voice changed from labored to annoyed. Pastor Stovall felt the change in the room and he knew that things again were about to get uneasy.

"Will, I need you to calm down."

Will didn't like that request. He thought about what was about to happen, and he didn't quite understand how Pastor Stovall could expect him to be calm when he knew that his life was about to change forever.

"How can you tell me to be calm when my life is at stake? Would you be calm?"

Pastor Stovall knew that his answer would have been no. But his goal was to get Will to develop a game plan because this was a situation that could and would get out of hand fast. He knew that in this situation the cooler head would prevail.

"Will, let me tell you a story. I was your age; in fact maybe I was a little younger. I was married and I was still out there but the Word had found its way into my heart. I knew that I wanted to be a preacher and that I wanted to build my own church and preach the Gospel throughout the world. But I also had this problem about having too many women.

It was fine at first. You know, I could have one on Monday and Tuesday and all the days. But, it never stays fine. They always start to overlap and then stuff gets messed up. I ended up almost ruining my marriage and I almost lost my career over something that wasn't worth it.

I was able to get damage control over the situation and developed a plan that allowed me to keep everything under control. Developing a plan helped me to keep it from blowing up in my face. I want to help you develop a plan, but you have to trust me on this one... Like you have never trusted me before."

Will looked Pastor Stovall in the eyes for a few minutes and didn't say a word. He just couldn't believe that it had come to this. With all the stuff that was going on in his world, why now, this? Why did his skeletons have to fall out of the closet at this particular moment in time?

All he could think about was how was his daughter going to take all of this? And what about his mother and father? Their son, the whoremonger preacher? His mind was taking him on a roller coaster ride with all of the twists and turns that you would expect.

Then there was Stephanie and Tamara. What would they say? Stephanie was not a real possibility, but this would definitely end the slight chance that he had there. Tamara wouldn't be seen with a Pastor that was about to lose his church. Who would? How would he explain the chain of events that were about to happen to him?

"Son, I know this is a lot to take in. I didn't know any better way to tell than to just tell you. I want you to know that this is not the end. I believe in you, and my wife believes in you. We just need to come together in order to make this work. If we don't, it will not go well for you. And if it doesn't go well for you then it won't go well for this church. You are the new face of this growing church. Rise or fall, I need you to make it happen."

As much as Pastor Stovall was telling, he wasn't going to say who the person is that has ratted out William. No, because in saying who that person was he would create a firestorm that he would have a hard time putting out. Two Pastors fighting against each other? His blood born son versus his spiritual son? Not the type of controversy that one wants to add to an already controversial situation.

Nonetheless, William did not miss that he hadn't said who the snitch was. He knew that it was Lil Junior from the beginning of the conversation. He had already answered him in so many words. William was determined though, to move in the direction that would make it possible for him to continue being the Pastor of that great church. He knew what this was about.

'Revenge runs deep in the blood of the scorned'

That was a phrase that he remembered well from his seminary studies. He never thought that he would see the application of that phrase against him in his lifetime. William realized that this revenge was greater than him. It was greater than being a Pastor against a Pastor; or ideologies clashing. This was about a father and a son. This was about a choice and the consequences of that choice. This was about approval and redemption, or the lack thereof.

"Pastor Stovall, I will do whatever you want me to do. I will work with you on making this plan happen. But, I am not stupid and you can't pull the wool over my eyes. I know that your son is up to this. I know that, whether you say he is or not I know that he is. I feel it within me. Revenge runs deep in the blood of the scorned. You know the phrase. He is fulfilling it right now."

Pastor Stovall closed his eyes and meditated on what Will was saying and then it clicked. The Book written by James Edwards called 'The Lighthouse" was used in seminary. In it there was a quote by the father in reference to the fact that his son was seeking vengeance against a father that had subdued him all his life.

"And for my son to return with fire for my flesh I do understand; there is a vengeance in him. I must admit to my treachery. Therefore I do understand that revenge runs deep in the blood of

*the scorned. So I too, must have that which I have done returned
to me. For I am not above nor below the path of retribution."*

"Will, I have done nothing but love my son. You know
that. I know that. He just has his own opinion of you and of
everything. This I cannot change. I just want him to finally
see the error of his ways before he brings everything down in
everyone's life who is involved in all of this."

Pastor Stovall paused again and thought on those words.
Poignant, pointed, and piercing were they to a father's heart.
He could only feel pain from the thought that it had come to
this. He the father, versus his only son.

"I knew that you would figure it out. I know that we can
prevent him from having his way with this one and destroying
all that you and I have built in the process. I want what is best
for First Baptist. I have known for a while that having you as
Senior Pastor is what is best for this church. I know that if he
wins and we lose that it will not only hurt us, but it will destroy
First Baptist. They will not follow him. This I know."

What Pastor Stovall said out loud was what Will knew
in his heart. They weren't going to follow Lil Junior because
he didn't care enough about them. They had never been his
focus. And they never would be. The entire situation was about
power and struggle for that power. Not even direction or what
was right. It was really just about power. Who has the power
to run the congregation known as First Baptist Church? Sister
Betty Stovall walked in and whispered a word into the ear
of her husband. Pastor Stovall nodded in the affirmative and
focused his attention back on Will as she left. He had some
disturbing news that signaled that there would be no playtime
for them. It was about to get ugly and ugly quick.

"Pastor Wright, I know that we have a lot to talk about, but I
am going to have to get back with you on this tomorrow. I need
to retire for the night and make some things happen before the

new day wakes me up. We will make something happen really soon. Do I have your word on it?"

Will looked him again straight in the eyes and said with confidence, "You can count on me." As Will walked out of the room, Sister Betty stepped in and had a few words that she wanted to share with him.

"Pastor Wright, I have known you long enough to say that when this is all done with you will be alright."

As comforting as those words were to Pastor Will Wright, his mind wouldn't allow him to believe them. The faith of a man of faith was being tested in so many different ways. The very idea of getting through this newfound situation just seemed far-fetched, he thought. In a lot of ways he knew that he would but what would he have to lose in order to get through it?

"Sister Betty, I know that you are right. I know that I am going to get through this. I know that God is going to work all of this mess out in the end. But I just can't see that end right now. I am just dealing with so much and I have so much on me that I just can't see that end right now."

In saying that, he has acknowledged within himself that this was all his fault. After all, he had been the person that was in the middle of all of the mess for as long as he has, so he thought. Maybe it was high time for the chickens to come home to roost. Maybe like Jacob, the supplanter, he needed to wrestle with the angel in order to see his way to the promise.

Sister Betty continued, "I know that things don't look good right now. I know all about your stuff and how you have acted. I don't care about any of that. That is for you to figure out within yourself." Sister Betty paused for a moment. She could tell that she needed to say more, but she wanted to make sure that her words were right. Then she continued.

"What I do care about is your faith. Your faith in God, and your faith in the church. Now, people are going to be people regardless. Don't worry about what they say."

William gave her a funny look as if to tune her out after her last statement.

"I know that may seem easier said that done. Just remember that God knows your heart and what you have been through. People don't care. But no matter what happens, remember that He cares about you and will always care."

"I understand that. I am glad that you care as well."

Sister Betty stared into his soul.

"I said to myself that I wasn't going to say anything, but I feel that I need to. My husband and I love you. You better fix this."

If no other words had motivated him and bothered him at the same time it was those. He was used to being looked to by church member and the like. But those words, from a lady that didn't pull punches when it came to how she felt made him stand up straight and move forward with a vengeance.

He could see the tears in her eyes when she said what she said. If he didn't actually see those tears, then the slight tremble in her voice would have given it away. It was as if the situation, out of all the other situations that had taken place in the last months, would be the one to cause the fall. And hearing the shudder added to the clear nature of how quickly and how terribly thing had gone with him.

Will finally thought to himself the thing that he should have thought a while ago. It was time for him to tell his mother and father.

Will got up in haste and made a quick dash for the door.

"Sister Betty, tell Pastor that I will have to talk to him later. I need to go home."

Sister Betty just waved and went back in the house after Will pulled away.

As Will drove away he began to run through all the things that would and could take place in his mind. This private information that he had kept that way for a very long time was now about to become public knowledge. Public to his congregation. Public to his family. His mind could not help but wonder how? How does he handle this situation without all of the collateral damage?

His mother would not take this well. At that point the cold winds of reality chilled him to his bones. He got goose bumps for fear of his parents' reaction.

And then, almost simultaneously, he realized that the one thing that he never wanted to disappear had. It had just clicked in his mind the real reason that all of this was happening now. He had lost his diary. That thought made his already troubled heart beat faster and harder than it had before. For a man that was about to go through the most trying time of his life, this diary represented everything that he was for the last fifteen years and beyond. He had his every secret thought in that diary, every dirty little secret. Every lustful image. Every woman that he had ever slept with in sequence.

His pulse began to rise as it became ever so clear that this was a situation of immense complexity because there was no way for him to deny what was in that diary. He had been so meticulous in his writings. So descriptive in his depictions of how curvaceous this woman's body was or what sexual position this partner enjoyed. It became so clear to him that, yes, his chickens were about to come home to roost. And roost they would.

Chapter Twenty

The ride from the Stovall's in Decatur was a long one, especially, if you had a million things running through your mind. Tina's words floating through his mind like a newfound curse on his life. She was right, he thought. He was about to get his. But in a lot of ways this was really what he wanted. This was really what he needed.

As crazy as the future looked to William, it was forcing him to do something that he had refused to do for so long. It was forcing him to finally deal with the demons of the past that had been haunting him. That which he enjoyed so much had also become his prison. As much as he wanted a fulfilling relationship, his desires had become skewed. His ideas when it came to relationships were unhealthy. He knew this. So, as much as he wanted to continue the way that he had been, he knew that he couldn't.

The main thing though, that was flowing through his mind was the thought of his diary. He was deftly afraid of what might happen. There was too much information in it for it to be in the wrong hands. And he knew it was in the wrong hands.

"Damn it! I can't believe this!" He said slamming his fist to the steering wheel as he drove. The horn honked quickly from his thrust as he passed cars to his left and his right.

"Lord, why now? Why now? Don't I have enough going on in my life? I can't understand why I just can't have a little peace. Is that too much to ask? I mean I have been a minister for a while now. I can't get one day of peace?"

The car was quiet and there of course was no answer from heaven to his question. After a few minutes, the cell phone rang. Will picked it up on the first ring.,

"Hello?"

"William this is Stephanie."

His heart started beating with a pace of fear. He didn't know what to think. Why would she be calling him out of the blue like this on a Tuesday night this late, he pondered within himself.

"Hi Stephanie… How are you doing?"

She caught the pause in his question. She knew something was up. She could hear it in his voice.

"Is there something wrong, Will?"

He couldn't help but think, how do I answer that? Of course the answer could not be yes over the phone.

"No. Everything is great. I was just thinking about you."

He defers, hoping that she won't pick up on the fact that he had changed the subject.

"Oh, really… Then why am I the one who called you?"

"Because I thought it would be too late to call someone who is getting married and has a fiancé. I respect you and your husband to be, just like I would any other married, or rather, soon to be married couple."

As he finished those words, the phone went silent for a minute. In fact it went silent for so long that William questioned whether or not she was still on the phone.

"Hello… Stephanie? Are you still there?"

"Yeah, I am still here. Any way I need to talk to you about something important. Can I see you tonight somewhere?"

The time was already 10:00 pm and most of the normal places in the City of Atlanta had closed. With Stephanie living in Marietta and Will living in the West End, It seemed as if the best place for them to meet would probably be the Waffle House.

Will still a little hesitant to answer because of the calamities of the day, decided that maybe that wasn't such a good idea.

"I don't know if tonight is a good night to meet up with you, Step. I have not had a good day. In fact I have had a bad day and I am not in the best of moods to be talking. I know I could use a friend right now. But, I believe that my best friend right now is my bed."

Stephanie got quiet again. She was disappointed by that answer.

"I need you, Will. I don't ask you for a lot. I need you to be here for me. Can you just meet me please?"

Will had never heard her so desperate to talk with him.

"Ok, I will meet you. Is the Waffle House on Northside Drive ok?"

"Ok. I will be there in about ten minutes." Stephanie replied.

"I will see you soon then."

"Ok, Will... bye."

"Bye."

As Will hung up the phone a sigh hung long on his lips. This meeting with Stephanie only added to all of the things that he had to deal with in his now tumultuous life. He had once talked about Al and all that he was going through and dealing with. Now his life had more drama than a soap opera and he was not, in his mind, cut out to deal with it. He never thought that it would be this way for him. Oh, what a tangled web we weave when we practice to deceive... ourselves Will said to himself. He chuckled sarcastically within himself because he knew that he had brought it all on himself.

While he was thinking about Al, Will decided to give him a call. But then he realized that including Al in on all of this right now would not be the best of ideas. Al had enough going on still in his life that bringing him in on this while it was hot and fresh would only make the situation worse. He knew that was not the answer. Besides, he was already there anyway and he saw her car sitting in the parking lot so it was time to deal with the task at hand.

Will got out of the car and walked slowly and softly to the door legs weary and weighed down with fear. It was unusually cool for that time of the year and with it being late spring the cold air was a great backdrop for the unusual events that were occurring in his life. He only took twenty steps from his car to the door but each one seemed like an eternity and yet each one seemed quicker than the first all at the same time.

In his mind he wondered, what could it be? It could be a number of things that she wanted to talk to him about. Yet, in the same breath, all of them seemed to point to the idea of something that he didn't really want to hear about. Things like her being pregnant, or jumping the gun on the wedding. He didn't know what he was about to get involved in. But hey, this was Stephanie. He would still walk on water for this girl and he knew that she knew that.

She was sitting in a corner booth on her cell phone, as usual. When Will saw her on the phone, his first inclination was to leave. His irritation was heightened because what she was going to tell him he knew that he didn't want to hear. So any excuse to not hear it was enough. Besides, he thought, what did she need him for if she was already on the phone talking this over with someone else? He was never one for being the second fiddle. Will, always had to be number one, especially with her.

"So, do I need to just leave and let you call whoever that was on the phone back?" He asked as he sat down at the table.

"Don't start. I was hanging up as you were coming in." She said as she politely placed her phone in her purse.

"I mean, I can go home if you just want to get whatever is wrong with you off your chest with the person you called. My bed is calling me, anyway." He said with his signature cynical charm.

"Will, I didn't come here to fight with you. I really wanted to talk to you about something that has been on my mind and the things that I have been going through. I think of you as a friend, even though we don't always agree on things." She said as caringly as she could.

Her careful nature with her words added to Will's already fearful inclinations. Will swallowed hard, clearing his throat to prepare for whatever was coming.

"Stephanie... I am here for you. Tell me what's on you mind."

"Will, I am pregnant."

And the words that he did not want to hear caused him to sink in his seat. He felt pain and then numbness. As if he had been shot in the heart and each second after was a moment in time before he realized that he was already dead. If hearing that she was getting married was pain, then this was indeed death.

"Con... Congratulations Step...I am happy for you."

His response was forced at best. Happiness was far from the sound, pitch, and tone in Will's voice. What was more was that she knew that he wasn't in the least bit happy for her.

"You are not happy for me. You don't have to pretend. I am not even happy for me."

Will's ears perked up on that last comment. As dramatic as the first words were, those words were truly unexpected.

"I don't think that I heard you correctly. Did you say that you were not happy about being pregnant by your future husband?"

Stephanie eyes didn't blink when she said it, and when she repeated it again they did not blink.

"I am not happy about this, at all."

William was still confused. He knew that they were about to jump the broom and he knew that she was ready to get married. Why wouldn't she be happy?

"You know my mother told me all that glitters isn't gold...I wish that I had listened to my mother."

As hard as she may have seemed, Stephanie was having a breakdown of her own.

"What is going on with you Step? I thought you guys were on the fast track to marital bliss. What changed?"

One tear after another danced slowly down her face as she began to explain the unraveling of her not-so-perfect world.

"He wasn't what I really wanted. More than that he wasn't what I really needed. After you and I and everything with that, I just wanted something different and something that wasn't you. I needed someone to need me and to want me and to let it be all about me for a change. You had so much going on in your life and you had so much that you had to deal with that I felt like I was just there. Then, there was that whole deal with you and you-know-who. I was not going to fall into something like that again."

Apparently, stress had not affected Stephanie's appetite. As she wiped her face and ordered her scattered, smothered and covered hash browns and waffles she continued with her story. Orange juice was more than enough for Will.

"Problems began early. He lied. You all lie!"

Will coughed as her voice echoed loudly from her yelling her last statement. Lucky for them there were only the cooks and servers in the place. And their stares were enough for Stephanie to realize that she was a little loud.

"Stephanie, can you bring it down a notch, please???"

Stephanie acknowledged his requested and brought her tone down a notch or two as she explained the predicament further.

"His lies, though, were over stupid, stupid, stupid stuff. He didn't even know how to lie. Then he just wasn't a man. He didn't have good job. He didn't have any of the aspirations that I would think that a man of 31 years old should have. Why is it ok to be living with a whole bunch of roommates at that age? Why is that ok?"

Will interrupted Stephanie with a question.

"Why get engaged then? Why do that?"

Stephanie paused. She wiped the tears from her face again. Cleared her throat and answered with words that he did not expect.

"I wanted to hurt you."

Those words stung like a bee to his neck. To Will, it all just seemed laughable. What the fuck, he thought. His thoughts were as fluid as water rushing over a cliff. He played all the scenarios out at that moment. Anger and frustration, determination and intensity flushed his face. He turned red, if it is possible for a dark skinned man to do so.

"You wanted to hurt me, huh? Seems like you winded up doing a number on yourself, doesn't it? That is really messed up! And I am supposed to be your friend. That is how you do a friend, huh? You go and get with someone and marry him to hurt your friend? That is how you do it?"

Stephanie just looked at him for a minute as he ranted. The more he spoke the harder she looked at him. Until finally he realized what she was about to say and stopped talking.

"William, Do you not remember what you did to me? Have you forgotten what happened between us? You don't remember the lies and all the bullshit that I have had to deal with from you even after our break up? I have trusted you and you have constantly betrayed my trust. You have belittled my friendship with you. You have even slept with one of my girls; who I don't even deal with anymore because of that shit!

What do you expect of me? Do you just think that I will just let you walk all over me and we just be, like the closest of friends, and I not want some kind of revenge?"

The truth quieted Will. He had expected so much while giving so little.

"I see you don't have an answer, do you? It figures. You don't have to answer. Your silence speaks volumes."

Then Will decided to do what most men would do. He decided to say something stupid.

"I was just saying."

"What were you saying Will? What were you saying? That it was ok for you to fuck my friend? That it was ok for you to lie about it? That it was ok for all of that stuff to take place? Then, after all of that, for us to just brush it aside and be cool?"

Stephanie asked that question and then all words between them turned silent. The sound around them engulfed their area as people began to enter the Waffle House. The crowd had taken an upswing from the time that they had gotten there to then.

Will decided to break the silence.

"Look Stephanie, I know that I was not the best person in the world when we were in a relationship. I probably will never be able to live that down. But please know that I have been your friend and been there for you when you have needed me. I haven't dropped you like a bad habit or left you high and dry. I am here for you and that has not changed over the years. It won't."

"Will, I am not saying that you haven't been there for me. I am just saying that I loved you. You hurt me and expected me to be ok with that. You were wrong for that and I was wrong for what I did. I am not trying to make you out to be a bad person. But good people do bad things sometimes. You did it. So just admit it."

As she ended her statement she began to sip ever so slowly on her hot cocoa. She looked over the brim of the cup to try to decipher the expression on William's face. Stoic or nonchalant was the question in her mind.

William was ready to move on in the discussion. He didn't want to dwell any longer on the fact that he had been such loser in that relationship. That was obvious to everyone, including him. No need to continue to gnaw on that bone.

"So, are we finished or is there something else that you need to tell me? Oh, and before you do… Let me get my heart ready because I can never know what to expect from you." Will said as he sipped his coffee.

Stephanie had more to tell but she still was afraid to say it. She wanted to find a way around it but she had come there for that specific purpose. To let him know how she felt.

"I came here to let you know what I told you. I am pregnant. You know that you are not the father but I need to know something… I need to know what I should do."

Will looked at her as if he didn't know what she was talking about but he did.

"Stephanie, what are you talking about? I know you are not talking about abortion, are you?"

Stephanie answered him short.

"Yes."

"Well that is not an option. Why would that be an option?" Will replied.

"Because, I am not going to have a baby with someone that I am not in love with and I am not going to marry."

In his mind he couldn't believe that all of these revelations were being made at this one time. William was having a hard time wrapping his mind around everything.

"So, not only are you not getting married and pregnant, but you are not in love with this guy? I just don't understand. That is what bothers me about all of this. You are with this guy. You introduce him to me like he is everything that I am not and then you end up not even being in love with this guy. I don't get it."

Will shakes his head after that statement. Things for him just didn't add up. He thought she was having one of those infamous pregnancy mood swings that he had heard so much about when his daughter's mother, Tawanna, was pregnant with Kristian.

"Does he know about all of this?" Will asked.

"He packed up and moved about a week ago. Don't you see what I am saying? William, I am all alone. I have a baby on the way. I am not getting any younger and I don't want to raise a child by myself. If I wanted to do that I would have done it at a much younger age. I think that an abortion is my only choice. It's not the choice that I want, but it is the one that I've got."

"You don't have to do that. There is always another option."

Immediately she chimed in with her question.

"Like what? What are my options? And then how would it look? How would it look for me to be as caught up in the church as I am and then have a baby out of wedlock?"

William, again, quiet because he could see her point.

"You see my point? That is all that I am saying. So what should I do? What should I do?"

"I can't tell you what you should do on this one. I know that this is a very hard decision to have to make at this time. Trust me I know what you are going through. All I know is that you shouldn't end a life to save your reputation. Your reputation will bounce back and you will survive. Trust me, I can speak from experience. You will."

"Would you help me?" Stephanie wanted to see what his answer would be regarding this knowing that there would be a lot of questions with regards to their relationship.

"You know what, I sure would. I wouldn't even care either. There is so much that I can't tell you but know this, my drama will make yours pale in comparison."

"What's going on with you, Will?"

The words formed in his mind yet Will knew that saying them at that moment wouldn't help what he was going to have to go through anyway.

"Like I said, nothing that I can talk about now. But you will see. Unfortunately, you will see."

Will finished his coffee and waited in silence for his food. He tried to ignore the stare that Stephanie was giving him. He knew how she would do it how the next few minutes would proceed.

First, there was the staring. He had always been able to get through the staring, even though she would continue to stare until he looked at her. This, of course, was soon followed by the questioning. This repetition would take place until finally he answered her. If that did not work then usual the final solution was: the silent treatment. That final solution worked every time.

Unfortunately for Will, he never made it to the silent treatment. As soon as the questioning began he would start to tell his part of the story.

"So, Will, are you going to tell me, or what? I need to know. I have told you all that is going on with me. Why won't you tell me?"

Will looked at her and said to himself, I am going to hit her with it and see how she takes it. So he did.

"Stephanie, the church is going to know about everything about me and you and everybody that I have had sex with in the last 15 years. They are going to know about what happened between us. They are going to know about Tiffany and our sexual relationship."

Stephanie's squinted her eyes as he spoke. It was as if his words were hurting her ears.

"Stephanie, someone has the diary. And that someone is Lil Junior."

The stare had changed. He could see in her eyes that maybe he shouldn't have told her. He knew that she knew about the diary. In fact she knew about the diary before they dated. But Stephanie also knew that he guarded those things with his life. She couldn't believe that anyone would have been able to get their hands on that; because he had never been careless with it before.

"How? How? I don't understand. How? What?"

She could not even get her words together.

"I have to go. I can't look at you right now. I have to go!"

Stephanie got up and ran out of the Waffle House as fast a she could. He didn't even have time to call her name. She was gone. He tried to get up as she left but his mind would not let him. There was nothing that he could do that would explain how this had happened that would be legitimate to anyone.

He was worried, though. If anything were to happen to her he would have lost his mind and his faith. He called her on her cell phone but there was no answer. He called again and still no answer. The worry became larger as the minutes went on.

He paid the check and got up and walked out with everything that had happened that day on his mind. He knew that there were a lot of things that he could have done differently, that he would have never ever done knowing what he knows now.

"Time is the greatest of friends and the cruelest of enemies." He murmured to himself as he walked out the door of the Waffle House.

As he went to get into his car, his cell phone rang. It was Stephanie.

"I am at home. Don't call me! Don't text me! Don't speak to me! I don't want to have anything else to do with you! I am leaving the church and I don't want to have anything else to do with you!"

Then the phone went dead. A perfect end to a perfect day, Will thought. He started his car and drove home.

When he got to the house, he called to check on his little girl to see if she was ok. He spoke to his parents to see how they were doing and to let them know how he felt about them and how he was so thankful for everything that they had done for him. His heart at that point just couldn't take it anymore. He finally broke down.

He cried for about fifteen minutes on the phone with them uncontrollably. They didn't know what was going on. His tears were necessary. Even as a man, he needed that cleansing. He hadn't known how he was going to get through it. But God had gotten him to the place where he needed to be. He was ready to deal with the challenges that he was about to face. But he needed to lose himself in order to gain a new relationship with God and be the leader that he needed to be.

So, as he cried those tears about everything, the strength that he needed was beginning to grow within him. Strength for today and tomorrow, and that was what he would need in order to press on.

Chapter Twenty-One

S tephanie awakened to a new day as the morning light softly warmed her face and invited her to begin her new day. The night had not been the best, to say the least. As she journeyed home the night before, the revelations of future persecutions played ping-pong in her head. Will and her former life with him, was about to be made public through his diary. Her baby and her future decisions with it were about to become the forefront of her thoughts. Tears, anger and frustration, were her companions for the night, but a new day was a new possibility in her eyes. She was very interested in moving past the things that had transpired the night before. Today was the beginning of a new life for her.

As much as she thought all of that to herself, she couldn't help but still feel the hurt of it all in her chest. Maybe it was the hormones or maybe it was just all that had happened over the years that set her off. She didn't know what it was. What Stephanie did know was, that she didn't want everyone that she had ever known, to know about what had or was going on between her, William, and anyone else. She especially didn't want anyone to know the fact that he had also slept with Tamika. What was more prevalent in her mind was how this would affect his daughter. She had been going through so much that she didn't need this to be a part of all that she already had to deal with.

She looked at the phone sitting on the nightstand next to her. No new messages. No words of comfort from her ex fiancé. No words of joy from her ex boyfriend Will. No words from no one. Only the loneliness of reality, which fought vigorously against her strength to subdue her. But she was not going to let despair become her morning meal. Because as sure as the sun was bright, the burdens of the night past, would not become the depression of day present, she said to herself as she arose.

William also awakened from his slumber with the rising of the sun. The sounds of jaybirds rustling leaves in the front yard and singing their songbird's song filled his empty home with morning noises. He wiped cold and crust from his eyes as the rays of light peeked through the curtains in his bedroom window. Will's thoughts began with the same tone as Stephanie's. His night had been filled with so much startling new information that he didn't even want to think about it. But, reality would not allow him the opportunity to ignore the situation at hand. The reality of how he had endangered himself with his own actions; how he had placed his entire family in a very precarious situation all for the sake of his ability to chase tail. This thought, was the reality of his hindsight vision. He had not thought about it like that until then. After the fifteen minutes of tears from the night before and the scolding of a father and mother that had defended him and protected him. A family that had helped him along all the way after Tawanna had passed. And as he thought about it more, the idea that their repayment would be his and their public ridicule, laid heavy upon his heart.

Then there was an explanation that was due his daughter. Though his house was empty, the thought of how he would explain all of this to her filled and plagued his mind. She, too, had been through a lot in the last month. So how does a father explain that he has been a hypocrite? How does a father explain a checkered past and present to a daughter that he is trying to teach to live at a higher standard?

As he rose from his bed he remembered the words that his mother said to him. "Whatever is done in the dark will come to the light. God is not mocked. You are reaping your seeds that you have sown. This is your mess, you are going to have to fix it."

She had been more disappointed than angry. He could tell that she seemed like she felt used but she didn't respond like she would have. Maybe it was just so soon, he thought. Then he remembered that he had cried for as long as he had. Maybe she just felt a little sympathy. Maybe...

His father had no words. He had just handed the phone to his mother and let her talk to him. As much as his father had been a loving man, he was also a very private and proud man. He never believed that his son would have been capable of behaving in such a fashion. In Will's father's mind, Will had received all that God could have given him. All Will had to do was to follow. But when you are hurting on the inside, and no one can see your pain, it is hard for people to feel sympathy.

Lil Junior awakened as well at the rising of the sun. He was lively, knowing that everything that he had planned was playing out like he wanted it to. He knew that by then his father had revealed the things that would take place in the not-so-distant future. He knew that his father would not be happy and would be planning how to make things right within his congregation. The only thing he didn't know was that his father had no plans on getting rid of Pastor Wright.

In Lil Junior's mind, the idea of a womanizing, promiscuous, whoremonger of a Pastor as your Senior Pastor was not the poster child of a vibrant Holy Ghost-filled, Bible-based, Spirit-led Baptist church. He was right. Will wasn't the poster child for that church. What Lil Junior didn't see was the fact that even though this man had done all that he had, he still had touched lives of so many in that congregation that they wouldn't let him leave if he wanted to, or at least that is what Rev. Cleveland Stovall, Sr. thought.

The more Will thought about the things that had happened over the past few months he realized how it all pieced together. He remembered the break in and why it seemed like they didn't take anything but went through a lot of effort to get into his office. Why he remembered thinking that his diary was missing and how he just didn't even think about it any more. How he and Lil Junior had gotten into the argument at his parent's house and how things went down then. There was always motive right in front of his face and he just hadn't noticed it. It was as if he had blinders on and the person that was ready to cause him the most harm was right in front of his face and he couldn't see him.

Problem is that he already knew that Lil Junior was dangerous anyway. He had made his case with Rev Stovall, Senior about his son. He had made his case known and was ready to have him removed from the Pastoral staff at the church anyway. That was it! He knew.

At that moment Will figured it all out. He realized how it all worked together. He knew that he was about to be ousted. How do you defeat a Pastor? By adding scandal to his name!

Will was infuriated by that thought. He realized that he had created his own monster by trying to remove Lil Junior. Even though Lil Junior needed removing he never would have thought that these would be the lengths that he would go to in an effort to reverse it. But no one would go to these lengths. That couldn't be the only reason. It had to be something else.

Will got into the shower and thought hard on what else there could be. As the hot water washed away the residue of the day past, his mind still couldn't understand the why. Even though his hypothesis was good, it still just didn't seem like it was enough. There had to be more to cover the complexity of the mess that Lil Junior had stirred up. He had to know. So he did the unthinkable. He called Lil Junior to set up a meeting, and to get his diary back.

As he picked up the phone to make the call his phone rang

in his hand. He looked at the caller ID on the phone to find out who it was. Stephanie. He figured he better take it because there was a possibility that this would be the last time that he would speak to her.

"Hello?" Will asked laboriously.

"Will, it's Step. Can I talk to you for a minute?" She said softly.

It sounded like she had been up for a moment. She sounded like she was sad but he could tell that she hadn't been crying, just sad.

"What's up, Step?" He asked nonchalantly.

"Well, I have been thinking about it all. You know everything that happened yesterday and… I want you to know that I take back what I said. I take it back. I don't want to throw away our friendship."

Will took a sigh of relief on that one. He knew that she would have been justified if she did. He did have one the greatest leaks of information that one could ever have in their life. Some things just shouldn't be written down he thought at that point.

"I am saying this to say that I forgive you for everything, and I want to help you to get through this. I know that there may not be much I can do but I am willing to help you if you need help."

Will was glad that he had answered the phone. It was time to put her money where her mouth was.

"Step, we both know who did this. Lil Junior stole my diary… Now, I want to find out why." Will said.

"Well, what did you have in mind?" she inquired.

So they began to discuss what Will thought would work. They discussed her issues with the whole situation as well. Time began to fly as they continued to conjure up scenario after scenario to try to get the root of the problem. The problem was they already knew the answer and it just didn't seem to be the likely conclusion.

"Will, there is no need to even go over this anymore. This is all about power and respect. He wants to be in charge and run the show. He also wants to make you look like a fool and ruin your reputation, as well as your relationship with his father and your family.

You ended up giving him everything he needed to with that damned book of yours! Why would you write so much in there in the first place? Who wants to remember all of the stuff that you had in there? Who does stuff like that?"

Stephanie asked a question that only Will could answer. In her mind, no normal person does that kind of stuff. But, to Will, being the sentimental person that he was, wanted to remember everything that happened verbatim. He didn't know how to be any other kind of way. It was a reminder of his flaws and his fault. A reminder of the transition that he had hoped to make; from being the whore to being holy. But as time passed the lists and the depravity only grew. So the diary became a chronicling of his conquests rather than a book of his transition. That was truly the end all be all of it.

"I wanted to write my life in my own words. As I lived it, as I thought it. I wanted to have a living testimony that would be able to be here long after I was gone. I wanted to be able for people to see that I overcame and I had my ups and downs just like everyone else. I just wanted to have a lasting and real testimony of my life. I know I have made some mistakes. Maybe I was a little too descriptive about my sexual experiences…"

"Ya, think?" Stephanie interjected.

"But, this book was my book. It wasn't even meant to be seen by anyone outside of me until after I was dead and gone."

Stephanie gave him that you are so stupid look.

"I know that may seem far-fetched. But I have kept it out of the hands of others up to this point. You had never been in it because I never let you. And you didn't even know the extent of the contents of the diary, until I told you yesterday."

"You are right." She said.

"But none of that matters at this point. Think about it, Will, you don't have it and we know who does. So the problem is getting it back before the damage is fully done."

"I don't think that getting it back is going to undo what has already started." William said shaking his head as if she could see him doing it.

"But letting him keep it will not be what is in your, nor my, best interest." She said rebutting his statement.

"He is going to use it as ransom at some point because he knows that you have a vested interest in it. The primary goal is to cut you. However, the secondary goal is to get you to ask for it."

As he said that Al beeped in.

"Step, hold on. Al is calling me I am going to three way him in."

He clicks over to talk to Al.

"Hello."

"Will, what's going on with you?" Al said as chipper as usual.

"A lot." Will said.

"Al, I got a lot to tell you so I am going to three way you in."

And they continued their conversation.

While they were making plans to get the book out of Lil Junior's hands, he was making plans to be on the agenda at the next board meeting. He had already spoken to the church secretary and she had placed his name on the provisional agenda. This agenda had not yet been seen by the Pastor and had to be approved before it could be called the agenda.

Lil Junior was no fool, though. He knew that if the Pastor saw his name on the agenda that he wouldn't allow for him to speak. He instead, placed his ministry on the agenda for the purposes of reporting on the growth in that department. There was no way that he could turn down that request. There would be no merit to it and Lil Junior's rebut would be that he had his request in, in time to be on the agenda.

He was also smart enough to have his request submitted by his assistant, Deacon Walter's Wife, Tylese. She was oblivious, or at least she seemed oblivious, to the rants of her department head. All she knew was that he had requested that she submit his request the church secretary by the time that he had requested. She did as she was asked and she was happy about it. In her mind if there was some good to be done in the outreach department, and some soul winning had taken place, then she wanted the whole church to know.

The stage is set, thought Lil Junior. He said to himself, 'I have pieced it all together. Now it's just a matter of a few days. Just a few days...'

Chapter Twenty-Two

"You know what?" Stephanie asked.

Morning had slipped to afternoon and the new day had aged enough for them to be reminded of the fact that they were human. Like every other animal on God's green earth, they needed to eat something.

"What?" Al and Will replied in unison.

"I am ready to eat. I have a baby on the way, and I need to eat something."

"A baby?" Al asked, in complete and utter shock.

"Yeah, Al… I forgot to tell you about that part. She is pregnant." Will said as an afterthought.

"Oh, yeah and…"

Stephanie cuts William off.

"Don't talk about me like I am not here. I can tell him, myself, you know. Al, I am not getting married. I am going to take care of this child on my own. He was not the man for me. Blah Blah Blah. Let's move on, shall we?"

"Alrighty then… Moving right along now…" Al said as only Al could.

"She is right. We do need to move on but this is something that I have to deal with on my own. I need to deal with this head on myself."

Will made that statement. The phone was silenced for a minute.

"I mean… I am the one who started this mess with this diary to begin with. A Pastor's diary, I thought would be a sacred thing. I thought of it as being my own bible- my life's book. I mean I know I was a whore but so was Solomon. I didn't do his numbers."

That statement was enough for Stephanie to chime in.

"You did enough."

"You are right, Step, I did. But I have to confront him and let him know that I know what he is doing and I am not going to take this lying down."

"Why can't we help you on this one?" Al asked.

"You need all the help you can get. This is for all of us. We are all affected; one way or another."

William's pride wouldn't let him let them take part in this.

"I have brought down too many already. I need to deal with this myself. If I need you guys, I can count on you, right?"

"Of course…" Al responded.

"Do you even have to ask?" Stephanie blurted.

"Look, it is already 2:00pm and I think that we have to do a lot today. I will let you guys know what the deal is going to be. So let me be, and I will figure it out and I will let you know how things go. If I need you I will let you guys know, ok?"

They respond with a yes. Not to their liking, but they couldn't argue against his point. He was a grown and capable Pastor. All the help that he would need will come from the Lord anyway. All that they could do to help was to make it easier for him to accomplish his goal.

As soon as he hung up the phone, it rang again. Will answered it immediately, without realizing who it was.

"Hello, Pastor Wright speaking." Will stated.

Little Junior had beaten the Pastor to the punch.

"I believe that I have something that you want, and I think that we might have some things to talk about."

As much as William wanted to talk to Lil Junior, the sound of his voice was enough to make his skin crawl. For Lil Junior this was all a part of the plan though. He knew that the Pastor would want what was his eventually. Even if only for the purposes of saving the very thing that was causing him so much grief.

"Where do you want to meet me?" William asked.

"Let's meet up at your regular spot. Let's meet up at Paschal's today at 6:00pm. You are buying, so come prepared." Lil Junior said with a cocky tone.

Junior knew that he had an upper hand in this case and he planned to use every bit of it to make William feel the pain.

"I will be there and I will be waiting." William replied.

William hung up the phone and proceeded to finish getting dressed. He ran to his closet and threw on the first pair of jeans and shirt that he could find. This was not a situation where he had to be looking his best. But he did want to look inconspicuous. No suit and tie. The Sunday's best idea was not what he wanted to convey. If anyone saw him, he didn't want them to recognize him. It's kind of hard not to be recognized when you are the Pastor of a church so close to the place that you are going to meet someone.

Time was not on his side either. He had been on the phone so long with Stephanie and Al that the day had slipped right passed him. His rituals of prayer and study had long been forsaken for that day. He was running on borrowed time and the problem was that he was supposed to be meeting up with his family to talk about the upcoming board meeting and how things would probably be going in the near future.

Weighing the two was difficult because as much as he wanted to believe that meeting with Lil Junior would end the situation, he knew better. Even if he could get the book back, quail the noise, and refute the accusations, his right mind would not let him believe that Lil Junior didn't have something up his sleeve. But most importantly, he would be able to see what all was in his little book.

He had written so much in there that he had forgotten a

lot of what he wrote. He never really thumbed through it just to get a peek at the past. He just kept writing forward. His idea was that at the end of each year he would do a year-end review of what had happened and what he had written. The problem with that was that he didn't do one in the last year. He just kept going.

The phone had become the source of most of Will's problems and again it was ringing. William looked at the clock on the chest in his bedroom. 5:21pm. He knew that he didn't have time to answer the phone, nor did he want to, but he was a Pastor still before all of the drama in his life.

"Hello, Pastor Wright speaking."

"So did I do something to you or what?"

As sweet as her voice was, it was a voice that at that time he did not want to hear. Tamara had become a figment in the distance. As much as he liked her and wanted to be with her, there was just too much going on right then in his life. Her voice was even more of a shock to hear than Lil Junior's.

"T-Tamara…I have been meaning to call you…" William said stuttering through his sentence.

"You don't have to lie about it. I understand. I never thought that I would be dissed by a Pastor and especially not my own Pastor. I can read the writing on the wall, though. I was just wondering… Why not the decency of a call to let me know that you weren't that into me?"

As Will was dealing with the call he looked precipitously at the clock. Time was not in the mood for the conversation as it continued to tick away at what would seem to be a much more rapid pace. William was not pleased with time and did not have enough of it to finish this conversation.

"I know that it seems that way, and I am sorry that it does. But you are going to have to trust me that I am not dissin' you. I can't talk any longer about everything but I will give you a call at another time."

Tamara was tired of feeling as if she was second tier.

"Tell me now or don't call me." She demanded.

"I can't tell you now and I have to go." Will said as he slammed the phone down.

William wasn't angry but he just didn't have the time to go through all of the gory details. There were bigger fish to fry now in his life, so he thought.

5:50pm: Will hopped into the Accord and headed down Lawton towards Ralph David Abernathy. He knew that he had only ten minutes to complete a trip that normally takes 15 to 20 in leisurely traffic. Not enough time in a day, he thought. He was right.

As he swung a left on Lowery he realized that he was not going to make it to his destination on time. He hoped that Lil Junior would give him some grace time, but considering the facts, he decided to call him and let him know that he would be late by but a few minutes. He made the call and Junior did not pick up the phone. Whether on purpose or not, he knew that Lil Junior had not answered his phone to know that he was still coming. William knew that this opportunity to get this diary back without incident would not present itself again. So he had to think fast on what to do.

All was not lost though, as William had thought. Lil Junior had not arrived yet either. In fact Lil Junior had planned to make him wait. So in all of William's rushing he would be the one that had to wait. And wait he would do.

William could not come up with the right words to approach Lil Junior with for being late. So Will had fixed his mind to just give him the truth. As he parked the car at the restaurant he ran as fast as he could to the front door. The hostess for the day asked him to wait to be seated and he did as scanned the room for Lil Junior. As the adrenaline began to subside from his body he began to realize that all that extra effort was unnecessary. Lil Junior wasn't there.

As he began to wait it became clear that maybe this had been a setup all along. That Lil Junior had no plans on coming after all. So the waiting began. First five minutes became ten and ten became twenty. Then one hour had passed. He continued to call but still no response from Lil Junior. William was beginning to get frustrated. Then, finally his phone rang. He picked it up quickly because he had been waiting with baited breath for something to happen.

"Hello, Pastor Wright speaking."

"I figured you would wait until the cows came home to get this back, would you?"

The number came up private on his phone, but the voice was as familiar as ever. Lil Junior's voice had not changed. But William's temperament for having his time wasted had.

"So this is some kind of a game to you? This is my life and it is the only one that I have right now so would you please not waste my time?" William asked.

"Will, do you really think that I care? Do you? After all that has happened I don't care about you or your life. Anyway, I will see you in about 30 seconds." Lil Junior ranted. His breath blew cold with every word as if his blood ran through his veins cold.

And thirty seconds later Williams was finally facing the accuser of the brethren. Anger buried itself in apprehension, as these were the prominent emotions that William knew at that moment. And though he tried his best to hide what he was going through emotionally, it was written indelible on his face.

Lil Junior basked in his moment of triumph. He truly felt the cold knife that was revenge. He knew that at that moment he held the Pastoral career of William Fitzgerald Wright in the palm of his hands. He had never been so empowered. His heart fluttered ever so slightly from the irony of it all. On one hand, the Bible, being the Book that had empowered William to become a great man. On the other hand, his own words in a book, his bible, to be the book that would destroy him.

A cold stare was all that was mustered between them as they sat face to face. A waitress interrupted that stare to ask them for their orders. For William, his traditional coffee with cream and sugar would suffice. Lil Junior on the other hand had his usual, which was good old fashion sweet tea.

As they received their beverages, the words that William sought to express were clouded by the words that he was burning to say.

Yet, soft words were going to be needed in order for William to get what he wanted so dearly.

"Why did it have to come to this? What have I ever done to deserve this from you?" William sounded desperate.

"What haven't you done?" Lil Junior rebutted.

"You have been successful in pulling the wool over the eyes of thousands in our congregation but I have seen the truth and I know that you are not the one to lead our church. You were never the one. My father was wrong, and now I am going to show them where they erred!"

"How is that going to help First Baptist? How is that going to help you? You know that they do not have the confidence in your abilities to lead. This does nothing for your cause. You are not the minister for First Baptist. You know that. Just let it go."

Those words got under the skin of Lil Junior.

"You don't know a damn thang about nothing! I helped build that church with my own sweat and tears. I was there while you were still in seminary trying to figure out how to preach, so don't you act like you know what is best for my church! I built that church! I know what is best!"

Will knew that he better think about what he was saying before he made his next statement. It was his ass that was on the line and Lil Junior still had his book and had a firm grip on his future, as well.

"Lil Junior, I am sorry for what I just said. Look, I know that we can work together to make First Baptist a better church. But in order for it to become what you think it should be we need to work together. I am willing to put everything that has happened in our past aside, so that we can work together on getting this church spiritually together. I am just asking you to be willing to work with me and to not do what you are trying to do."

Lil Junior took a sip of his tea and chuckled a little.

"Lil Junior, what did I say that was funny?" William asked sternly.

"Just find it amazing how all of a sudden you are so diplomatic when it comes to our relationship. It just reminds me of how much of a snake you are. Do you really think that I want to work with you to do anything? No… Let's be real. Do you really think that I think that you really want to work with me?

You are just trying to save your ass just like anyone else would if they were in this situation. Just don't try to play me and think that I am stupid. I know what is going on and I don't care. You know that you are going down and I do too. You are going to have to do much more than that little gesture to get me to not put you out there."

Will looked at him and knew that he was right. He still thought that he had the upper hand in this situation but he didn't. This was one of those times when he would just have to count his losses.

"Junior, I am not going to mince words. We don't like each other. I know that you want me gone but I am not leaving. So what do we do? Do you put that out there to embarrass the church and me like that? Is that what you want to do to our congregation?"

Lil Junior placed his coffee cup down for a moment and he cleared his throat.

"I want you to listen to me, William, for I will not repeat myself. I am going to crucify you. I knew that one day I would have a handle on how to deal with you but never did I believe you would make it so easy for me. I would like to express my thanks for a job well done."

He picked up his cup and took a quick sip as William stared hopelessly.

"I am going to give you this book back; your precious diary. You should learn to keep up with it. That way fools like me wouldn't have to ruin ego-maniacs like you."

Lil Junior reached into his satchel and placed William's diary on the table. As he slid it to him he leaned in real close, and whispered something very softly.

"William, I promise you will never forget my name..."

And as quickly as he had come to sit, he left. He also did not leave a tip or pay his bill. He left all of that for his friend, William, to handle as he had brought him his book back in its entirely.

As William grabbed the book, he frantically combed each and every page. He noticed that it all liked exactly how he remembered it. The pages that were frayed were frayed the way that they were before he had lost it. But there was one addition that he noticed at the end. A message was written to him by yours truly, Lil Junior.

> *I have copied all of the contents, so I have no more need for the book.*

> *With Love, Your Successor*

William's heart dropped at that thought. He knew that the battle was far from over. It had only just begun. And he was not willing to fight in the forum of the public. He was beginning to believe that stepping down might be what is good for all.

Chapter Twenty-Three

"Lord, I am looking to you for my help. I need you for everything now. I want to believe, please help my unbelief."

The words out of the mouth of a praying Pastor named William Fitzgerald Wright. The sun having nestled its rays upon the bed, began warming his forehead as he prayed. The time and seasons are harder and more chaotic now that the rumors are all around. His daughter had asked about it. He had to tell his parents and that made it even a more miserable time for the Senior Pastor of First Baptist.

"I want to be the man, father, husband, preacher, and son... that you want me to be. That is who I want to be for you Lord."

He knew that this could very well be one of the last Sundays that he would be preaching before this his congregation of believers. A congregation that he had nurtured and cared for, for what seemed like an eternity.

"Lord, I know that I can only blame myself for this. I want to blame everyone else but I know that my back is against the wall on this. I have tried it my way and I haven't been very honest with anyone... Including myself. I need to know that you are with me on this one. I need to know that you have my back. I need a sign and I need one now. I need to hear you... I am on the brink, and I need to hear you... A word from you... Something!"

The only thing that he heard was the echo of his voice resounding throughout the house. His daughter was staying with his mother on the back end of all the new revelations that he had presented her with.

"I just want to hear a word from you, Lord. I need something to get me through this. But I shouldn't expect that considering all that I have done."

The realization of life is settling into the pit of his stomach. Never had he been so introspective and it was killing him. Life is not a bed of roses for anyone. William knew this. The idea that his sin would not be found out was built on a lie. And that lie was always his arrogance.

"Here it is, then, Lord. I have slept with all these women. I have. I have enjoyed it; even reveled in it for a while. I have not been very sensitive about anything. I have been trying to look out for the church and, in the same breath; I have been trying to look out for number one...me. I have neglected the relationship that I had with my daughter and I have not allowed things to go the way that they should have. I am glad that you have been there for her, because with everything that I have been doing... Well, we both know that I haven't been the best parent. Better than some, but still not the best."

Pastor Wright's eyes began to well up with tears as he struggled to fight them back and to finish his prayer.

"I know I have been trying to say something, Lord. I don't know if you will answer me back, but, Lord, I need something bigger than myself right now. I have believed enough for everyone but myself. Show me what to do and I will do it."

This time no phone calls, just the sounds of the morning around him. He understood that for the first time in a long time, he was alone in the world. He had to deal with everything alone. That had been his fear all along. The great problem that he had never solved, the great situation that he had never dealt with, was his fear of being alone.

Since Tawanna passed away, whenever he felt the need,

or felt alone, he would always be able to find someone to lie in his bed with. Or some ear to fill up the empty spaces in between. When he became Pastor, his story of how she was killed became the stuff of legends. He had no problem with pulling women that were just touched by his charisma and moved by his perseverance through it all. But now there was none of that. No one to listen to his stories and no one to keep his bed warm. No, this time he would have to face the world and all of his problems alone.

He had spent the previous night listening to old sermons and preparing for the day's message with that thought in his head. He knew that a quiet had fallen upon the church with regards to the delivery of his message. He also knew that there was to be a board meeting that evening at church after service. He needed to look at the agenda to see what was on it because he had no idea what was being discussed or the like.

His life had taken a toll on his duties and responsibilities as the Senior Pastor. So much so that he had delegated a lot of his responsibility to Pastor Al Williams. As much has Al tried to keep him abreast to the situation at the church, William's mind was constantly elsewhere. There were so many things left unresolved that he couldn't focus on any one thing to get it resolved.

There was the Stephanie situation; there was the Tamara situation; there was the trying to sit down and talk to his daughter about all of this so she won't look at him like a hypocrite situation. Then there was the greatest of them all. How do I remain a Pastor after all of this? How do I get through all of this alone and deal with the questions and the requests to have me ousted.

His typical response was the one that got him into this mess to begin with. Sex was still a drug that he had not fully overcome. As with all people who are addicted to something, the withdrawals are the hardest part; especially when you are going through. So Pastor Wright was having one hell of a time.

"Lord, I am going to do what I can. I don't know how this is going to play out. I don't know what else there is to come. But, I do know that I am going to do my best to trust you. Let me believe and obey. In Jesus' name I pray, Amen."

Pastor Wright's mother was praying her prayers as well. This Sunday morning presented Cecilia Wright with all of the problems of other days but with a new twist. How do you explain this situation to a granddaughter that has already been through so much in her lifetime? How do you do that? That is the prevalent thought in her mind. And she knew that her son, the mighty Pastor, had done his best to explain it painlessly. But, she was the closest thing to a mother that Kristian had. And she knew that there was only so much that Kristian would let her father know about how she was feeling. So her priority was to find out and make sure that her granddaughter was ok in all of this.

Kristian was praying, too. She was praying about the situation that her father had told her about. She was crying because she had wanted her father to feel what she was going through. Then, when he told her about what was going on in his life, she felt like she had been the cause of it all because of her prayer. She felt guilty, to say the least.

"Lord, I am sorry. I love my dad but I just don't think that he listens to me. He has dealt so much with the church that it just doesn't seem fair. I need him sometimes to just make me first. To let me know that I am his baby girl even when I don't want to be her. I really miss my mother sometimes, and in some ways I miss my dad too. I always feel like I am alone and the only time I can get his attention is when I do something wrong.

I know I am not supposed to be happy right now, Lord, but I feel like this going down will free him from all of his duties and maybe we can talk like we used to. I feel like all he can do now is argue with me."

She pauses to think of what else she wants to say. There

are so many things running through her mind that she doesn't always know how to begin or end a prayer.

"Lord, would you please let my mom know that I love her. I know that she is sleeping in you. I believe that I will see her again one day. But if you could in some kind of way, let her know that I miss her. Let her know that my dad misses her too. You don't have to let her know about all of this. But just let her know that we miss her, ok? In Jesus' name, Amen."

Pastor Wright's mom came in to speak with Kristian right after she finished her prayer. Kristian was in her closet picking out the clothes that she was going to wear to church that day. Though they had acknowledged each other, they had not said a word. The quiet was enough for them. Though they both were dealing with everything that had happened over the course of the last six months; quiet now was better than conversation could ever be.

Al and Sharon were up early that morning. This was Al's time again to shine because he knew that he would be the one to fill in for the Pastor if things were to go south; which is how they seemed to be going. So Sharon asked him the questions about everything that had been rumored.

"I heard that Will slept with over fifty women in this church. Is that true?"

Al looked at his wife like she was someone other than his wife, asking him a question that was none of their business.

"Sharon, if he did would it change how you looked at him?"

"Yes." Sharon answered immediately.

"Look, I know that he is your boy and all but if he did then he is a whore that has been pastoring this church under some false pretenses. I don't..."

Al stopped her before she could go on to her next sentence

"Let me tell you something about the man that you are calling a whore. Whenever I have needed him for whatever the cause he has been there for me. When people call him in the middle of the night with their problems whatever they may be he is there. When some of the parents have children that go to jail and they need a character witness he is there. When there is something going on out of town, whatever function it is, he is right there.

Ok, so he is not perfect. He has slept with some women in this church. He has done his thing in that respect. But who among us can cast a stone at anyone? All I know is if I was going to believe in someone I would rather believe in him than to believe in anyone else because I know that he has my back!"

Sharon had no words to respond with because she knew he was right. She had seen all of the work that he had done for that church and all the changes that had taken place since he was the Senior Pastor. She just didn't understand how he was able to do all that he did as a Pastor and still have all of these illicit relationships.

"Ok, Al, you are right. But, help me understand something. How did he have all of those relationships? I just don't understand that part. I don't."

Al thinks for a moment before he answers her back.

"Sweetie, I don't know. He just has a way with women and he has been doing what he does for years. He is smooth at it but I couldn't be him for a minute. I have enough problems trying to work through our issues. The stuff that he is going through right now, man, I would go crazy!"

For that is all that he could think of in that moment. The things that were going on in Will's life were much more than what Al would ever have to deal with. He was, for the first time in his life knowing William, glad that he wasn't him.

William left the house to meet Al as they always did on Sunday mornings. Paschal's was the place and the time was always 9:30. Will had so much on his mind that he knew that today would not be the day for him to preach and he needed to let Al know that he would not be on the pulpit for today. A phone call would probably have sufficed, but he would rather see his friend than to have to call him. Seeing him would be much more personal and it would do him good he thought.

Al gave his wife a final kiss and hopped in his car and headed to Paschal's. He knew that he had not spoken to Will that morning but their ritual had not changed for a Sunday. It was Paschal's and it was 9:30 always. Not even this situation would change the ritual, thought Al. And he was right.

As all entered he said William sitting in the usual booth at the usual end of the restaurant but looking different. He noticed that he was not in his suit and that he looked like he was really going through. He could tell that he was not going to be preaching today, which was what he thought anyway. As much as he didn't want to ask the obvious question, he felt that he needed to.

"Will, are you ok?" Al asked as he sat down at the table.

"Al, I am not ok... I am not." Will murmured.

"I am not going to be on pulpit today. I have some things I am going to have to attend to... Within myself and with others. I hope you will forgive me for dropping this on you today. But I need to deal with some stuff. You understand don't you?" Will said.

Al looked at him and if he didn't understand before that, he understood it right then and there.

"Dude, I understand. I do. I am just going to pray for you, man, because I have never seen you look like this. I don't know if I will ever really be able to understand what you are going through. But I am just going to keep you lifted up. And I want you to know that God loves you and that you are going to get through this. Please believe that."

Those last words struck a nerve with Will. He had been looking for God but he couldn't hear His voice. He couldn't see God's face. God was not communicating with him. All he could see was his situation that was eating away at him daily. So Will had a question for Al.

"Where is God, Al?" Will asked calmly.

"What?" Al replied.

"Where is God?" Will repeated.

"He is everywhere Will… you know that." Al added.

"Al, I haven't seen God since I have been alive. I have never smelt His fragrance. I have never touched His hands. I have never had a full-fledged conversation with Him that I received a response back, yet but I am a purveyor of God. I am a spokesman for the Almighty. Have you ever seen Him, Al?"

Al looked at him and knew where he was going.

"You know that He is there Will. Try this on someone that doesn't know any better."

"No, Al, I am talking to you! We have spread this Gospel about how God is here and God is there and God is everywhere but when it comes down to it, when was the last time you saw Him in your life. I mean with all the shit that you have done, it should be even harder for you to say that you know Him because you are worse than I would ever be… you know with the fucking around on your wife and all.

So, tell me Al, where is God?"

Al just looked at Will. He knew what he was trying to do, but Al was not going to let him do it to him. Not this day or any other day.

"William, I love you. I will not let you turn me against you today. I am going to leave you to your own devices. But know this; God is real and you know Him just like I do. You need to come to grips with your sins and move forward with your healing."

Al left his money on the table for his breakfast and proceeded to walk out. He didn't look back to see if Will was crying or even if Will was attentive to him as he left. He just knew that he needed to leave a man like Will alone, to deal with his demons by himself.

Desperation is quiet. Yet it wells up on the inside. That is the experience that William was having at that moment. A quiet desperation. As his friend was leaving to go and preach a sermon to the people that Will had been leading for quite some time, Will was dealing with his inability to be alone. And when all else failed he went to the place where he was always welcome: Tiffany's.

She lived in Decatur, off Glenwood Road, not far from the intersection of Glenwood and Candler. As much as he didn't want her to be the one for him, she was always there. That was just it though. She was just there when he needed something from her but she was not where he was in her life. They all had gone to school together and she was just never quite there when it came to what she wanted to do with her life.

To him, that was never his problem. He had tried to get her to go back to school and finish up her degree and get her mind right regarding that but she never did. She only had one child and she was doing ok but she just wasn't where he thought she should be. That is one of the many reasons why in his mind she just wasn't the one.

The other problem was the fact that she had given it up to him so quickly and so easily. That led to a trust issue with him. He knew in his mind if it was this easy for me then if the right brother came along it would be just as easy for him. She would remain in his mind the other woman until another woman came. She was always the backup but never the starter. Always the undercard but never the main event in his mind.

Going to her was always comforting to him. Besides the sex, she was an all around good woman. She catered to his every need. She did what he wanted her to do, sexually, she listened to his problems and she didn't care as much about the fact that he was with other women; except Stephanie. Bad blood between them had existed since college.

Going to her would be a vacation from the rest of the world because she was not so indoctrinated into all of the things that were taking place at his church. He could take a vacation and be at peace. But, Tiffany was not the kind of peace that he needed. She was the reason, in a lot of ways, that he was going through what he was going through. She was his piece that he would get to come over when he just need someone to talk to or he just needed some.

She came through and did her thang and then she left. But, when she did her thang, she did her thang. That is why he kept going back. He couldn't leave it alone. He was addicted to her. She had him pussy whipped. But that didn't keep him from trying others, others and still others. But it did keep him from being married and being happy and all the other things that he desired. He had never let her go, not even for God, and the lesson that he needed to learn he was about to learn it.

As he arrived at her house, he got out of the car dazed by the fact that he was at her house on a Sunday that he was supposed to be preaching. But he was still having his pity party. It was much easier for William to think about himself at this point than it was for him to think about what his actions had done to others. It was so much easier for him to drown himself in his own misery than for him to look at the consequences of his actions.

He walked up to the door and knocked. No answer. William knocked again and still no answer. William knew that Tiffany was there. Her car was visible in front of the house as it always was when she was home. He knew that he should have called first but he was in need of whatever she had and he needed it right then and there. So he knocked again. This time someone did come to the door. And it was not the person that he had expected.

"Who is it?!"

An angry male voice came from the other side of the door. William knew that was not the voice of anyone that he wanted to talk but his pride would not let him just leave.

"William... I am looking for Tiffany."

Silence was the response. He paused for a minute because he just couldn't believe that someone else would answer her door. As he was about to knock again William could hear the latches on the door begin to unbuckle. As angry as he was, he was even more frightened by whoever it was that was on the other side of that door. Only a few seconds more and William was still pondering whether or not standing at that door still was a good idea.

Slowly he heard the clanking sound of the door unlocking. Apprehension in the form of a slight cold sweat swept over him for a moment. He had no idea what to expect or rather who to expect it would be that he would be facing at that door. His mind was just hoping for it to be Tiffany and not some man of hers. Then he had an epiphany. Why hasn't she told him that she has men on the side? His naivety became apparent to him at that point. She was entitled to have a life outside of him. In that moment he realized that he was still a very selfish man indeed. But that was still not enough to take away what he was feeling inside. After all, he had been sexing up Tiffany for so long now that he felt she at least owed him an explanation.

Finally, the door opened to find her standing there, looking the way that she always looked. She was always appetizing to his sense. Always slim, but with a figure; always bourgeois, but with a little hood. She was always sassy but had enough affection in her to make William's heart melt.

William knew that if he looked for too long that his mind would get caught up in the fact that he was there with her and not the fact that she had a man at the house with her.

"William, what is it?" Sassy as ever were Tiffany's opening words.

"What the hell? How are you going to come off like that towards me when some nigga is up in there answering your door?" William responded with a little attitude of his own.

"That man is my new man. Besides that, why are you here?" Tiffany blasted back.

"I thought that I would be able to talk to you about all the sh—"

William stopped himself. No need to stoop to that level in order to make a point.

"I just could really use a friend now and I was hoping that you would be that friend for me. I see that I am just going to have to deal for a while."

Then that deep voice that he had heard before, he heard again. Then he saw the man that was producing all that bass.

Her boyfriend, Hakeem, owned his own business and it was time for him to go and make his money. So she had no problem with him getting out there to get his paper. He had dreads, was artistic and about his business, all the qualities that she liked in a man. On top of that, was a tall, darker brother with light brown eyes which made him look all the more mysterious. He was a lot more striking that William, even in William's eyes.

"Baby, I was just about to leave so if he needs to talk to you, let him talk. But make sure that is all that he does." Hakeem said as he passed through the doorway and in between the two of them.

Then Hakeem hopped into his Ford Explorer and was on his merry way without another word.

William was just looking in amazement at the things that had happened to him just in the last month in his mind. He couldn't believe that all that had taken place just right in front of him. He just couldn't believe that his life had to be that difficult. But he needed the wake up call in order to wake up.

She was still standing in the doorway even after Hakeem had left. She was conflicted because she didn't know whether it was good idea to let him in or not. William couldn't believe that there was even a doubt as to whether or not he was coming in. He was getting more pissed by the moment. Finally he placed things in perspective.

"I know that we are what we are. But after all this time you aren't even going to let me in to talk?

"William, I know what you are going to say. You have said

enough in the past to make me come back I won't be talked out of it this time."

Tiffany had no idea that he was dealing with what he was dealing with. She just thought that she had been caught in the act and was being defensive for no reason.

"Tiffany, I didn't come over here for any of that. I don't care about that. If you have found someone that makes you happy then I am happy for you. I am not going to sit here and be like I like it, but I am going to say that I am happy for you. I know that I couldn't provide you with that happiness so I am just glad that you were about to have it with someone.

But I came over here because I needed someone to talk to. I am just dealing with stuff right now and you were the best friend for me right now. You are not biased because you don't even come to church anymore."

"Yeah, because of you and everything that went on with that bitch." Tiffany interjected.

"Well, I know. That is my fault." William continued.

"Anyway, I just wanted to talk."

Tiffany stood there for a minute as she gathered herself and thought about what she should do. She realized that he would not be there if he didn't really have issue that he was dealing with. She decided within herself to let her own feelings go for the moment to talk with him about whatever was on his mind.

She opened the door wide for him and motioned for him to come on in.

"You know, I am glad to be at your service, again as always." She said sarcastically.

William walked into a place that had been for him a sanctuary of pleasure and peace for many years. But, of course, that idea was far from his mind now because new revelations made for a change in his mindset. Yet, the burdens of days past, coupled with this new secret revealed, made the solace that he was so desperately seeking all the more elusive.

"Why didn't you tell me that you had moved on?" He asked angrily.

She looked at him as to stare into his soul.

"Why do you even ask these kinds of questions? You know that you have in no way been concerned about what I do, or who I do it with. So that's why. We have an arrangement remember?" She spouted with sass.

His only response to that level of truth was silence.

"You talked a lot a minute ago, what's up? Cat got your tongue now? IF you can't handle the truth then don't ask questions that require you to be truthful with yourself."

The more Tiffany spoke the more he realized that the truth hurts.

"Ok. You know what? I deserve everything that I am receiving right now. I deserve it. And I should have been a better person than I was. But think about this. Chew on this for a moment. You let me do all that I did, so you are just as much at fault as I am."

His argument made him feel better in his mind. 'Cause in all honesty she had been cool with the way that things were or at least that is what he had conned himself into believing.

Tiffany couldn't believe what he was saying. She knew that he had been delusional before but this statement had taken the cake.

"Do you really think that is what I wanted between us? Do you really believe that? If you do then I gave you way too much credit. I thought that you were intelligent."

Again silence in the house. For a quick moment the birds replaced the sound of arguing between them. Then Tiffany killed the moment to move forward.

"You know, Will, I understand that you have a lot on your mind right now. I understand that things are not going the way that you had expected them to go. But do understand that I have loved you and now I know that I must let that love go...

At least as a lover. I am now your friend; just your friend. And as such, I am going to be here for you."

Will stopped her before she could proceed.

"I don't need your pity party. I am fine. I didn't know that all this was going on over here. I will leave."

Will's pride was getting in the way of his pain. But Tiffany was not going to let him place that guilt trip on her.

"You know, I didn't tell you that you had to go. This is all you, Will. In fact, it's always about what Will wants. If it isn't Will's way then it's the highway. You know you need to get a grip. Life is not like that."

Will stopped her immediately.

"Don't act like I don't know what life is about. I have been living this life that is full of disappointment. Just shut up!"

Surprisingly Tiffany did just that.

Again the awkward silence stepped in and made itself at home. He knew that he was wrong so he knew what he needed to do.

"Tiffany, I am sorry. I just... you know that I have been through a lot..."

"And, took me through a lot." Tiffany interjected.

"I am sorry about everything. I really can't even explain everything. I never thought that it would end up this way. With Tawanna dying... the world was just changed. I was changed. I don't even know how to think sometimes. And with all of this happening the way that it is. I... I just... I really need a friend right now."

Tiffany walked over and gave him a hug.

"I am going to be here when you need me. But, don't get it twisted. The way that things used to be are not the way that they are now. You need to get your stuff together and figure out where you go from here."

William looked puzzled. He didn't know what she meant or if she really knew what she meant when she said your stuff together. So his eyes were telling on him.

Tiffany noticed that he stared like he was confused at what she said.

"Oh, you thought I didn't know about all the mess that was going on at your church. I know what you are and have been doing. People talk, especially about you. I have been praying for you, as much as I can. I know that I am a real sinner but I figured that you could use all the prayer that you could get."

Will realized that he had been so naïve to believe that no one knew.

"Who? How did you know?" He asked.

And Tiffany began to tell him everything that she knew about the situation. How she knew about the diary and how she knew about her name being in there. How he had chronicled in explicit detail his sexual escapades and the feelings that he felt afterwards.

She already knew about Stephanie, but more than anything she learned and told him that she learned a great deal about how much of a whore he was. That was when she came to the conclusion that she didn't need to play herself anymore.

"I just couldn't do it anymore." Tiffany said nonchalantly.

"I just began to realize that you didn't want me and it sank in. I mean, I realized that I didn't owe you anything. I didn't need anybody to tell me that you weren't thinking about me and my future with all the shit that you were caught up in. It just became clear that I should start looking for something more real than this fake shit that we were caught up in. Then I also realized that you weren't caught up in it. It was just me. So I had to get over the fake shit that I was caught up in."

William's heart dropped. He lowered his head slowly into his hands and sighed deeply. Tiffany continued with the assault as he dealt with the facts that he was being hit in the head with.

"William, I really feel sorry for you, but you brought this on yourself. Whatever you do, don't get angry with God over this. Don't be angry with Lil Junior either. This is your mess. You made it. You set it there for anyone to see if they looked hard enough. Yeah, be mad that you got caught, but be mad at yourself. Cause this is some dumb shit for real."

No pity party for me, William thought. No pity party. Tiffany was not going to let him off that easy either.

"So, what are you going to do? What is the next step? Because I am not going to let you come over here with that 'whoa, is me' mentality. I know that you are in a difficult situation, but you have been in plenty of those. What is the plan to get through this one?

Will sat up and looked at Tiffany in a way that he hadn't in a while. He knew that she was strong and that she had been there for him in the past. But she had never quite been this way to him and for him ever. She had put him in his place like no one had. She was right about everything and she did give him time to sulk.

What was his next move? That was a question that William had not fully contemplated.

"I am not going to just take this lying down. I guess my plan is to get up now and start putting the pieces of the puzzle back together."

She could see it in him as he started speaking. The change that she had been hoping would happen. The difference between grief and conviction. He was beginning to be the man that she had fallen in love with and that was enough for her to give him the support that she knew he sought.

"Now that you are back to normal," Tiffany said, handing him a pen and paper to write with.

"Let's write it down so that we can get to work. So, what's first?"

"First I have to meet with everyone that I can before we have this board meeting. I know what is about to happen and I am ready for what he is going to try. He is going to bring all the revelations regarding me out at the board meeting. So I need to meet with every officer that I can before then."

"When is the board meeting?" Tiffany asked.

"It's at 6:00pm." William stated with a slight chuckle.

With service going on as they were speaking, and the fact that he wouldn't be able to go back to church to make that announcement without bringing attention to himself, William knew that idea was out of the question. As he thought it he could see that Tiffany had already figured that out as well.

"So, since that is not going to work, what else can you do?" Tiffany asked next.

"Okay. We will just have to improvise." William said as he began to get his things to leave. "I know that I am going to have to suffer some of the consequences for my actions. But I believe that I can limit what Lil Junior does and how far he takes it."

Tiffany looked hard at William.

"Is that the same Lil Junior that has been there for forever?"

"Yeah." William said as he opened her front door.

"I am going to get back with you before it's all done. More than anything, I want to say… thank you."

Tiffany stood there motionless as he gave her a kiss on her frontal lube and dashed to the car. As she watched him become the go-getter that he has always been, she realized again why he was so hard to love. She also realized why he was so hard to hate as well. He was much more than just a minister to her. He was her best friend that she had lost and found again. But she knows that her place, in his life, is not to be the one for him but to be the one that would help him in whatever she could.

William's determination had changed and become what he needed it to. He was headed to where he needed to be headed. It was time to face the facts and to resolve a situation that he created. Even though he knew that he was too late to talk to anyone before the meeting. But he could be there and tell his side of the story. So the story would be settled at church, just like the story started. The irony of it all, William thought. The irony of it all.

Chapter Twenty-Four

Pastor Al had delivered one of his most riveting sermons ever. He had preached for about an hour and a half and closed out with more than twenty people coming forward for baptism. His passion was translated into a sermon that had touched on his personal convictions. The congregation had been impressed. His last sermon was good, and it elicited responses that were on par with that of Pastor William. But his performance on Sunday was by far the best sermon that they had ever heard.

Al had never had such a time in the pulpit. He had become comfortable with the congregation. The congregation had become comfortable with him. He knew that if William was going to be back, that this was going to end and end soon. So he figured that he might as well enjoy it while he can…

Lil Junior knew that there were only a few hours before we would be able to do what he need to do and finally make the church a place that was holy and sacred. His thoughts were as if he was the only one who could have thought up the things that he did. His mind was bathing in the future that would finally place him at the forefront of everything that his father had denied him from. He knew that he was meant to be the one. He knew that. There was no denying that he had the church's best interest at heart. But the problem was that he always thought that his best interest and the church's best interest was the same. He was about to find out whether that was true or not.

Sharon, Al's wife, was happy that her husband had been allowed so many opportunities to preach. She believed that maybe he would be the one to take William's place; a bitter and sweet thought for possibly the next first lady of First Baptist. She wanted it for her husband, but she had been used to the idea of not being caught up in all the hustle and bustle of running a larger than life organization like First Baptist. After all, she saw the pain and frustration that William had to deal with by himself. She didn't want that for her husband. She wanted him to succeed but thought that maybe the collateral cost was too much for her to take. And, as much as she wanted him to succeed, with all that she had recently had to deal with as a wife, she wanted him to fail too.

Cecilia Wright prayed hard for her son. She knew that no matter what, today was the day. The buzz had circled the church. She could see the looks and know. Maybe it was her intuition or maybe just everything all together. As much as she wished that she could escape the fray, she knew that she needed to be there when her son could not. After all, his father was done with the situation. He felt like he had embarrassed them enough. But she knew that even after everything that her son was still human. He was capable of making mistakes. She knew that she wasn't perfect. Nor was his father, for that matter. So as stupid a mistake it was that he made, he was still human. He would bounce back. She knew it in her heart. And she prayed it in her prayers.

Stephanie had heard the commotion. He had heard the whispers. She had seen the looks. One woman even asked if it was as good as they say under her breath as she passed by. Stephanie almost showed her other side at church but she let it go. She knew that if she was dealing with the rumors as bad as she was that William must have been catching it a lot worse. Then there were the questions of why he had not called her. The first person to come to mind was Tiffany. But that just didn't seem likely since she already knew that Tiffany had finally gotten her a real life boyfriend. That was probably one of Stephanie's most prayed prayers.

So she wondered, what was the problem? She knew that all the plans that they had for solving the current situation that he was in would not work. The only thing that would work would involve the board meeting of that day. She knew that he would be there if not anywhere else. But she just wanted to know what would the plan of action would be?

Jimmie Davis had been laying low. He didn't even want any of his involvement in everything to come out- ever. He just wanted to wait and see what happened. He was just ready for it all to be over. It was as if the time had dragged on to this point. He had known for weeks that the bomb was going to be dropped on that day. But everything was just becoming overwhelming. He had become anxious and he knew that if asked the right questions by the right person that he would talk like a parrot. He was glad that he had not been pushed to that point. He really felt sorry about everything. He just wanted to do what God wanted him to do. He didn't want to be involved in all of the political mess. But he was stuck between the past and the future, as Lil Junior put it. And he was just trying to hold onto all of it.

Cleveland Stovall, Senior, the great Pastor of First Baptist was quiet as ever. He had been very quiet for weeks and the day that he had dreaded to think about was finally upon him. He was about to have to deal with the one thing that he had never ever known how to deal with... His son. He knew that he had to choose sides on this day. There was no escaping this moment of choice. He had already made up his mind, though. That was probably the hardest part of the ordeal for Rev. Stovall. Him knowing that he was going to have to go against his own flesh and blood so that his legacy would not be destroyed or completely diminished.

Worry and retirement should not have to go hand in hand

but they did. He didn't know how this would go but his faith kept him believing. Reverend Stovall believed in the power of God to right wrongs and to bring restoration. He also believed in William probably more than he believed in himself. He had seen the work of God in him. He knew that perfection was not an aptitude that any of us are capable of in ourselves. Years of believing in the 'press toward the mark' theory led him to believe that the mark was unobtainable. But, because it was unobtainable, should we stop pressing toward it?

Kristian's life had been complicated before, but nothing like this. Nothing like this. She had not had to experience the cold stares that were aimed at her father. She had not experienced the separation that she had experienced then. Separation from her friends and her family. Her father was not himself anymore. Neither were her grandfather and grandmother for that matter. She felt more alienated now than she did when she thought she was pregnant. And that whole ordeal was still in her mind.

All of the uproar, all of the pomp and circumstance, all of the noise that was made with her situation, only to find that he was so much worse than she had ever been. Hypocrite. She could see what his motives were. Maybe he just didn't want her to end up like him she thought. She was so hurt in so many ways. But this was her daddy that had always protected her. So, if anyone were to come to her with that mess, she would set them straight, and was not afraid to get ghetto in order to prove her point. Don't mess with my dad.

Tamara was done with him. He had just become that possible mistake that she was glad that she didn't make. She knew that he had been that Pastor whore that everyone hopes isn't the leader of their flock, but she never thought that it would come to this. She knew that he had problems but everyone does. She just never saw all of this unfolding the way that it had. She thought that maybe, just maybe, she would have been able to break up the mess to help him become the better man that she thought he was meant to be. But as time had slipped forward to this inevitable moment, she realized that she was just not fit to be with him. Let alone try to change him as he went through this mess. She had realized that she was just better off with out him.

Still, intrigue led her to stick around the church for the board meeting. This was an opportunity of a lifetime. There was a buzz around the church about things that were going to happen. Church folks talk entirely too much about the wrong things and so rumors were running wild. Everybody was trying to stick around to see what was going to happen and Tamara was not going to be one of those left out in the cold. She wanted her say too. In fact for this board meeting to be only for the board, there were a lot of people trying to stick around to see what the end was going to be. Rumors always have at least a hint of truth in them.

William had made peace with everything. He had come to his senses with Tiffany. He just accepted what might happen and is working in faith on what he hopes to happen. He knew that he was wrong and now it was time to face the consequences. He would not take them lying down, but he would take them. His mind thought more than anything about the trouble that this whole situation had caused his family that had been through so much in the past few months that he was sick of it. He had hoped that time would heal the wounds that his family and he, himself, had experienced. But as fate would have it, this was a situation that he must face head on. There was no dodging this battle, no outrunning this issue. The bottom line had become the situation that he had to face now. He was as ready as he would ever be. Once he arrived, it became clear that he would be up for the challenge of his life. But, he had always been a praying man. And as he prayed his last prayer before he went into a place that made the man that he was, He knew that no matter what, this is how it was supposed to end. He had finally made peace with it all. And that was enough for him.

Chapter Twenty-Five

"Lord, here we go." said Pastor William Wright as the anxiety of the moment caught up with him. As much as he had been prepared for this moment, he was still not prepared enough.

"I am still just a man and I need you to be more that I am for me right now. I know that I have made so many mistakes that I don't deserve another opportunity. But, Lord, I am trying to make things right. I need to know that you are able. I am scared but I know that you are still going to be there when this is all said and done. I know that I will get through this but I wish I could just avoid this part. I really wish I could."

The fellowship hall was located next to the sanctuary and was setup in its usual way. The Pastor felt different in his usual seat waiting for everyone to show up. He didn't have to wait very long though. This meeting was highly anticipated. This would be the final battle for the future of this church and as much as it was a witch-hunt it was to be a battle of wits.

All of the board members were present and accounted for earlier than they had ever been there. In fact, it was almost standing room only. Pastor Wright forgot that even thought the public could not vote at a board meeting they could attend. There weren't enough chairs for the extra two hundred and fifty people that showed up including his parents. Stephanie was there too. She waved at the Pastor from across the room.

He also noticed that Sharon, Al's wife, was there in support. He felt a little better with some of his friends being there. Tamara was there too. That was an unexpected surprise if not a welcome one. He didn't necessarily want her to have to experience the problems first hand that he was about to experience. But she wanted to know what the real deal was. She wanted to see firsthand if the rumors were true. She would soon know.

Lil Junior was the last to walk in. He walked with a confidence that he had never exhibited before. There was a twinkle of contempt in his eyes that exemplified his arrogance. He knew that he had what he wanted. He knew that there would be a vote that day that would change the tide. He knew that he held William in the palm of his hands. He also knew that there was nothing that William could do to stop him.

Everyone felt the uneasiness in the room. For as many people that were in fellowship hall for this meeting, there was an unusual quiet that blanketed the whole room. William felt it. He could sense it. Under his breath he began to pray "Lord, be my strength… Lord be my strength."

As Lil Junior sat down the meeting was called to order. Pastor Wright stood up and addressed the multitude that had gathered.

"I believe that this is the first time since I have been a minister at this church that the whole congregation showed up for a lowly old board meeting. I am proud of you, good job." He said sarcastically. Normally, there would have been a lot of laughter. The sound that he heard was more nervous laughter than anything.

"Well, let us stand and look to the Lord as we open this meeting up."

Everyone stood up quickly and bowed their heads as to get the meeting started with haste. Pastor then proceeded to bow his head to pray.

"Father God, we thank you for this day and for the Word

that was brought forth today through your manservant Al. Now, Lord, we ask that you would forgive us of our sins, both seen and unseen. And Lord, allow us to let mercy be our guide and the recompense. Let us look to you for guidance, judgment and for justification. We know that in ourselves none of us are perfect. So let us who are imperfect look to the examples that you have set forth in your Word to be our guide for the decisions that we will make today. We thank you for all that you have done. Continue to bless our past, our present, as well as our future. We speak these words in Jesus' name, Amen." And they all said amen.

As William finished the prayer, he noted in his mind the fact that Pastor Stovall, Sr. was missing in action. William questioned, did he forget that today was one of the most important days of his life?

William proceeded as he would at any board meeting. He asked his secretary for the reading of the minutes from the last board meeting.

She stood slowly as if she was afraid to read them. She had been eyeing the situation and she could tell that things were going to get tense when she read the agenda for the meeting.

"These are the minutes from that last meeting. We discussed the budget presented by the Treasurer. There were areas in the budget that needed to be reconciled and they were tabled at that meeting because of there were questions that still need to be answered regarding it. We all discussed the old business regarding our policy as a church when dealing with youth/ teen pregnancy. After discussing this issue thoroughly we voted and the vote stood for censorship when dealing with this issue. These are the minutes from the last meeting."

She sat slowly, as well. She knew that Pastor was oblivious to all of the ramblings that had taken place while he was busy doing whatever it was that he was doing.

William reviewed what she had read and compared it to

what he had received. It all seemed to match up. And, as always, he asked if there were any questions regarding the minutes.

"Are there any questions? We are only going to spend a minute or two on this so let's make it quick."

There was no noise from the fellowship hall. It was understood in everyone's eyes that this was just the undercard and that the main event was next. They wouldn't dare waste too much time on this. It could all be worked out later.

William noticed the silence and responded by moving forward as swiftly as possible.

"Is there a motion to accept the minutes?"

"So moved." Said Pastor Stovall AKA Lil Junior.

William swallowed hard and moved to continue.

"Is there a second?"

"Seconded." Said Sister Stovall, convincingly. She wanted him to know that she was there in support and that she was on his side. He could see that he had everyone that he needed with him for the ride.

"Alright, it has been properly moved and seconded. All in favor of the minutes being recorded say 'I'."

The I's resounded. And it was carried.

This is where things got a little crazy. In the haste and hustle, the Pastor had not looked at the agenda for the day. He had realized that his Pastoral life had been on the fritz and that there may be a discussion of what was going on with him and all the rumors. But apparently Lil Junior had completely rearranged the agenda without his knowledge. Now this did not bother him that much. But what did was the fact that it had been approved by his best friend because he was the only one that would have been able to allow it to go through. The same best friend that he had left in charge of running the church while he dealt with things. The same best friend that had just stabbed him in the back without a word. And at that time there was nothing that he could do to stop it.

William Fitzgerald Wright looked at his best friend as if he had seen a ghost at first. His heart was broken. He had been set up. In fact it was going to happen whether he had been there or not. They were going to discuss the accusations and make a decision on the direction of the church without him. He just couldn't believe that his boy would hang him out to dry like that. Just place him on the stake at that point.

Then in the same moment the anger set in. Not only was he about to go through the inquisition but he also he had to deal with the fact that the one that he had looked out for all these years was the one that was going to take him through the inquisition. Then that song from the O'Jays popped into his head.

> 'They smile in your face
> All the time they want to take your place
> The back stabbers, back stabbers.'

It had become clear to him that his friends were no longer his friends and that he had to reevaluate who was a friend and who was a foe.

Al recognized that he had just noticed the agenda. He just closed his eyes and put his head down as to imply that he was praying. He just couldn't look at him. He knew that the decision had already been made but he needed for things to go through smoothly. He wanted it all to work out the way that he felt it should. It was time for a new era to begin and that era would involve him as the head and not next to the head. An opportunity had presented itself and the whole time William was focused on Lil Junior, Al was the one that was making the moves to become the next Pastor of First Baptist.

"Are you serious? Is this really the agenda?" William asked with a hint of laughter.

Al lifted his head up and faced William. It was time to deal with this, he thought.

"As serious as we will ever be, Will."

Their eyes locked for the first time since the meeting had begun. The stare was as if they were looking at each other from a new perspective. For the first time in their lives they were on different sides of the fence. They had never faced off before and now they would have to in front of all of these people.

"Al, you really don't want to do this, do you? You really don't want to do this. This will not be good for you." William said with a cocky laughter. He knew that he had all of Al's secrets locked up inside his head. Al knew that too and was willing to let the dirty laundry be aired. He had already talked to Sharon about some of the things that would be said at the meeting. She said that she would support him as she always had. But he still didn't mention the prostitute thing and that was something that he had forgotten that William would remember.

The first item on the agenda was the vote of no confidence in the residing Senior Pastor of First Baptist Church at West End. Since the agenda had placed it at the forefront, it was good for the Pastor be there to defend himself. After all, he thought to himself, who would have defended him if he had not been there? Definitely not his best friend who was placing him under this big bus, he said to himself quietly.

Al took over at that point in the meeting.

"Since I am the presiding Pastor, and since the purpose of this meeting is and was to discuss the issues that have plagued our Pastoral staff in the weeks that have preceded, we will continue this meeting with a discussion on what will be the right decision regarding this issue." Al said standing up as to call things to order.

The murmurs were still heard throughout the Fellowship hall even as he was speaking. The main event was finally unfolding before their eyes like a movie.

"We are really here to clear up all of the mess that has been caused by our Pastor and his messy ways. I don't like having to put all of the things that will be discussed tonight out into open. But I don't want us to continue to speculate and bother the minds and hearts of the saints with these rumors. Therefore, questions will be asked of the Pastor and he will have to answer them or he will have to be sat down. This is the will of this board and the will of the church at large that elected this board. Of course, nothing is ever final until this board returns its decision back to the church body and asks them for their decision."

All of this was going to take place whether he was there or not, William thought. He was just astonished at that fact. They were going to oust him whether or not he was there that day. They were going to oust him without hesitation.

William wanted to leave but he couldn't. This was his only opportunity to make things as right as he could. His feelings, sure they were hurt. But the bottom line was that he had to keep himself in check in order to make his case. And he felt that he had one heck of a case to make in front of this condensed version of his congregation.

"You know it is interesting that when you speak of my messy ways, you speak as if you all don't have messy ways of your own." William said as he stood up to address his accuser. He knew quite well that they were completely out of line with the way that they were handling things. The board meeting was never to be an open forum for things of this nature to be discussed. The business of this church was meant to be handled in decency and in order. But nevertheless, he would continue his case in the forum in which he was propelled.

"Am I on trial?" He questioned.

"No, you are not on trial." Sister Betty responded.

"But you do have to answer these allegations that are constantly being brought up against you. These rumors are becoming a nuisance to the church and to the experience that is First Baptist." Al interjected.

"This is a witch-hunt." William continued.

"You are placing me at this board meeting and blindsiding me with these allegations of rumors that are unsubstantiated and I am supposed to just answer them. Is that what I am supposed to do?"

Then in the blankness of their stares he knew the answer. William at that point had found himself alone. He needed to answer the question to lay doubt aside and let it be known from that point forward who he truly was. So he did what he had to do. He answered the question.

"What question do you really want me to answer?" William asked.

"You know the question, Pastor Wright." Al returned.

"So, now I am Pastor Wright to you, huh, Al?" William asked.

"I am just amazed at the fact that my closest friend, my best friend, would be a backstabbing backbiting bastard after all this time. I would have never guessed that."

Those words created a still in the air. It was as if for that moment, the air left the fellowship hall. His mother finally broke the silence.

"William!" she said.

"I am sorry. I would like to apologize to this board and to the community of believers that have come to this meeting today. I know that the words that I have just said may have offended some of you, but I have just been faced with the fact that the man that I loved like a brother has become to me what Judas was to Jesus. The only difference is, at least Jesus knew he would do it. I never saw this coming."

Al slammed his Bible to that table to gain the attention that he felt he deserved. He was tired of this intermission. He wanted for them to deal with the inevitable.

"Answer the question. Have you been sleeping around with women in the church? Have you? Put the rumors to rest. If you have, say you have. If you haven't, say you haven't."

Lil Junior was eating it all up. He could barely contain himself. He knew that everything was just working out the way that he wanted it to. And he felt it was his time to add a little spice to the conversation.

"Board of auxiliaries, and church leaders, I won't let another moment go by without stating what I know about all of this. He is what they have been saying he is. He is a whoremonger and a disgrace to this church. I have read his diary. I know what he has been doing. He slept with so many of these women in this church that it is a crime. And how can we, in good conscience, allow him to continue to be the hypocrite that he is!

It is our duty as believers, to bring correction to our parishioners but if the head itself is in need of correcting, is it not the responsibility of the church to be the head of that correction?"

Lil Junior's speech was enough to continue to stir up the rumblings of the board and of those that were there to observe the actions of the board.

William's rebuttal would be strong and pointed.

"How can you judge me? Who are you to be my accuser? You are the same one, who if given the opportunity would sell your father up the river just to be the head of this church. You do not want to go here with me, Lil Junior. You know that I know your secrets just as well as you know mine."

Lil Junior cracked a sinister smile and then finally brought forth what he had been waiting to do for what seemed like an eternity to him.

"If we are going to talk about secrets, let's talk about your diary. Let's get to the root of the matter. Your diary says that you slept with about well it doesn't say how many. It just names a few. Would you like for me to name names?"

Playing to the crowd of church folks that are sitting with bated breath on his every word, Lil Junior asked a that question of William as to challenge his pride and his integrity as a man. The question was rhetorical though, because his intentions were very clear. He would be the one to name names.

William's pride wouldn't let him ask or in William's mind,

beg him to not to say what he knew for certain that he would. William would not even respond to the question.

"So, you don't care if I put it out there that you slept with at least ten church members some of which are in this room?" Lil Junior said.

William didn't care about the fact that he was calling him out. What bothered him more was that Stephanie and his mother were about to find out what was really in that diary. Everything that was in that diary. He thought to himself again, some things are just not meant to be written down.

Lil Junior turned his focus to Stephanie knowing that this action would twist the knife a little more.

"So Stephanie, I know that you are pregnant, right?" Lil Junior asked.

William raised his voice.

"That is enough!" He said.

"If this is my inquisition let it be my inquisition. But you leave her out of this. This is about you and me Cleveland James Stovall, Jr."

Lil Junior smiled again.

"Ok, she is not the one in the hot seat. After all she is in love with you and pregnant by someone who doesn't love her. So I will stay off her. Let's focus on you again. I think that I am just going to read aloud a little entry from your infamous diary."

And so as Lil Junior went through his bag and pulled out the diary, William's heart dropped. He could feel but would not acknowledge the eyes of his mother and Stephanie burning holes in his head. Dread and misery were about to become him. But he still had his secret that he was going to share with the class when this was all said and done.

In two minutes he found exactly what he was looking for. And Lil Junior began to read it.

"My initial intent was to paraphrase but I believe that this is best read so that your church can hear the words of their Pastor."

Junior cleared his throat.

"And it reads… I am just beginning to think about all of the consequences for my actions. I am going to have to answer to Him for everything. All the women: Tanisha, Tawanna, Mia, Sandra, Stacey, Shrameka, Sanji, Rebecca, the White girl, Lolita, Maceyanna, Marquita, Laqushina, Stephanie, Tiffany, Alexis, Julia, the White girl, Victoria, the stripper, Ronnell the stripper, Adrian, Ann, Shante, Mary, Kim, Yolanda, Sylvia, and Sylvia's cousin, Denise, Jasmine, Sherri Ann, Sheryl Lynn, the sisters that were White, Nisha, the crazy one, Nishe the sane one, Tisha, Rita, Robin, Nia, Vivian Lee, the darkest, prettiest girl that I have ever seen. There are others but the list goes on and on."

Lil Junior closed the book to dead silence in the fellowship hall. Some of their friends were on this list. Some of the women on the list were married. And some had been in long relationships that had just never led to marriage. There was no stopping it now; the shit had finally hit the fan. But Lil Junior's triumph was not over yet.

"So there they are. You have strippers in the bunch. You have everyone in the bunch. And still you could not settle down. Not with Stephanie. In fact, with all of those women, it is a wonder you don't have HIV or something. You are not a representative of the living God. You are a representative of Satan. You have misled all of these women into believing that they could have something solid with you. That is, according to you. And now we have people that won't even come to this church because of you and something that you did to them. Like I said before, if the head is corrupted then the whole body is corrupted. I don't believe that I am the only one that believes this. We are not perfect, but how can God be pleased with this?"

And it was at that moment that William could not hold back any longer. He had tried to stay above the accusations and everything. But he had had enough. He knew that he had done wrong. But he would truly be damned if he would allow him to lead this church when he had secrets of his own that needed to be outed.

Yet in Lil Junior's eyes there could be nothing that would take away from his moment of triumph. If only he knew the words to come out of the mouth of Pastor William Fitzgerald Wright.

"I can't take any more of this! I have let you sit here and accuse me of this and of that. But let's get real Cleveland. You have secrets of your own, don't you."

Lil Junior looked at him with puzzlement.

"Yeah, you are talking about all my stuff. And I have done my dirt. But you are not sharing with the class that you are not fit to lead either are you?"

Lil Junior had no idea what he was talking about. And in a flash it came to him. He knew. He couldn't have known but he knew. How did he know?

William could see him melt. He could feel himself began to feel joy but he really didn't want to do to Lil Junior what he was doing to him. But he had no choice. There was no other way to get this man to stop outside of outing him. And that is what he was going to do.

"Ahh... Umm... William, can I talk to you for a minute?" an exasperated Lil Junior asked, stumbling over his words in an effort to quail this situation that he thought he had under control the whole time.

"You had your turn, Lil Junior. You had your opportunity. You have put me out there and I applaud you for doing that. I told you that and I told Al that this not something that you wanted to do. I tried to be a Christian about this. But I have had enough of this. So since all the cards are being put on the table let's put them on the table."

Then William stood up with fire in his eyes and with everything that he would say, clearly scripted in his head. He said to him self at that moment. I built it with the truth and I will leave it with truth no matter how much it hurts.

Al looked up and said "Oh, shit."

He knew that it was about to get really ugly. He looked at his wife with that 'he is about to go there' look. She looked back at him with that 'I hope that I am going to be ok with you after this' look.

"So, let talk about morality Lil Junior, shall we?" William said with a determined and vengeful look in his eyes.

"William… can we talk about this?" Lil Junior said again.

"Why, Lil Junior is it that you are not with your wife?" William asked.

"William can we talk about this… Please." Lil Junior said.

"No, you wanted to take me down for my moral ineptitude. You wanted to take me down for my dirt. So, we are going to talk about morals and values that are consistent with the church of the Living God. Isn't that what this whole meeting is about?"

"But, William you don't have to do this, man."

It was as if the tables had completely turned at that moment. No one knew what was going on. Al had no idea what it was that William could have over Lil Junior that would cause him to be that afraid. In fact all Al knew was that he had his drama that he could be outed on, and he didn't want that to become public knowledge. But the old saying was so very true, 'people in glass houses shouldn't throw stones.'

Everyone was holding on to find out what it was that he was going to say. Because no one had ever seen Lil Junior look that way. He looked almost pale, and considering that he was a golden brown color, that was hard for him to accomplish.

"What is all of this going to accomplish?" said Sister Betty.

She was enjoying all of the theatrics, but she had grown tired in her older age of the show. She knew what she needed to know and would vote according to that.

"Are we going to just sit here and let this circus go on? I

love the Pastor. I know that he has done wrong. He has to be punished for what he has done just like any other member of our church. I understand that. But this is a trial and he is not on trial. We are not a court of law. And even if we were, this mess would not take place like this. Someone needs to stop this before it goes on into another hour. And I for one am tired."

She was right. They had been there already for thirty minutes debating- basically crucifying, their Senior Pastor.

"So, Pastor," she said boldly "spill the beans or close the jar."

And that was all that he needed in order to say what he needed to say.

Chapter Twenty-Six

"I am going to say this and I have to because I will not allow only part of the truth to be placed on the table without the rest being put out there as well." William said.

"I never wanted it to be this way but I wasn't given a choice in this matter."

"You have a choice." Al and Lil Junior both said simultaneously.

"No, I don't." Will rebuked.

"See, the men with the most mess going on in their lives are the ones that decided that they wanted to oust me. It's funny to me because I know their secrets and now I guess they know mine. I was always willing to go to the grave with theirs but they wanted to use mine against me."

Then he said the words that produced a silence that could only be experienced to understand.

"You see the reason that Lil Junior's wife left him is because he... is gay. That is the reason. That is also the reason that his father never made him the Senior Pastor of this church. That is also the reason that he resents his father and me. He has been on the down low for so long that you would never know. He didn't even know that I knew but I do.

I think that he figured it out when I started to say what I did. You see we have a gay Pastor that wants to be the Head of our church. And this same gay Pastor, is charging me for my sins without ever looking at his own. Now how does that work? Is he without sin? He has a boyfriend that has been to this church. He also has had other boyfriends up in here. But it is just funny to me that he would be bold enough to front me without thinking about the fact that he had all of these skeletons in his closet."

And then there was silence. At that moment, for everyone that was quiet in that church at that hour, it all made so much sense. Finally, it all made sense. It was as if a veil of secrecy had been lifted to reveal how everything really was. The greatest of lies had not been the fact that William, a single Pastor, had slept with several women at the church. No, the greatest of secrets was reveal in the homosexuality of Pastor Cleveland James Stovall, Jr.

For Al, his face spoke of his disgust. He could not believe that he had turned his back on the one friend that he had had for so long, all on a lust for the power to be the one running that church. He just couldn't believe that he had followed after Lil Junior only to find out that he held the greatest of all their secrets. He never would have guessed in a million years that this would be the secret exposed when he came to the board meeting that day.

The face that really mattered was that of Lil Junior's mother. She didn't want it to come to this but she knew that Pastor Wright had to do what he had to do. She loves her son, but she knew in her heart that this had been more about the vendetta that he had with her husband, his father, than with leading First Baptist. She knew that her son needed her but she had to stand with her husband. He had made his bed hard she thought. It was time for him to wallow in it.

How does a father deal with having to sell his son up the river for what was right? That was a question for Pastor Cleveland James Stovall, Sr. His son had placed him in a position that almost destroyed his legacy. As much as he loved his son, he could not allow him to do that. And as much as he loved his son, he could not allow his gay son to be the leader of God's church. In the end, he had never accepted that his son could be both a man of the cloth and a homosexual. As much as his son had hidden it from the congregation for as many years, his father knew.

His masquerade of marriage only lasted long enough for her to find out about his male lovers on the side. She wasn't there long enough to be known but was there long enough to be noticed. Everyone knew that he had been married for a year or two. And everyone had seen her at church with him, and around at times. But the reality of who he really was would overshadow every aspect of their lives together. She didn't want to believe what she saw in him. She didn't want to accept that she hadn't seen the warning signs prior to the marriage. But she had ignored them all. She had been in denial. She was not willing to continue to be that way though, and neither was he.

He had just accepted that the mask of marriage was just too much for him to take. He knew that he didn't love his wife. And he even resented his father for suggesting that to him. Senior knew that it would be more obvious to an ever watchful congregation if his only son was single. He just wanted his son to be normal as a Pastor.

"I… I don't know what to say." Lil Junior said in a subdued voice.

"There is nothing that I can say. I am sorry…I just, I just have to go."

He got up and walked away from the table and head out of the fellowship hall door to his car. His body was limp. His steps labored. His posture, arched over. Pride had fallen and he knew that the respect that he held was no more. He had no snappy comeback for the truth. No thought provoking revelations that could negate the lie that he had been living. In a way it was a sad relief for him. Yet it was one that he would not, and could not appreciate for years to come. His sexuality and his faith did not fit into the same box. And no congregation in the black community would allow him to lead them with that scarlet letter affixed to his chest.

Again, his mother wanted to run to his aid as she had before. But, she couldn't. She had seen him be wrong in all of this. She knew that it never even had to get to this. Even though her mind understood the situation, her heart grieved for her son. Her tears could not stop falling.

Stephanie could not believe what she had just witnessed. Her worries about Williams' position in the church and how things would go had just been eliminated. She was more worried about whether Lil Junior would be suicidal after what just happened. She was never his fan, or his friend for that matter, but that was just a lot for one person to have to take. Yet, she still cared more for William than for Lil Junior, and she could see that William clearly did not want to have to stoop so low. They gave him no choice.

Sister Betty spoke up again.

"So with that said and done, I guess we can move forward with the more pressing issues."

She seemed to be the only one that was concerned with the pressing issues.

Al refused to continue the meeting. He knew that things were not going to go the way that they, he and Lil Junior, had planned. But, William wanted to finish off his accusers.

"I move to adjourn this meeting." Al said.

"I move to continue this meeting because of unfinished business." William said in rebut.

There were no seconds on the floor for either motion. This had truly become the greatest show on earth.

"So what are you going to do William? What are you going to say? Are you going to put me out there like you did Lil Junior? Are you going to air my dirty laundry, as well?"

William looked at Al. He looked hard into his eyes and he almost began to say what he had promised that he wouldn't. But then he remembered his promise. He remembered Sharon's eyes and the girls. He didn't want to bring shame to his best friend's family. He didn't want to undo everything. The bad blood had been shed enough, he thought. It was time for him to just let it all die down.

"Al, you and I both know that this is not how things are supposed to go. We have been friends, and I never thought that my best friend would turn his back on me like this. But, I am not going to turn my back on you. I am not going to place you under the bus the way that you have done me. I refuse to let this situation make me bitter, evil and not the person that I am.

"Al, you will always be my brother and my friend. I am upset and I will continue to be upset. But that is not what this is about. This is about what is best for First Baptist. I know that I need to be set down for some time. I am willing to accept that. I believe that I have been out of line and that I have sinned. I am praying that God will forgive me and set me free from that bondage. I am at the mercy of you, my constituents and colleagues, who can make the decision.

I know that God will forgive me. I only hope that this church can forgive me and let me continue to serve in some capacity if not as the leader of this body."

"Well, with all that we have heard today, it going to be hard for us to trust anyone. I mean I am starting to believe that all of you are just a bunch of crooks anyway." Sister Kincaid said boldly.

She said what they all had been thinking the entire time. What in the world was going on at First Baptist?

"How would it be any different if you stay than if Lil Junior did? You were both in the wrong." said Tylese Walters.

Her husband was Deacon Tyrone Waters. He was the head deacon and he was sitting there with her as all of the nonsense was going down. Her husband and Lil Junior were friends and he would always go to bat for him if anything came up. William would always refer to them as the thorns and thistles.

William was about to speak but Al cut his sentence short.

He knew that it was time for him to stand up for the person he should have all along. Even though the damage had been done, it was never too little or too late to do the right thing. And so he did.

"William was never trying to crucify anyone for gain. He was just trying to defend himself. I was wrong too. We all have been wrong. While we are talking about it, half of the gossip that goes on in this church comes from you and your family so you should know what it means to be wrong."

People began to chuckle with that statement. The Walters were not amused.

"This is more about what God would have us to do. I know that I have done wrong in the sight of God. I am not excusing my wrong. I am at the mercy of this church and I will seek counsel with God, and I have already sought counseling with Pastor Stovall. I pray and hope that the church will forgive me and allow me a role, whatever that role might be."

He spoke with more sincerity than anyone had heard from him that whole day. His voice trembled slightly because of the seriousness of the situation.

"So, we have really had a lot to deal with tonight." Jimmie Smith said lightheartedly.

He had figured out that it was best for him to keep himself out of the mix as much as possible. He realized that this was not a situation where taking sides would make for good consequences. So he listened to the voice of reason, and the voice of the Lord. It seemed to have worked out in his favor.

"I believe, Pastor Wright, as a church we trust you. Even after this, we trust you. But we need for you to get yourself in order and make sure that your focus is on living in accordance to God's word.

And the fellowship hall said "Amen!"

At that point Founding Pastor, Cleveland James Stovall Sr. stood up to say something. It was the first time that he had allowed his voice to be heard.

"Well, I know that you all must have been waiting for me to say something about all this commotion. I know that everyone was expecting me to step in and say something about this little ruckus that you had here tonight." the Pastor said with what would seem like a chuckle to most but to those that knew him, it was a tell tale sign that he was not pleased.

"But, I wasn't going to. I wouldn't do it to save my life. Not even to save this church. See, I am the founding Pastor of this church, but God, He is the head of this church. And I believe in God. I don't believe in Pastor William Wright. I don't believe in my son Pastor Stovall Junior. I believe in what God says and what He will do."

He squinted his eyes closely together as he looked around the room in contempt for the display that he had seen that evening.

"You have shown me who you believe in. Not in God. But in yourself, with your little witch-hunt. You have shown me that you as a family of Christians do not know how to care for one another. And pray for one another."

He took a deep breath after that. Once again, the hush that had once enveloped the fellowship hall did so again.

"You know I feel like I failed you as a Pastor." He said looking down at the table in front of him. In himself you could see how this whole incident had made him repent the fact that he had even started the church up.

"When I started this church, it was my goal to make it a place that the whole Spirit resided. A place where people would be able to find a refuge from the storms of life, and to expect a word from the Lord."

Again, he paused. He tried his best to hold his emotions at bay, but this was his church. If no one else loved it or cared about it, he did, more than anyone.

"I never thought that this would be a place where backbiting and bickering, and all of this nonsense would be the way to go."

His face was not as bright, nor his demeanor as at ease as it was before. At 70 years old he looked as if he was going to cry. And that is what he did. Not a sob, but a tear. A tear, which reminded everyone of the great sacrifices that he made for that great church; sacrifices that came with reward and with loss.

"I am disappointed in my son. I am disappointed in my successor, and I am disappointed in my congregation. I love you as a church but we have to do better. I am not going to reassume the roll of Pastor. But I will be working with the Pastors of this great church to put this mess that we, all of us who go to this church have created, behind us."

Pastor Stovall always had a way of making you feel a lot better even after he had blasted you for being the sinner that you are.

"You know I am not perfect. I mean, sometimes I can't even remember how to put my pants on the right way." He said laughing slightly when he thought of it. Everyone there followed suit with slightly nervous laughter.

"But as much as I am imperfect. I am looking constantly to the Master, for my help. I am not focused on what everybody else is doing, I am focused on Him."

As he was about to sit down he made one last point.

"You know, Pastor Wright came to me with all of this before it got out and I was about to judge him. I thought of how wrong he was and how out of line he was. But, I was reminded of two things. One, I was him when I was younger."

The confusion that he created with that statement was written on the faces of everyone that was in the fellowship hall, except that of Pastor Wright and Sister Betty.

"Yeah, I know. Hard to believe but so true." Stovall said as he finally sat down.

"I will not go into details but know that just because I am who I am today, does not mean that I wasn't somebody different yesterday. That is what I mean about pressing toward the mark."

He sipped his water and took another deep breath to prepare his next statement.

"The second thing that came to mind was Jesus on the ground. When the Pharisees and the Sadducees came to accuse the woman that they found in the very act of adultery, Jesus sat on the ground drawing. Now we don't know what He was drawing but we can assume that when He said 'he who is with sin', that He had drawn their sins on the ground right there in front of them."

Pastor Stovall took another long sip of his water amidst the silence.

"So, I would like to ask you one question. Who is without sin among you?"

At that point he got up with his water bottle in hand and began to walk toward the door. He had nothing else to say and he had no more to listen to with regards to the meeting. Sister Betty followed him shortly afterward. But she first had to take care of some unfinished business.

She went over to Pastor Wright before they commenced with their discussion and whispered something in his ear.

"Don't forget that we love you and God does too, my son." She said.

Then she kissed him on the cheek and followed her husband out the door. Privileges that only being an elder is lucky enough to have. Of course after having smacked everyone back into the reality of the real world, they would decide to jump ship so that they could remain dry. But his points made sense, and they reverberated in the minds and the souls of everyone there.

"Maybe he is right." Al said as he watched Sister Betty make her exit.

"I think maybe we need to just let this be it for the night. I am tired and I don't think that I could take any more surprises."

That wasn't a very welcome statement to the many that were left to find out what the end would be. After all that had happened, they still expected a show and there always has to be a spectacular finish for any good show. Not so with this particular show.

There was still too much to be discussed. And with everything that need to be discussed mending needed to take place. That would help to decide what really needed to be done next. No one wanted to continue the actions of the day before. Because everyone listened to what the founding Pastor said. And as it had been said before, he was right about it all.

Chapter Twenty-Seven

Al, William, Stephanie, and Sharon stared at each other sharply as the throng of people slowly filing out of the fellowship hall. As close as they physically were, after all that had transpired that afternoon, they were as far apart as they could have ever been. Their eyes told the story. Distant and weary, hurt and discontent; they wore resentment and disappointment in their eyes.

Sharon, still in herself, wondering what the secret was that William still held onto. She wanted to know because she almost felt as if her marriage depended on it as well as her life. With all of the diseases and things out there she just felt like she need to know the truth, the whole truth, and nothing but the truth. Even if it made her the unhappiest person in the world.

William, still in disbelief that his friend, his closest and dearest friend, would be the one who would turn his back on him. Stephanie, just in disbelief of it all. How would she explain all of this to her child? She felt like she was in a fix in the midst of all of this. Still being in love with someone with such a jaded and twisted past and present. Then on top of that, all the drama with her child and her child's father that she had to think about. The apprehension of it all made Stephanie sick to her stomach. Or maybe it was the pregnancy.

Al could only recollect, and with a regretful heart ponder it all. How could I have been so stupid, he thought. And then, for what? There had been no worthwhile change. No newfound glory to be had. An opportunity to be the head of a church that did not embrace him? His stomach cringed a minute at that thought. He had been willing to sell his soul to the devil for nothing. He gained nothing in the process and he lost his best friend.

They lingered still until most of the noise had cleared the fellowship hall. They all knew in their hearts that they had unfinished business that wouldn't allow them to leave that room. Not even for an instance. Friends and lovers they once were and yet they sat across from each other as distant still as they had ever been in life.

"So, what do we do next?" Al said, noticing the stalemate of stares. "How do we fix this?"

"I don't think that we can." William said as stood up and headed towards the door.

"Only if you don't want to fix it!" Al snapped back.

"I am not the one who broke this, Al. I am not the one who started this mess. I am not the one who came out against the person that they called their best friend. That was you!"

William stared hard into the eyes of his friend. Al stared back glancing down every so often because of his guilt.

"You want to fix this Al?" Will questioned.

Al knew that it was a trick question, but he felt compelled to answer it honestly.

"Yes" he replied.

"Then tell your wife about everything. Right here, right now."

He looked up quickly at William. He couldn't believe that he brought it up again. "Why would he do that?" Al thought.

"Yeah Al, tell me what he is talking about." Sharon said. She had been waiting for this to come up.

"I mean it is only fair Al, since you have sided with my enemy, and you have tried to get me ousted with the mistakes that I have made in my own life. I want you to let your wife know about all of the philandering that you have done. You know all the women that you have been sleeping around on her with. You know that kind of stuff. Let her know about that."

Stephanie looked at Will. "What are you doing?" she asked.

"I am just saying. He wanted to put me out there and he did. Why don't we just clear the air?" William said whispering under his breath.

"So Al, you have been cheating on me?" Sharon said, with the question choking her slightly.

Al was hesitant to answer but Will was ready to answer in his stead.

"Yeah, he cheats on you."

"Will, don't do this." Al said pleading with his former best friend. Will ignored him.

"He has cheated on you so many times and each and every time I have helped him cover it up. I have tried to tell him that it wasn't worth it but he hasn't figured out how good he has it. That is until now. See now he knows. Because he sees all the mess that I have had to endure and he realizes that I have really done him a great service by preventing all of the stuff in his life that I am having to endure in my own."

Al's nostrils flared in anger and in shame. He knew that he brought this on himself but he was mad that his friend would not be as much of a friend to him now as he wanted him to be.

"Why William? We couldn't we get past this? We couldn't just let some things go?" Al said.

Sharon just sat there and took it all in. Stone-faced and in wonderment she just sat there and absorbed it all.

"William, I think that is enough." Stephanie said in a feeble attempt to intervene. But William was determined to get it all out.

"No way Stephanie. There is no way that I am finished. This was my ace. I brought him to this church and I placed my license and my character on the line for this guy. I believed in him and this is the thanks that I get?"

William then looked at her with flame in his eyes.

"If his ambition allowed him to destroy my reputation, then in order to repair our friendship I think that we need to get a lot of stuff out in the open. So that is what I am doing. I am venting!" William said with a long release of air afterwards.

"So, where was I?"

Al had to stop him because he knew that this would be it for him and Sharon. There were just too many things that he could come up with at this point that would just basically kill their relationship.

"Will, I am begging you. Stop!"

William looked at him again.

"You know what, Al, I am going to stop. If I told anymore, I don't think that there would be an opportunity for you and your wife to work things out. So I am going to leave you with that. When you patch that up, when you figure out how to be really honest with that loving woman that has made you happy for the last I don't know how many years, then call me. Her happiness is way more important than our friendship."

And on that note he began packing his things to the sound of pure silence. That was the kind of silence that lets you know that you are in a place that you don't want to be. Sharon was still staring forward and Stephanie was hurrying William along so that she could have a friendly or not so friendly word with him about his behavior. But William had one final message to make before he finished. He turned to Al and Sharon before he left.

"Al, I will always love you as my brother. I know that I am going to forgive you for all of this. But you really did a number on me. I thought we were better than this. Out of everyone in the world, I would have never expected this from you. But, we are all human and we make mistakes. Take care of what needs to be taken care of. I will get over this, but things will never be the same. Never."

And William walked out with Stephanie, leaving Al to sort his new found, or rather old found mess out with a wife that was totally unaware.

Chapter Twenty-Eight

When Stephanie got William out to the parking lot she let him have it.

"What the hell was that?" she said yelling as loud as she could.

"What do you mean?" he replied playing the dumb man role as best he could. He kept walking towards his car even after she asked him that question. He had his things that he brought to the church with him that he wanted to take home. He had placed them on the table when the meeting was taking place so he was just going to take them to the car and leave them there.

"You know what I mean!" Stephanie said again screaming.

"You didn't have to do this! Why did you do it? They have enough to deal with in their lives for you to go and fuck it up with that news break in there!"

"He did this to himself." William returned.

"Why wouldn't I do this? Why not? He didn't care about what he had done to me? He didn't seem to be that concerned about the loss that I was about to experience. Why not give him a little loss of his own?"

In his mind he couldn't understand why this was even a question considering what had just happened. He didn't recognize how selfish he was being, but Stephanie did.

"Whose side are you on, anyway?" William asked angrily,

as he placed his laptop and some of his books in the car. The more he thought about it, the angrier he got.

"I am on the side of right." She said.

"Ok, so who was on the side of right when I was in there being crucified by all of them? Where was my, 'on the side of the right' time?" He said with his tone elevated to the side of anger.

"You weren't right, William." Stephanie responded.

"I don't care what you may think about all of this. You weren't right. That is the just the truth."

That was not what he wanted to hear.

"You know what, Stephanie? I don't even care right now. I am just glad that he is getting what he deserves."

Stephanie looked again at him hard. She couldn't believe that the same person that was just shown a little bit of mercy would be so merciless only a few moments later.

"What did you deserve?" she asked. Her voice trembled with the heartache and anger that his words had invoked.

"What did you deserve when you lied to me? What did you deserve when you cheated on me and all the while you preached about this or that? What did you deserve when you were out there fuckin' all the women that you did? Did you deserve to catch HIV or Herpes or some other disease that you can't get rid of? Did you deserve to get sat down then? Did you deserve that? What did you deserve, William?"

Her eyes welled up with tears as she thought more and more about what she had heard. She was right and he was so far from being right that he didn't even get it when he was wrong. He had forgotten how much hurt that he had caused in all of this. Then, at that very moment in his mind, entered the thought of the things that his daughter was going through.

"I", he paused for a moment. He had to figure out how to say what he really wanted to say. An apology was the best thing that he could come up with.

"I'm sorry."

She knew that he was sincere but what she had heard in the board meeting that day had just opened up so many old wounds that didn't heal properly, if they healed at all.

"William, I know you may not know this." she said with tears still streaming down her face.

"I still love you. I haven't stopped loving you. But I have tried to stop being hurt by you. And apparently I can't stop that either."

William looked at her in disbelief. He knew that she had just been in a relationship so he didn't know if they were trying to work that out.

"Stephanie", he stated heavily but she wouldn't even let him finish his statement.

"William, what I said was how I feel and that alone. I don't expect you to tell me how you feel or even try to explain to me why we can't or won't be. I was just letting you know how I felt. That is all. I love you. There I said it."

And with those words she left him to ponder that truth.

He watched her every step away from him as she made her way to the car. She purposed her steps slowly to give him every opportunity to let her know that he felt the same. He wouldn't though. As much as he would have liked to have made that connection. As much as his heart melted at the thought of having that relationship back to where it should have been, he couldn't do it. Maybe the guilt of knowing that even after everything she still loved him was much too much for him to bear. Or maybe it was the fact that she was pregnant by another man. Still his heart was pounding from the thought of losing her. When he decided to take action, she was already gone. Too little too late he thought. But he had reaffirmed his belief within himself. And he had finally admitted to himself that she was the only one for him.

Sharon sat there at the table looking at Al as if she could see through him. She knew deep within herself that he was still that guy. That he was still that nigger that she was told to stay away from in college. She knew that he was still that nigger that her girlfriends told her was no good. The same one that had no problem with sleeping with sisters; she knew that was who he was. What she had hoped, for all the time that they had been together, was that she had been able to change him with her love. She had hoped that the kids had changed him; that all of the shit that they had to endure had changed him. That the house, the car, and everything in between had changed him. But, more importantly, she wanted to believe that God, Himself, had changed him.

But as she looked blankly into his beautiful flirty brown eyes, she realized that nothing had changed him. He was still that man that he had always been. The thing that had changed more than anything was her. She had become blind to the facts of the matter. She had become blind to the late nights that were actually covers for his apparent secret rendezvous with these women that William was talking about. She had become blind to the stares that she could remember. From all these women, and she never ever understood why. She knew why now. She had been lying to herself. She was the one who had changed, not him.

Her pressure began to boil with each passing moment. She just couldn't believe how stupid she had been. She couldn't believe that she had stuck around that long to deal with everything that he had put them through. For this she said to herself. To have it all come crashing down.

Al just sat there. What could he say after all the dirt that he had done on that day? What would his comeback be? What excuse could he give as the reason why he had cheated on his wife? After all, he knew she was a good woman. He married for that reason alone. She was everything that he ever wanted in a woman. The problem was, he always had another that he could see being with. It is hard for a man to stop doing something that he has done his whole adult life. And old habits die hard. Harder than marriage and children and a family for that matter; we are after all, creatures of habit.

"I don't have any words that can say what I really want to say. All I can say is that I am sorry. I have said it a million times, and if I have to I will say it a million times more. I am sorry, Sharon."

He stood up slowly. You could clearly see the burden of this conversation was like a weight on his shoulder. He wanted to make amends but he knew that there was so much that she didn't know about and so much that he didn't want to have to tell her but he knew that she needed to know in order for this to finally be done in his life. So he told her. Everything and about everybody.

He told her about the prostitute that was really a cop and how William had to get him out of Jail. He told her about the women at church that he had messed around with when they were supposed to be concerned about the relationships with their husband, only to be at home alone waiting for him to get there. Mind you, none of the women that he had affairs with went to First Baptist. But, they would make the occasional visit just to see how he was doing. He told her about some of the out of town "crusades" that were actually opportunities for him to get reacquainted with some of his old "friends".

And the more that he told her, the harder it was for her to listen and maintain her composure. She did a very good job of it though considering everything that he had done. Once he had finished with all the gory details he let out a sigh of release and of apprehension. The moment of truth had presented itself to him again. What would happen from this point?

As Stephanie drove away she had so many things running through her mind. She was trying to figure out why she had done what she did. Why even spend to time to tell someone something that they were obviously not interested in knowing? Why even waste the breath on someone that really couldn't possibly be in love with her the way that she was in love with him. But she knew that the thought of continuing her life without having let him know how she felt was worse than what she felt right then and there. She knew that she hated the way that she felt. But she just couldn't continue to go on holding that in. Love has a way of shifting things. So her mind had to now shift to that which she had control of. And that was the new baby on the way. Six months to go. Six months to go.

William got in his car and sat for a while. He took deep breaths and concentrated. After a day like that, with all of the revelations, this was the first time that he had to gather himself. He focused on the steering wheel as he thought about what had just happened. Al and his betrayal. Could he forgive him for what he had done to him? Could he let it go? Lil Junior. That worked out like he thought it would. He knew that he had enough on him to make his case in the end. But why was it so easy for a church that he had headed for that long a time to turn on him?

He placed his hands on the steering wheel at 3 o'clock and 6 o'clock, still breathing in and out trying to calm himself down.

"Focus on the issue…" He said as he turned the key in the ignition to start the car.

"Focus on what you want now William."

He turned the car back off. He just sat there for another moment or two. The night had settled in around him. As he was sitting there he noticed that Al and Sharon's car was still in the church lot. What Stephanie said regarding that situation was right. He had been shown mercy and it was time for him to show some himself. In fact he came to accept that everything that Stephanie had said was right. He was beginning to finally let things go and accept it for what it really was.

As he had that thought Sharon came out of the building. She was clearly upset from the look that he saw on her face. As he watched her, she noticed him. He tried to lower his head but she was headed towards his car so he had to acknowledge her when she got there. As she got closer he thought he better get out of the car because he knew that he was in a world of trouble for all the mess that he had stirred up. She came up close to him and then the verbal assault began.

"You two deserve each other." she said enraged.

"I was just trying to help him and you at the same time." William replied.

"So, helping me is lying to me? Helping me is covering up all of his bullshit, while he goes and fucks around with whomever he wants to? Is that helping me?"

Sharon poked William and with each poke she broke down more and more until finally she was in his arms crying. He held her close, confused but comforting her as much as he knew how. She was awash in the moment and all that she wanted then was to be held and be told that the moment would pass. That things would go back to the way that they were. That all of these revelations would not change the way that things were with her husband. Yet, the reality seeped into her fantasy and even that moment of comfort was not nearly comforting enough. She felt safe in Will's arms for that moment. And the safer she felt the more that she was reminded it was the very man that was holding her that was one that had helped to perpetuate the foolishness all along.

"What do you want from me, Sharon?"

With that question she pulled away quickly and looked up at him. As much as she was hurting, she didn't want to say anything or do anything that would make things worse. Revenge was on her mind but her children and getting her life back on her terms were much more important. Her answer reflected her motivation.

"Nothing, William…You have already given me more than my husband did."

She turned around and walked to her car. As hurt as she was, she had her pride. Pride would not allow her to shed a tear more before moving forward. And that is what she did. She wiped her eyes, got in her car and made her exit from the parking lot. Leaving all of the tension and problems where she felt they belonged. In the church that caused them.

Chapter Twenty-Nine

"So, are you happy now?" a weighted down Al asked not in anger, but with the sound of exhaustion.

Will had walked back into the main sanctuary to pray because of the day. Al's words echo throughout the church, loud enough to wake the dead.

"Were you happy when you placed me under the bus and then ran over me with Lil Junior at your side?" Will fired back.

"Well, Will, that was never the way that I wanted it to be. But he sold me a dream and I believed it. I believed in that dream more than I believed in you."

Those words stung a little. But, that was no different than anything that he had to hear that whole day. In his mind, Will thought, nothing else could really hurt him from that point forward.

"You know what Al, I really can't even be mad at you anymore. Yeah it was really messed up what you did. In fact it was fucked up, but I have to forgive you the way that you have to forgive me."

Al agreed.

"Will, I am really sorry about how all this went down. I know that I really did wrong you. I was just ready to make that move into, you know, the top spot."

Will look at his boy and thought maybe it was time.

"Al, you are still the my man, you know that, right?" Will said.

Al was hesitant to respond.

"You do realize that it is ok for you to say yes right now, right?" Will said.

"Yeah. I got you. But, it's hard for me to say that we are boys comfortably, after all of this."

Will looked at him again with a look of reassurance.

"Let's just say that after all of this is said and done, we are really going to need each other for the times to come. I have known you for forever. I am not willing to let this mess get in between what we have as friends. So let's put it behind us and move forward. Trust me, there is so much mess coming up that we have to deal with. We might as well deal with it together."

Al nodded his head in approval. He knew that he would have never gone this route after everything and that is what really made them different. Different was what made William an excellent orator and Pastor. Different is what made Al a good evangelist and a good youth Pastor. And different was what made them work well together. Different is good.

As William and Al parted ways, Will began to think again about the next phase of his life. How would he accept the decisions still left to be made about his relationship with the church that he loved? And more importantly, how would he tell his daughter about it all? After all she was the only one that was left out of the loop regarding everything. And she is the one that will call him the hypocrite in the end.

And the thought of that conversation left a bad taste in his mouth if any conversation did. It was always easier to accept the responses of adults that are going to do what they want to do anyway. William was always able to give advice and accept it when they ignored his advice. But to now have to tell his child just how wrong he had been and what the consequences might be for his actions. Well, that was not something that he had ever wanted to have to do. But life doesn't play by the rules that anyone may place on it. Life has a mind of its own. Sometimes you just have to go with the flow he thought. Sometimes you just have to go with the flow.

But that thought made for a sleepless night at his home. He arrived, exhausted and ready for bed throwing his clothes on the floor as he made his way up the stairs. He knew that he would be home alone that night and that idea bothered him a little. After the beating that he took that day, he would have wanted some tender loving care in the arms of some women. In fact, it didn't at that moment matter what woman it was just as long as it was a woman.

Interestingly enough, he understood that to be the problem. As much as he wanted to be taken care of he knew that he needed this moment of solitude in order to move forward. He had surrounded himself with women for so long that it seemed as if he could not operate without them. This was partially true. And as much as it pained him to sit on that king sized sleigh bed by himself, he knew it was what he had to do.

As midnight approached, to his surprise, the phone did not ring. There was no knock at the door. There wasn't even an email sent to his email account. There was silence. The sounds of the night surrounded him but none of the sounds that he silently hoped for. No, for the first time in a long time he was truly alone.

As unfamiliar as this state was for him, he had felt this way for a while. His mind drifted to sleep as a way of relieving the stifling feeling of alienation that had come over him. But sleep would not last long enough for him, especially when the mind has wrapped itself around the name of a woman. His mind was lost in that last moment with Stephanie.

He kept replaying it in his head like an old scratched record that would replay the same part over and over again. He knew that his opportunity to make things right had come and he blew it. As much as he felt that he may get another one, he really didn't know if that were true or not. And more than being alone, the thought of losing her bothered him. She had been there in the past and he didn't want her to stop being there. They had their separation, but it seemed as if this was their time. There, he thought. He had said it to himself; this was their time. Now he could approach the situation and make something happen.

Al, having revealed everything that he had to his wife, now had to deal. To deal with his wife who was already hurt by the things that she knew before everything. To deal with his children, who were going to wonder why Daddy wouldn't come home anymore. To deal with reconciliation in all of it. He was glad that he had avoided the public embarrassment that his friend had just endured. But, the loss of his family faired way worse in his mind than losing his church. The truth was that Alfred Williams' life would never be the same. That much he did understand. How to make things right, better, those are questions that he has yet to be answer.

Monday morning sprang forth with the sounds again of birds and of people. It was another day like any other day and the only thing that had changed was the way that William, Al, Sharon, Stephanie, and the rest of the faithful members of First Baptist would perceive it. The truth sometimes is the worst weapon. And all of them had been its target.

William woke up thinking about Stephanie and what to do next. Al woke up to the sound of a wake up call from the front desk of the Hampton Inn that he was staying in. Stephanie woke up to morning sickness and a call from her ex-fiancé. Sharon woke to the sounds of an alarm clock reminding her that for the last Monday in this school year, it was time to get the kids ready. All of them fully aware that things were so extremely different, yet all of them acting, trying to maintain the façade that things were still the same.

Lil John too, woke up with this mentality. But it was short lived. He could not stop thinking about it. He knew who he was but he couldn't believe that at that moment, everyone else knew too. He was still bitter. The wound was still too fresh to hide from himself. As much as he wanted to forget, it was as a tumor in the forefront of his mind constantly reminding him of the error of his ways. But, it is hard for a man with so much pride to believe that he is the one that is wrong. It is hard for that kind of man to find humility and to move forward. Even though he was a homosexual, Cleveland Stovall, Junior was all man. And there is no greater satisfaction for a man than to be able to seek revenge. For Lil Junior that is all that he could see in the future.

As William started his day his phone rang. It was 8:30 on a Monday, so it wasn't quite unusual for him to receive a phone call at that time. What was unusual was the person on the other line. It was his daughter. He had not prepared himself to even talk with her but he had forgotten that he promised her that he would take her to school every day for the last week. With all of the drama that he had been living, little things like his word, had become things forgotten.

"Kristian, I will be on my way, ok?" He said as he made haste putting on his shoes and a wrinkled shirt.

"Am I going to be late for the last week, Daddy?' Kristian asked impatiently.

"No, No. You know that I am going to get you to that school on time. Why would you even need to ask? I always come through."

So he drove to his parents' as quickly as he could to pick up his daughter.

The trip was quiet out side of the pleasantries at the start of the trip. He knew that he did want to make any reference to the events of the day prior. He was hoping that it would not come up but as luck would have it, it did.

"Daddy," she said coyly, "you don't have to worry about telling me anything. I already know and I am sorry that you had to go through what you did. You were right about consequences."

William felt his heart drop through the floor, never to return again. He only nodded because the only audible sound that he could have made at that moment was the sound of collapse.

Kristian understood that he would not say a word, so she did not say another one until she was about to get out of the car at school then she would let him have it.

"Daddy, just remember that no matter how hard it is for you to overcome your sins, I will always love you."

And at that moment she gave him a kiss and he thought that he had died. He had no words. He had to fight hard to swallow back the tears that were forming in his eyes but those words would always be in his mind from that day forward.

He wanted to call his parents and give them a piece of his mind but he couldn't. Why would he? Everyone else knew, why not her? She was going to have to deal with it anyway. The more that he thought about it and the task of telling her, the more he realized what a great service that had done for him.

The morning continued and he lunched with Al as they discussed everything and continued to try to get over their issues. Al's wife came up in the conversation and he just couldn't see them working out.

"She has never been this mad." he said drinking his uptown, a combination of lemonade and sweet tea. They decided to lunch at a new location because things for them were new too. Plus, this wasn't their usual Sunday meeting. As he continued to sip he reflected on everything and then proceeded to give him the reasoning behind his thoughts.

"She doesn't answer the phone. Then, if she does she says I don't want to talk to you and then hangs up the phone. I am telling you, dude, I think this is it. And on top of that I just don't see it ever being right after all of this."

The anguish was clear in his tone and body language. He had given up. Not moved on, but given up.

As much as William wanted to help that situation, he was in almost full agreement. It seemed pretty bleak and time hadn't passed enough for her to be over it as well.

"Al, you may just want to give her time. I know that things seem very, very... damn bleak. But you are just going to have to give her time on this one. You know that she just found out a whole lot of stuff, and quite frankly you don't deserve another chance. And I know that I was the one that caused the problem. But truth is you are just going to have to wait on this one."

As much as he didn't want to understand, Al knew that Will was right.

"You know this is all your fault, right?" Al said jokingly.

"Well I think that there is enough fault to go around right about now." Will responded.

"You know you are talking about Sharon, what are we going to do about the church? What am I going to do about Stephanie?"

Al looked at Will like a deer in headlights.

"Wha... What about you and Stephanie?" Al replied.

William forgot to mention all the stuff that had happened with them and the whole fiancé thing.

"Al, long story. Anyway, how are we going to move forward with the church? Our legacy will depend on how we bounce back."

Al realized that Will had ignored his question but he chose to go ahead and ask it again.

"So, you and Stephanie are back at it?"

Will repeated his question as well.

"Al, my question. Moving forward with the church? You know, the legacy that we are leaving at First Baptist."

Al knew the answer to that one.

"That is not our decision." He said.

"That decision rests squarely in the hands of the board and church. The only choice that we have is to accept the decision of the church. More than anything we need to make sure that we aren't called to order regarding our license."

Will had forgotten about that. If the Georgia licensing board decided to, they could lose their license to preach because of all the mess that this church has been through. They ended their lunch on that note.

Chapter Thirty

Pastor William Fitzgerald Wright stood in front of a mirror about three hours before what was to be his last sermon as the Pastor of his great church. Three weeks had passed and the church had voted to make him one of the associate Pastors but that Al would be the interim Senior Pastor for the church until a selection was made to find someone new. As much as this hurt William to his heart, he understood and accepted the decision of the church as a whole.

There were several recommendations on the floor of that meeting. Some, to have him completely removed from the church that he had helped build to the point that it was. Other calls were to have him not only removed from the church, but also banned from preaching anywhere. But, the greatest calls were for him to remain and to help with keeping the membership intact. And above all, that is the only one that would be approved by the founding Pastor. He still carried a lot of weight, and agreed that he needed to be punished just so that people would understand that especially in God's house you cannot sin and there be no consequences.

As Pastor Wright stared into his own eyes, he remembered all that had transpired over the course of the last year and how his life had changed. He knew that there was no one to blame but himself for everything. He had begun to finally understand the difference between being arrogant and being holy. God had given him a gift, he thought. He had not used his gift for the full glory that God had commissioned him to use it for. To whom much is given, much is required. And the longer he stared the more he realized that he had been given too much to be so ungrateful.

"Sometimes I wish that I could have taught you something long before He had to teach it to you." He said to himself as he pointed up.

"I think that we have learned enough to last a lifetime."

He was wearing his best robe already. He had shaved early that morning. By six o'clock he was already at the church on a Sunday morning long before the dew had burned off the grass. The sun had barely crested above the horizon and he was going over his sermon. This was his last moment and as much as it was a very sad day for him, he wanted to leave with a good sermon. One that would be remembered for as long as he was there.

He walked through the empty and quiet sanctuary one last time as the Senior Pastor, enjoying the solitude of his thoughts. He felt chills down his spine when he thought of all the sermons that he had spoken to a packed sanctuary. To him he could feel the presence of God in that place for the first time in a long time. He still had a burden and as he stood in front of the pulpit, in front of the altar, he kneeled down and began to pray.

"Father God, in the name of Jesus, I pray that you would forgive me for all of the things that I have done to disgrace the commission that you have given to me. I know that greatness was placed upon me not for my own purposes, but for the purpose of spreading your Gospel and promoting your love. I am sorry. I have been in hell in myself and my sins are always before me and you have made me aware.

Lord, you have given me another chance. I know that you still love me and that the enemy has been after me everyday since the beginning. I know that I have done so much more against myself than the enemy has ever done. I am just glad that you have allowed me an opportunity to come back home and be with you where I really wanted to be all along.

I miss Tawanna. I know that I have to get over that and I have gotten over a lot of that. I still miss her but I know that I have to move on and I have. I want this church to grow and prosper. Whatever I have to do to make sure that souls are saved that is what I will do.

I know that I have been a whore. I have. I have been a lot of things that were not what I am supposed to be as a child of God, let alone a Pastor leading a flock. I know that I do not deserve to be anyone's Pastor but you have been still so merciful to me. So now Lord, I ask that you would be with me in this, my last sermon. When I speak, Lord, speak through me.

Lord, let the words of my mouth and the meditations of my heart be acceptable in thy sight. Oh, Lord, my strength and my Redeemer."

He opened his eyes and the quiet let him know that he was still there alone. But as much as he was, he felt a closeness that he had not felt before to his Heavenly Father. He was glad that he could have this time but he still wished in his heart of hearts that he didn't have to go through all that he did in order to get to this point.

Al was up early too. Now that he and his wife were separated, his life had become a series of activities to keep his mind occupied. He went running at six. Started on the elliptical at seven, and wrote a sermon at eight.

Things had changed a little for Al and Sharon though. She allowed him the opportunity to see his children. He could come over there on the weekend and see them. She would always answer the phone now but her response to him was still distant. But it was better than nothing.

Al called Will on his cell to see how he was dealing with everything.

"Will, are you already at the church?" Al asked.

"Yeah, just going over things, you know what I mean?" William answered.

"I know this has to be hard for you. I know it does." Al sympathized.

"Yeah, but I am cool. I am just trying to deal, you know? Just trying to deal."

And as a moment of silence set in, Al and Will understood each other in a way that they hadn't in quite some time. Al understood the struggle that this had to be, and William understood his struggle with being alone. They had been growing closer ever since the event, but this was their first 'I understand you' moment. It made Will feel good to know that he really had his friend back.

"You know, man, this might be a good thing for me." William said with a chuckle.

"How is that?" Al quipped.

"Because now I don't have to be in the pulpit all of the time. I will leave that to an old pro like yourself. I get to ride the bench now. You are the star quarterback."

Then, William had another thought.

"This will be my last game as the quarterback, so I want to end it on top. Then ride off into the sunset like an old western hero."

"Do you really think it will be like that?" Al asked sarcastically.

"Well I…"

Al cut his answer short.

"You haven't died and you are not retiring. This is a transition. Who knows how long before you are the starting quarterback again? The point is all this is where you belong. You belong here. Nowhere else. This is your church home. Whether you are the Senior Pastor or just a regular old pew warmer. You live, eat and sleep First Baptist. Your life hasn't been the same since you briefly left us. And it definitely won't be any better if you leave for good or stop being who you are to this church."

Will was surprised to hear all of this but he appreciated someone saying it for him right then and there. He was feeling a little depressed on the fact that he had to be demoted. He never thought that it would end the way that it did but that's life.

"Al, you are right and I thank you for being my friend in the midst of all of this. I am glad that you are going to be the one for a while. Now, maybe when I get in trouble…"

Al interrupts him.

"There will be no more trouble for us. We are too old of all the mess that we have had to deal within the last year. Me with the prostitute thing; you with, well you know. I think that it is time for us to just move forward with stable and happy lives. Don't you want happy. I mean all…"

"Al?" Will says cutting him off.

"You are right, man. I was just kidding, dawg. I know. I know. We know better so let's do better, right?"

"Right." Al asserts.

"Well, Will, I am going to have to get going because I don't want to be late myself. So I will see you in a minute, aight?"

Will responded with his usual response. Since Al was notoriously late, him saying a minute meant about an hour at the earliest.

"I will see you when you get here, Al."

And William hung up the phone feeling a lot better than he did when the conversation started. He felt good to the point that he needed to just tell the Lord was on his heart. For the first time in a while the burden was one of joy and not of sorrow or questions.

"Lord, I know that you love me and I know that I am going to be ok. I know that this too will pass and I am going to just deal with today as much as I don't like the way that things have worked out. I love my brother, Al, and I want you to bless him to be better at being the head than I was at it. I want you to try and work things out between him and his wife, if you can. Lord, whatever I need to do for them or for you or for anybody, help me to do it. In Jesus' name and for his sake I pray. Amen."

Time passed quicker than he had expected and the next thing that he knew it was already 9:30 and the church was already almost filled to capacity. There was an expectation for the sermon that they would hear that Sunday. It was almost as if this was some popular Pastor had decided to come into town and he would only be there for one Sunday. He found it hard to believe that all of that attention was for him.

When he thought about it, he realized that his confidence had been lowered by everything that had happened. The cocky Pastor that he had been had been replaced by someone who questioned everything and especially himself. He knew at that moment that he would be able to do what God wanted him to do because he identified for the first time that he was not going to be doing it to impress anyone. He was doing it to please God and God alone.

The more thought on his sermon, the more that he thought on his commission and on what he knew then. The more that he wished that he had come to this conclusion such a long time ago. But he realized that everything has a season. That time that passed before was not the season for him to understand what he did then. He began to understand that God had been speaking to him the whole time. That every question, ever prayer had been heard and answered but he was not listening with ears that could hear. He was not looking with eyes that could see. But now, as he reflected he could see and hear everything that God had already told him. And just being able to see the Lord at work began to give him the confidence that he needed to say the things that God wanted him to say.

He came up with the title of his sermon at that moment. 'The seasons and the times.' He would be taking it from Ecclesiastes. As God had allowed him to see what he needed to see, He was also talking to him through his friends. His phone started to fill up with texts from all of those that supported him to let him know that they were there for this last sermon as Senior Pastor.

Old friends from college, and old colleagues from ITC and Morehouse had all come to hear what he had to say as he made this transition from being the star to being what God had called him to be; a very good Pastor.

10:30 rolled around and there he stood. His game face was on as it had always been in the past. Alfred Williams ran in his office followed by the rest of the Pastoral staff and deacons. It was his last opportunity to lead the prayer before service and there was a lot that he wanted to say as they embrace for the circle of prayer.

"I would like to say first, thank you to all of you that have served with me since I have been the Senior Pastor. I believe that we have done a good work. We have saved some souls along the way. We have fought some battles and I believe that God is working everything out the way that He wants it and needs it to be for this church."

As he made that statement, Lil Junior walked in and joined in the circle. Everyone looked cautiously at the man that had been the enemy of this pastor from the very beginning, everyone looked except the Pastor. No one knew but he had invited him to be on pulpit with him and the rest of the Pastoral staff for this time because he was a part of his Pastoral staff. William also knew that it was time for their problems to end. Lil Junior had gotten what he wanted, but it was at a cost that was high for Lil Junior. William understood that as much as they had their differences, Lil Junior was as much a part of First Baptist as the building itself. It was time to change the seasons he thought and changing them would be making things the way they ought to be and not leaving them the way that they were.

"Now, I know that some of you may be wondering, what in the world is Lil Junior doing here?" He said as his eyes connected with everyone in the room.

"I wanted him here because this is where he belongs. Here. Right Here. He is a friend to many of us. He is a loving Pastor to a lot. And whatever ought that I have had or you have had with him, it is time for it to go down into the grave with every sin that we have all committed.

"I am not going to hold any grudges." William continued.

"But believe this, I will be angry if on this my last day you treat him any differently than you would treat me. We are a family in Jesus Christ. And we will be a family today for His sake. So if you have any ought and little things that you need to let your brother know about himself today. Let him know now. If you are angry at me or anyone for that matter, get it off your chest now. Because after this I am going to pray and we are going to move into our new season."

He made that statement, and it was understood that the man that stood before them was different than the man that they once broke bread with. They could see that God had made him different in a short period of time. They were at a loss for words. And since no one said anything, William moved forward.

"Since everyone is ok. I am going to pray." He said as he abruptly bowed his head.

"Father, it is in the name of Jesus that we come you in prayer. We know that you are an awesome God and a forgiving God. So, Lord, we as you that you would forgive us all of our sins and our shortcomings and blot out all of our transgressions as we come before you.

Lord, you know our hearts. Teach us how to forgive and lay our hurt feelings and egos down so that we can serve you in spirit and in truth. Let us move in love going forward and try to forget the things that have separated us through these years.

I know, Father, that I have wronged you so many times that I don't even deserve forgiveness. But Lord, I believe that you are a loving God. I know that you want what is best for all of these brothers and for this church. So bless them, Lord. Bless them from the crown of their heads to the soles of their feet. Please bless them so that First Baptist can be blessed. So that the community of believers that surround this church can be blessed. So that the world that we live in can be blessed.

Lord, we need you more now than we ever have needed you. So we say these things expecting miracles in our live because we know that you love us and are here for us. Lord, move in an awesome way and we claim the victory in your name. In the mighty and wonderful name of Jesus, your Son, we do pray. Amen"

And as he finished his prayer they felt as if they had all been touched by the Holy Spirit. The power of his words were different. The intonation and pitch was different. The boldness of his speech was different. It was an experience. For Lil Junior, it was almost a frightening one.

He hadn't had that much contact with the church in the weeks that had passed since the infamous board meeting that changed all of their lives. But for him just the way that he took up for him and made him feel like he was a part of it all, even just for this last time, was a very big deal to him. He just knew that the Pastor was basking in the defeat of his greatest foe, namely him. However, in light of everything the Pastor had just come to accept everything and God had given him a better understanding.

As they began to line up for the entrance into the sanctuary, Lil Junior got Pastor William's attention.

"Pastor, I just wanted to thank you," he said as they filed out.

"I really appreciate you having me back and I know that you didn't have to do that. In fact if it was me, I don't think that I would have done it."

Pastor Wright grabbed his hand and spoke softly in his ear.

"No matter what we have been through, and even after everything that has happened, I forgive you. God has been good to the both of us. We are brothers in the faith, and we have to learn more than ever to forgive and move forward.

Remember; it's a new season and God is going to move in that new season of faith. So I am asking you for the same. Forgive me and let's move forward together."

And as they walked in he knew that he was ready. As he stood in front of pulpit he could feel something that he had not felt in a long time in the air. It was the feeling of peace. He felt right at home with all of his congregation and all of his friends in front of him. He knew that this would be a high time in Zion for him to close out what had been his only church.

He was not one for doing things out of order, but this day would be his last time to be in that position as the head. So he took some liberty in breaking the rules and making a statement before the doxology.

"I know that I am stepping out of line, but I am just so glad to be in the house of prayer one more time."

He said as the Spirit-filled congregation greeted his words with a hearty amen.

"Now, I know that some of you may be wondering what is going on and all that. Well, I just wanted to tell you to stick around. You know we are not going let you believe that the mess that we have had is the end all and be all of this great church that Pastor Stovall has built. So just remember that this is a new season and God is going to move in this season to make this church. Amen?"

And the church resounded with a hearty amen.

As he took his seat, he looked to his left and to his right. Lil Junior sat to his left and his friend Al, sat to his right. His mind just wondered throughout the church. He looked out in to the congregation at his smiling mother who looked so supportive. He looked at his father who he knew that he had to repair his relationship with on the back end of everything that had happened. He looked at Sister Betty, who had been there for him through all of the trials and tribulations of the whole ordeal. She smiled at him with a smile of approval. She had never given up on him and he appreciated that.

Then he looked at his mentor who sat next to Al on his right. The man that built the church from the ground up to where it stood then; the man who had been like a second father to him; the man to whom he owed everything. Pastor Stovall looked back at him. And at that moment he just understood him better. He understood the calmness and the wisdom that he had. He knew from right there that there was an experience with Jesus that the Pastor had gained, that was not something that was from speaking but that was from living. Pastor Wright was beginning to gain that same experience, and that is why Pastor Stovall let things play out the way that they did. He could have worked it all out for the Pastor. But the bottom line was that he had to go through this experience in order to become a better person from it. He needed to be a better person in order to become a better Pastor. And only experience can create the growth that he needed. It became clear that God had allowed him to go through the storms that he went through in order to become the man that he needed to become.

The choir sang and the deacons collected the tithe and offerings. The announcements were read and the scripture was presented. The song of meditation was sung by the Pastor's favorite singer, Tylese Walters. Her husband, Tyrone, is a deacon has been a friend of the Pastor for years. He has helped them through a lot of difficult moments in their marriage and they had babysat for him in the past.

She sang "Great is thy Faithfulness" as the meditation song. She took it very slow and bellowed in the way that only she could. Her voice always reminded him of Mahalia Jackson whenever she would sing. She had a very deep and strong tone. She projected her voice very well and she held notes that no one else would dare.

As he looked out into the congregation for one last time before he was to get up and preach, he didn't see Stephanie. She was the only one that he had not seen in all of his canvassing with his eyes. He had seen Tamara, and all of his family. He had seen friends from the past and new friends alike, but no Stephanie. As much as he was ready to preach, he wanted her to be there to support his last effort before stepping down.

As Tylese finished, he kneeled in front of his chair and prayed his traditional prayer. "Lord, let them see you in me. Lord, let me see you in them." This prayer would always calm him if he was nervous because he was always nervous when he preached. As long as he reminded himself about Who he was really looking for, he would be ok.

He stood in front of the podium and waited as the congregation calmed after such a spirited rendition of the song. She gave him what he needed and his glance at her signaled his approval of her performance. He gathered his thoughts for a minute or so more as she returned to her seat. He made sure that his notes were in order as he began.

"God is so good to us. Great is His faithfulness," he said. They responded with amens and applause.

"And despite how I may feel today. Despite how you may feel today. Despite everything that we have done in our lives, God is still faithful!"

There were a few that stood to rejoice and agree with him. He could appreciate the excitement but in his mind this was just the beginning. He gave them another minute to settle down and then he began his sermon.

"First, I would like to give honor and praise to God who has always been and will forever be the head of my life. I would like to thank Him for bringing me to this point where I can just be so thankful and so full of praise to Him that I just don't know how to contain it. I know that I am blessed so that is why I can say all of this. Because there is no one else who sustains me but Jesus!"

Again he riled them up but that was heartfelt. That was not something that he had written down on a sheet of paper. That came from his heart and it was the result of everything.

"Turn if you will in your Bibles to the book of Ecclesiastes Chapter 3:1-8" he said.

As they flipped their pages, he saw someone walking in the balcony in his peripheral. As he looked up from reading, he noticed that it was Stephanie. She was late, but she was there. She looked at him and he looked at her and she gave him the final support that he needed to preach his last sermon.

"and it reads…"

He went on to preach that sermon. He talked about how God had moved them into this new season. He spoke about how sometimes when the seasons changed there were storms that would come to help usher in the change that was about to happen. Change was inevitable though, he said.

Then he spoke about the change that had taken place in his life.

"You know I have been through some changes myself. The last year has had a few storms for me. I have seen the lightning flash and I have heard the thunder roar and I know what the wind feels like. So, for those of you that are going through your storm right now just know that I am not immune nor is anyone from the trials that life can sometimes throw your way."

He turned on his lapel mic so that he could walk around like he liked to do. He was not a minster that would leave the pulpit much but he did like to be able to walk around the pulpit when he was speaking.

"I operated outside of the pattern that God had set forth for me to operate in. But, when you are a tree that is planted by the river of waters, you will eventually thrive."

As animated as ever, William expressed every word with his hands.

"I couldn't see where I was going when I was in that particular storm. I couldn't understand that God needed me to move so that others could move, so that we as a church could continue to grow. See, we have to understand that God will change our situations so that others will be able to move into the blessings that God has set aside for them in that particular season."

The congregation clapped and said amen thunderously on his last words. Then he did what he wanted to do for quite some time. He apologized to his congregation.

"At the end of my season as the Senior Pastor here at First Baptist, I would like to say that I am sorry for not being the Pastor that I needed to be at the end of my tenure. Some of you that have been closest to me know that I have counted on you for support, both physically and spiritually. So, to you I say thank you. We have been through a lot together. You have watched my daughter grow up. I watched some of your children grow into thriving adults in this community and in this world. So, now as this transition takes place just keep in mind that our new Pastor is not a new person, but is someone that you know and love. He has the passion and purpose that God needs for us to move in the direction that He would have us to go in."

As he returned to the podium with his closing set, he left them with his words of wisdom.

"Finally, I ask you my church family to trust in God. Know that the Lord is ready for you. In this new season we are going to need to lay aside every weight that has held us back from loving each other. We will need to lay aside every weight that has held us from trying to understand each other so that when He comes again we will be truly ready."

Will looked at his friend, his brother, Al and asked him to stand.

"Alfred Williams is one of the best men that I know. I know that he, himself, has had some tough times in his life but God is working things out. I pray that you will embrace him not just as a man of God, but as a brother. And as a friend. He has been here for you in the past. And you can believe me when I say, he will be here for you in the future."

As he closed out, Pastor Stovall, the founding Pastor of the church, prayed a consecration prayer over the new Pastor and a prayer of transition for the old one.

"Father, it is in the name of Jesus that we pray. First, we thank you for allowing us to be your vessels. We know that Lord we should not have to be used by you because we are not worthy, but Lord it is through your Son that we are made worthy so we say thank you. Secondly, Lord, we ask that you would forgive us of our sins and cleanse us from all our unrighteousness. Thirdly, Lord, bless these men. As they transition into the new roles in life as well as in leadership, Lord strengthen them. Where they are broken, Lord fix them. Where they have doubt, Lord give them faith. And allow their faith to be as that grain of a mustard seed. So that the mountains of their lives can be moved. So that they can calm the seas of turmoil and tension in their lives. I know that you are able Lord. So we ask this prayer not doubting but believing. In Jesus' name we pray, Amen."

And then it was over. His tenure had come to an end. It was very anticlimactic for him but he was so very glad to be allowed an opportunity for peace. Peace from being the mainstay in the public eye. Peace from the abuse of meeting after meeting with constituents within the church. But, more than that, this was an opportunity for him to try to rekindle relationships. A relationship with his daughter, the love of his life. A relationship with Stephanie. And that is where his mind would be in the coming weeks. His mind would be on peace.

Chapter Thirty-One

Over the course of the following few weeks, William moved all of his things to the other office located in the fellowship hall. The Senior Pastor's office was reserved for the Senior Pastor and since he was no longer that, he wanted to make sure he moved as quickly as possible. Al was in no rush but Will wanted him to enjoy it because he had earned the right to be there. Will, as much as he wanted in himself to be the head, knew that his role was to be supportive and to unite a church for the purposes of salvation.

As he was cleaning out his office he saw his lost journal in his desk drawer. He looked back through in for while just reminiscing on all the mess that had occurred over the last year and a half. It was amazing to him that God had just allowed him to live through all the things that had lived through. Even reading through it all he could see how God was trying to warn him but he just ignored all the signs throughout.

As Will neared the end, he noticed that there was still room for another entry. He sat there for about twenty minutes trying to decide if he should finish his diary with one last thought. One last anecdote, one last saying that just summed up all of the experiences that he had been through over the course of time that was covered in his diary.

As he was sitting there, in his former office, Stephanie called and asked him about dinner. He figured that he would just take it with him and ask her about it. He said Chantrelle's would be good, so they met there.

He decided that walking there would be better than driving and since it was one of those rare days of summer when the skies were overcast and the temperature dropped below 85 degrees in the city of Hotlanta. Plus, it gave him more time to think of what to say. It was no longer a question of whether or not he would write a passage, it had only become a question what to say. So much that he could say, but he felt that it should be short enough to be remembered, and long enough to make an impact.

So when Stephanie sat down at the table across from him she couldn't believe that he had that thing back in his possession.

"Isn't that the same book that caused all of the hell that you have had in your life recently." She said reaching to snatch the book out of his hands.

Will flinched and pulled the book off the table. He understood where she was coming from, but this was his testimony and he didn't want her to take that away from him.

"You know, Step, I understand where you are coming from. I do." He said placing it slowly back on the table.

"But you need to understand where I am coming from regarding this book. This is my testimony. These are my thoughts and I have a right to remember the way things were. There may come a day when someone somewhere has a question about me. They might want to know what I was like. In my own words they will be able to understand who I was."

She was ready to sass him but decided against it. Instead she took another route.

"Will, as long as you have a purpose for that book. I guess I understand. If it was mine, I would probably burn it."

"Yeah, well that is why you are you and I am me." He said still staring at that blank page.

She was kind enough to just eat and let him stare for a

moment. Then, her curiosity got the better of her. So she had to ask the question of the hour.

"What are you going to say?"

He slowly looked up at her as to indicate how absurd the question was.

"If I knew what I was going to say, I wouldn't be still sitting here looking at this page."

She had a snappy comeback but again she decided to take another route.

"Why don't you just say that you love me?" she asked with a coy smile, fluttering her eyelids playfully.

Will stared at her for a moment but the welling up of laughter inside of him prevented him from keeping a straight face. He busted out laughing and so did she.

"You know that I would put that down if that were what I needed to write. I just want to say something that would culminate everything. Something that could say what I really feel."

Will looked down again, slid his diary to the side and eat some more of his smothered chicken. He figured that maybe, trying to think on an empty stomach was not such a good idea. Stephanie decided that she was going to make her own entry. She snatched to book from the table as he was taking his fork to his mouth. There was nothing that he could do at that point but chew and watch. And that is what he did until he had fully swallowed his food.

Stephanie wrote something that was so simple, yet it exemplified what he wanted to say.

"I have lived. I have loved. I have learned."

As he finished eating that bite, he went and grabbed it back.

"What did you write?" He said as he thumbed through the book to get back to the page that he had left off at.

"Read it and see." She said smiling the whole time. She

knew that what she wrote on that page was profound enough to be enough for him to build on. As in everything, all he ever needed was a foundation. As he read what she wrote on that page, he realized that she was right. She always seemed to be that way. He knew that she would have been the best person to give him what he needed, and when he needed.

He got up after he read it, walked around the table, and kissed her. Enough for her knees to shake a little. Then he went back to his chair and started writing. She sat there in a state of shock. Pleasantly surprised but nonetheless surprised. She didn't know that he had in him.

He finally wrote his final entry and closed the book on it.

"Let me see." she said.

"No, this one is for the ages. It is my last testament for this diary. Remember it's a new season. And with that new season there will be a new diary. But the mess that I went through in the last year, that will remain only in this book. 'Moving forward forgetting those things of the past, I am going to press toward the mark towards the prize of the high calling'."

"Really, Will, as much as you make of it. It's just not that deep." She said sipping her lemonade.

"In the end, we are all doing the same thing just trying to be better than we have been before. Trying to be closer to the One Who made us. That is all that we all want. Whether you write it down or not, life is the testimony. And whether your life is in your Pastor's diary or not, God knows and will reward you based on that."

As Will and Stephanie sat there that Friday evening at Chantrelle's, he again basked in the wisdom that was the woman that he loved. She, saying the things that he needed to hear in order for him to grow. And Will at long last had found what he wanted in her and in himself. There was no more a need for all that he had done before. He closed the door on that life and locked the door with his final entry into that diary.

Chapter Thirty-Two

Entry number 106

I have come to the last page of this diary and as with all things in this world a change must come. I have not lived the most righteous life as a Pastor, but I am thankful that I can finally find the peace that I have wanted for so long. All the women and all the mess are out in the open and with that I am freed from it. I hurt so many people with what I have done that I can hardly believe that I am still here at First Baptist serving as a pastor if not the Pastor.

So what have I learned? I have learned that God is too good for anyone, but especially a man of the cloth, to continue to use Him as a cover for ungodly things. I have learned that I am not in charge, if I didn't know it before I know now. I was never in charge and I will never be in charge. God is always in control. I have learned that no matter how much I think that I know, God can always reveal to me a little bit more. I have learned that there has to be a change in order for you to see God. I have seen Him and He is more real to me now than He has ever been, and I am a minister.

I still miss Tawanna, and I always will. I have come to terms with that. I will never be without the longing for her. But I found someone that soothes my soul and her name is Stephanie. She is pregnant with someone else's baby but I don't care. She loves me and I love her and that is all that matters. As for rest, who knows? Only time will tell. But I do know that if we are working together it will work out fine.

I know that my best friend and my worst enemy were one and the same. But I love him still. Al and his wife have decided to get a divorce so I am praying for them. I am sad about it, but I think that they are going to try to work it out so that they can at least be friends. That is one of those things where you just don't know how to feel for them. I love them both, and I kinda feel like it is my fault. Al tells me not to hold that within me but I know that I had a lot to do with it.

My dad and I are finally talking again. He is not happy with me still. But at least now I can get a word out of him. We talked about it and he understood as much as he could. He didn't want me to even go into the gory details, and I would have never done that anyway. I was just glad that he was able to let it go so that we could move forward with being a family again.

Mom is always going to be Mom. She is always going to be there no matter what. She is the rock and she has always been that for me. She was still angry too but she supported me and she will always be there for me in the end and I know that and appreciate it from the bottom of my heart.

Kristian is a work of art. I never thought that she would be my biggest supporter but she was. We have talked and she has given me, her minister father, some great advice. I am glad that we are closer and I hope that we will stay that way. She still misses her mom and I do too.

Cleveland and Betty Stovall are still my biggest fans. Even though I am not the Senior Pastor of First Baptist, I am still their son. They have embraced their other son, Lil Junior, and their relationship is growing from nothing to something. I am glad that they were able to let some of the things in the past go to make a better future with their son. He is still hurt by a lot. And he is still working through a lot. So each day is a new day.

I am glad that I get another chance at being the minister that I was called to be. But, I am sad that all of the things that took place had to. I am praying for Lil Junior, as he is trying to leave the life that he lived behind. I know that God is able to help him. The amazing thing about how it all went down is that Junior would have never come out of the closet if it had not been for that board meeting. And I would not have been able to overcome my sexual addiction, if it were not for that board meeting. And none of this would have ever happened if it wasn't for you, my diary. So as much as I have been angry about even having you, I know that you were a tool of God. 'Because all things work together for the good of those that love the Lord and those that are called according to His purpose.'

As I move into this new season, I pray that I will continue to become a better man and a better believer and follower. Lord, help me be the man that you have always wanted me to be.

Sincerely Yours,
Pastor William Fitzgerald Wright

Printed in the United States
By Bookmasters